I0690484

Nights at Mata Hari: Book 1

EVERY BREATH YOU TAKE

ROBERT R W WINTER

Books by Robert Winter

Pride and Joy series
September
Asylum (coming in 2018)

Nights at Mata Hari series
Every Breath You Take
Lying Eyes

Vampire Claus

Discover more about the author online:
Robert Winter
www.robertwinterauthor.com

Nights at Mata Hari: Book 1

EVERY BREATH YOU TAKE

BY ROBERT WINTER

A Publication from Robert Winter Books
www.robertwinterauthor.com

This novel is a work of fiction. Names, characters, and locations are either a product of the author's imagination or used in a fictitious setting. Any resemblance to actual events, locations, organizations, or people, living or dead, is strictly coincidental or inspirational. No part of this book may be used or reproduced without written consent from the author. Thank you for respecting the hard work of this author.

Every Breath You Take
© 2017 Robert Winter

Cover Art
© 2017 Dar Albert

Author Photo
© Brad Fowler, Song of Myself Photography

Cover content is for illustrative purposes only and any person depicted on the cover is a model.

All rights reserved. This book is licensed to the original purchaser only. Duplication or distribution via any means is illegal and a violation of international copyright law, subject to criminal prosecution and upon conviction, fines, and/or imprisonment. Any eBook format cannot be legally loaned or given to others. No part of this book may be reproduced or transmitted in any form or by any means, electronic or mechanical, including photocopying, recording, or by any information storage and retrieval system, without the written permission of the Publisher, except where permitted by law. To request permission and all other inquiries, contact Robert Winter at robertwinterauthor@comcast.net or www.robertwinterauthor.com.

Second Publication November 2017
v. 2.0
Print Edition

ISBN-13: 978-1626227668 (Robert Winter Books)
ISBN-10: 1626227667
Printed in the United States of America

Dedication

To Colin James, for his friendship and his help in my writing adventures

Prologue

WHEN BRIAN GALLAGHER stormed out of the bar into a cold February night, he failed to notice the door open again behind him. A man with silver-framed glasses emerged slowly and focused his eyes on Brian's retreating back.

Brian twisted his scarf around his neck and then yanked up the zipper on his red puffy jacket with trembling hands. The zipper stuck, and he muttered, "Shit," but kept tugging until finally the slider moved and the teeth closed. The parking lot was mostly full. People came and went from Mata Hari, the newest gay bar in town, and the nearby dance club Pyramid. He stomped across the lot toward P Street and pulled out his phone.

"Hey, kiddo." Sandra sounded cheerful when she picked up the call, even though she probably guessed what was coming. "Whatcha doin' calling on a Saturday?"

"I'm going home already because I'm having a shitty night." Between his own anger, the pulsing beat from Pyramid, and the chatter of men scurrying from car to club, he practically had to yell into the phone. "Talk to me and make me feel better, please?"

"Aw, baby, wassup? I thought you were gonna hook up with that guy again."

"That's what I thought. Well, it's what I *hoped*, anyway. We were so hot last week. I was sure he'd want to get together again. He wasn't even talking to anyone important, just this guy. But when I walked up, he shut me down."

"So… you didn't have a date. You just surprised him?" Sandra asked.

"Well, you know." Brian was aware he sounded whiny. "He wouldn't give me his number last week, but I still figured he'd be happy to see me." He emerged from the parking lot and headed up P Street toward his apartment. "The sex was just spec-*tac*-ular. Like 'once in a lifetime' great. And he was so nice to me. I thought we had, like, a connection."

"Baby, did he say he wanted to see you again? If he didn't give you his digits, then that sounds deliberate…."

"Okay. He did say it was a one-time thing, he doesn't do dating, blah blah blah. But come on. We had sex twice that night. *Twice*. Like, I never gave it up so fast before."

"Bullshit. You're as easy as they come," Sandra said, probably to get a laugh, but it didn't work. Brian just got mad again.

"That asshole. Who does he think he is? God's gift to men?" he fumed. "Yes, he's gorgeous, but come the fuck on. Like, I got so pissed that I threw his own drink at him."

"Well, he'll remember you, then, no question. But I'm sorry he hurt your feelings."

Brian deflated suddenly. "What's wrong with me, Sandra?" he asked as he turned right onto Hopkins Street, where he lived. "Why do I keep going for these guys who treat me like shit?" The streetlamp on the corner was out.

Oh, fucking perfect.

His footsteps sounded loud to him once he turned off busy P Street. His quiet block was dark because of the busted streetlight.

"Nothin', baby. You just get close too quickly because you've got a big heart and you want a big love," Sandra cooed in his ear.

"You always say the right thing," Brian sighed. "But I'm a goddamn mess. I know it, and you know it."

As he expected, Sandra kept talking and tried to persuade him the right guy was out there somewhere, waiting for him. He just needed patience. She'd given him variations on the same speech so many times she must have it memorized. But he loved her for it.

As he hurried down the street toward his rented garden apartment, he heard the scuff of a shoe behind him. He glanced back over his shoulder. A man with shaggy blond hair and glasses walked in the same direction but on the opposite side of the street. He thought no more about it and got out his keys. When he unlocked and opened the wrought iron security gate at the bottom of the stairs, the metal didn't squeal anymore. His landlord must have oiled the hinges.

"Thanks, Sandra." Brian locked the gate behind him and then unlocked the front door. He pressed the phone between his ear and shoulder as he pulled off his jacket and hung it on the coat tree by the door. "You have once again fulfilled 'Best Friend for Life' duties."

"You home safe?" she asked.

"Yeah. Home at ten on a Saturday night, alone," Brian groused as he unwound the scarf from his neck and placed it with his coat. "Guess it's time for, like, ice cream and a sappy movie." As an afterthought he flipped the lock on his front door and then turned on a lamp.

"You want me to come over, baby?" Sandra asked.

"Nah. That's sweet, but I just need some time to beat myself up. I'll get back out there again next week. Besides, I don't want you on the streets this late."

"I'll see you in class Monday, 'kay? Call me if you need to talk some more."

"Thanks for listening." Brian signed off with another sigh. He set his phone on the side table and then changed out of his bar clothes and into comfortable sweats. He pulled a pint of Ben and

Jerry's out of the freezer. Curled up on his small sofa. Searched through his Netflix queue. Finally settled on a really bad romantic movie he'd seen three times already.

Just to make sure I'm completely miserable.

.   .   .

ACROSS THE STREET the man with the silver-framed glasses stood in the shadows. He stared at the front window of the garden apartment and the back of his quarry's head as he watched a small flat-screen TV.

Time passed.

Eventually the head nodded forward and then jerked up. When it happened a second time, the creature turned off the TV and then the lamp and headed to bed.

The man waited for another half hour, his back pressed against an alcove formed where two brownstones met. The street was quiet. Almost no one walked by, and the lone person who came down the sidewalk failed to notice him in the shadows.

The man's breath grew hoarse, and blood rushed in his ears. His heart began to pound. He cultivated that sensation as he reached into his coat pocket for the screwdriver that rested there. He made himself imagine the creature's hands touching the Beloved's face. Stroking his body. He curled his fingers around the screwdriver and then clenched and unclenched rhythmically. Its thick handle felt rough against his palm because of the grooves and sharp edges he had chiseled into it. He had ideas for other implements that would serve his purpose, but for now, this would do just fine. *This* would make his point.

His throat was dry, and his eyes burned from focusing on the darkened window, but he felt invincible. The tension in his body climbed exquisitely. When he could take no more, he slipped across the street and stepped down to the locked gate. It opened easily with his small set of picks. The gate made no noise when the creature went through it earlier. He was confident and quick and didn't bother to lock it behind him. Child's play, he thought as he worked the lock on the apartment door.

The tumblers clicked into place.

He stored his lockpicks, slipped inside the darkened apartment, and then closed the door behind him as silently as he could. Streetlight came through the slatted blinds the boy had failed to close completely. He waited quietly. When he heard a faint snore from the back, he removed his glasses to tuck in an inside pocket of his jacket. The scarf his quarry had worn caught his eye. The man bared his teeth as he lifted it off the coat tree and tugged it tightly between his hands. It was well made. It would hold. He smiled.

He slid through the gloom toward the room where the creature lay sleeping. He was hard, and the blood in his erection pulsed in time to the pounding of his heart. That boy had dared to touch his Beloved. He had probably even been fucked. But that wasn't enough—oh no. He came back for more.

It had taken the man so long to find his Beloved and interpret his subtle clues. He finally understood what was required of him. The undeserving gnat must be chastised, and he would be the Beloved's angel of retribution. He was conscious of the weight of the screwdriver in his pocket, the scratch of the wool scarf in his hands, and the power in his arms.

He reached for the boy on the bed.

* * *

ON MONDAY, WHEN Brian Gallagher failed to show up for class, Sandra Yu went by his apartment. She found the gate open and the front door unlocked. After an anguished moment, she called the police rather than go inside. That was a good decision. The sight of her best friend—face down, naked except for a scarf knotted around his neck, his buttocks and bed covered with blood and other matter—would have scarred her for life.

Chapter 1

ZACHARY HALL ROCKED back and forth on his heels as he stared up at the sign that read *Mata Hari*. It was his first gay bar.

Ever since he accepted the new job in Washington, DC and knew he was finally—*finally*—leaving home, that was the milestone he'd looked forward to the most. Ogden had a few gay bars, of course. His buddy Fred and the others from his college circle frequently tried to get him to go. But the fear of being seen always held him back. If he were spotted, if word got back to his parents.... Well, he wasn't sure exactly what they would have done, but it wouldn't have been good.

Now, though, Zachary was in a new town, with his own money, a job he was going to love, and an apartment. And at last he was going to see what a real gay bar was like. Would there be a back room, like the setting of a lot of the porn Fred had shown him? Public sex? Men in leather? It was Saturday night, the lot was full, and he was ready to take on the world.

Zachary took a deep breath and made himself walk across the parking lot toward the entrance. Two men walked into Mata Hari ahead of him, hand in hand. He grinned and made a point of falling into step right behind them.

Bring it on, baby.

When Zachary entered the bar, he was relieved. Mata Hari was elegant, comfortable, and apparently respectable. He was relieved, but maybe a bit disappointed.

The main room was filled with club chairs, deep sofas, and small cocktail tables. The windows were covered in Roman shades of a cream silk decorated with stripes of red and gold. All the seats he could see were filled with nicely dressed people. Men mostly, but a few women here and there, sipped cocktails and chatted. The mahogany bar that framed the back of the room had an old-world feel. Carved wooden figures ran up and around a large mirror behind it. High-backed stools faced the bar, and most of those were occupied as well. The walls were decorated with an eclectic collection of art. Many pieces looked to him like actual oils rather than prints. Other smaller rooms branched off from the main bar.

A grand piano took up one corner of the room and a black woman with some gray in her hair sat before it. She played softly as she chatted with a few patrons who stood around her or leaned against the piano. Zachary could tell she was good.

The overall effect was of being in someone's home for a cocktail party. Whatever he'd expected or secretly yearned for, that wasn't it. But he loved it instantly.

Zachary checked his overcoat in the coatroom by the door, glad he dressed up for this first foray to Mata Hari. The online reviews had told him the bar was new and attracted an upscale crowd. He wasn't sure what that meant but figured he couldn't go wrong with black trousers and a nice button-down.

Now Zachary was there, now that he'd broken through the fear of being outed, he didn't know what to do next. He looked around at the crowd and tried to make his feet move, but he was suddenly nervous again.

It's just people, for God's sake. They're drinking and talking and having fun. You can do this.

Most patrons were paired up or in small groups. He did notice one man with shaggy blond hair and silver-framed glasses standing by himself in a distant corner. Zachary took a deep breath and walked up to the bar. He waited near the hinged opening in the wooden countertop for the muscular bald bartender to notice him.

Damn. That guy is hot. The man was probably late forties or early fifties and stood well over six feet tall. He had a face made up of hard planes and a nose that appeared to have been broken at least once. A bit of dark scruff framed his strong jaw. His broad chest stretched a fitted white shirt, which was tucked into trim black pants that curved over a meaty rump.

Woof. Serious muscle daddy, Zachary thought. *Straight off one of the websites Fred follows.*

The solidly built man was chatting with a customer. He leaned forward so his big hands and thickly corded forearms rested on the bar. Zachary glanced at the customer then and thought his heart would stop.

The man reclined casually against his bar stool. He had one arm extended so his hand wrapped around a rocks glass full of ice and amber liquid. The other arm rested on the back of his stool, and his long fingers dangled down. He was probably a few years older than Zachary, maybe early thirties. He wore a tailored black blazer over a blue dress shirt paired with black jeans. His dark wavy hair and his eyebrows were thick. A straight nose featured a slight upturn at the end, and his smiling lips were full.

He was the most handsome man Zachary had ever seen.

When the patron happened to turn his head a bit, he met Zachary's gaze. Large blue eyes crinkled at the corners, and he brightened the smile even more. Zachary blushed to be caught staring and quickly turned his head. He focused his eyes straight ahead at the liquor bottles along the back of the bar.

"What'll it be?" a low, gravelly voice said, and Zachary jerked his head as the bartender moved over to his end of the counter.

"Oh, um… can I get a seven and seven, please?"

"Sure, soon as I see your ID," the bartender all but growled, and Zachary fished it out of his wallet. The big man took the Utah driver's license in his thick fingers and scanned it. "Twenty-seven, huh? Coulda fooled me. I figured you for nineteen, maybe twenty."

The bartender's tone wasn't exactly friendly, but maybe he wasn't as scary as he looked either. Zachary licked his lips and shot back, "Someday that will feel like a compliment. Right now, I have to tell you that having a baby face usually sucks."

The bartender laughed—a deep rumble Zachary could feel across the bar. He turned to get the bottle of Seagram's 7 to make the drink. Zachary risked another sidelong glance at the handsome customer and saw he was in conversation with two other men. One appeared to be in his sixties with white hair. The other was a bit younger—maybe late forties or early fifties—and taller with brown hair. The white-haired man was effusive and gesticulated wildly as he talked. The brown-haired man had an arm around his waist, and Zachary smiled at the palpable connection between the two.

"Seven and seven. That's twelve dollars," the bartender said, and Zachary handed him a twenty. More customers waited behind him to order. Zachary took his change, left a nice tip, and carried his drink closer to the piano. Maybe he'd be able to get up his courage to talk to someone after he lurked a bit.

The woman at the piano nodded slightly at him as he approached, and he dipped his head as well. He took a swallow of his seven and seven and looked around the room. A flash of blue caught his attention. Focusing on that, he realized it was the shirt of the handsome customer. As the stranger rotated on his bar stool, he smiled in Zachary's direction—kindly, not in a patronizing way. He inclined his head to address the white-haired man.

Embarrassed to have been caught looking *again* at a man so far above his reach, Zachary turned squarely to the piano player. One of the patrons who rested his elbow on the piano started to sing a show tune. Zachary remembered it from his mom's record collection. The guy had a nice tenor voice, and Zachary leaned against the wall to listen. When the song ended, Zachary joined in a little applause. Another customer asked for "Moon River," so the piano player modulated right into that song. She encouraged those standing around to pick up the melody.

Zachary liked to sing. He wished for the nerve to step up to the piano and join in, but he went for silent observer instead. The drink in his hand helped his nerves as he sipped. He gradually relaxed against the wall and began to sing along quietly. He was enjoying it all, even though—or maybe because—it was so removed from the images of decadence he had built up in his head. No doubt they were placed there by his parents' diatribes on godless homosexuals.

"Excuse me, dear heart, but are you here alone?" Zachary turned to find the white-haired man from the bar standing next to him. In a soft voice with a Boston accent, the man said, "If you *are* alone, come join us. Really. Come join us. Lord knows there're enough people against us as it is," the little man lamented as he stretched out his hand. "Come along." Zachary smiled and took it. Then he let the man lead him to the bar.

As they crossed the room, the stranger said, "My name is Joe Mulholland. Now tell me, darling boy, do you live here or are you just visiting?"

Too late, Zachary realized they were joining the most handsome man in the world. His breath caught. He was distracted for a moment but made himself focus on Joe's question. "Oh, um…

I just moved here. I started a new job on Monday with the Treasury Department. I'm Zachary, by the way."

"What a *delightful* name. Now," Joe said as they reached the bar, "allow me to introduce my husband, Terry. Terry, this is Zachary, and he has *just* moved to Washington," Joe said with a lilt in his voice.

The brown-haired man held out his hand and Zachary shook it. "Welcome. I see my Joe has collected you, but I assure you he's harmless as a box of kittens." Terry had a slightly rounded and soft look to him, but mischievous brown eyes and a wide smile suggested he was a real looker in his youth.

Zachary chuckled. "I was happy to be collected. Thank you for coming over, Joe."

Joe smiled at him, and his eyes twinkled in the light. "I just hate to see anyone standing by themselves. Now, Thomas, this is Zachary," he said as he turned to introduce the handsome man.

The god smiled, stood up, and reached out a hand to shake. "Good to meet you, Zachary. I'm Thomas Scarborough. Do you need a fresh drink?"

The hand in Zachary's felt like it was burning his fingers because Zachary was so aware of it. He held on longer than necessary.

What I need is an oxygen machine.

Thomas was a few inches shorter than him. Face-on and standing less than two feet away, he was even better looking than he appeared from the other end of the bar. Zachary made himself say calmly as he released his grip, "That's very nice of you. Thanks."

Thomas turned his head and called, "Randy." When the big bartender looked up, Thomas twirled a finger in the air to signal a full round. Randy nodded, and then Thomas turned back and rested an elbow on the bar. He met Zachary's eyes with his clear gaze and asked, "So, Zachary, where did you live before DC?"

"I'm from Ogden, Utah. This is the first time I've lived anywhere else."

Joe exclaimed, "How interesting. Thomas, I recall you ski in Park City. That's in Utah as well, isn't it? Now, Zachary, it's perhaps indelicate, but are you a Mormon?"

Terry laughed. "I doubt he'd be drinking in a gay bar if he were."

Joe scolded, "Oh shush, spouse. Perhaps Zachary is drinking pop."

Zachary smiled and shook his head. "No, I'm not Mormon, though I grew up on the edge of a huge Mormon community. Talk about feeling like an outsider."

Randy arrived with their round of drinks and passed Zachary's to him. He had brought a shot for himself; he raised it to Thomas and tossed it back. Thomas's blue eyes met Zachary's gaze again as they clinked glasses. The blue reminded him of a summer night just as twilight set in. Zachary nearly melted under that intense regard.

"Welcome to DC," Thomas said in a toast. "I hope you'll enjoy it here."

"And I'm just sure you will," Joe enthused. "I have a sense for these things, dear heart, and I think you've found a home."

"Joe, you've certainly made me feel at home," Zachary said, and he noticed Thomas give a pleased smile. "Can I ask, what do all of you do?"

Terry answered, "I'm an accountant, and my husband here is a retired school teacher turned do-gooder. Well, he was a monk first, then a school teacher."

Zachary had to laugh. "A monk? Really?"

Joe spread his hands beatifically and tilted his head up slightly. "The halo may be slightly tarnished, but yes, I was once a member of the Franciscan order."

Terry chortled, "He had to leave, though, because he couldn't stick to the vows."

Zachary felt embarrassed. "Umm... you mean the vow of chastity...?"

"No, he managed that one quite well. The problem was they expected him to honor a vow of *silence*."

Joe swatted at Terry's arm. "Now you're just making fun of me. But Zachary, it's true. They put me in a simply untenable position. I was secretary to the abbot. How could I ruminate on the sufferings of the world? I had all this gossip to share, but instead they expected me to keep my mouth shut. I was fairly *bursting*. I'm sure it would have given me an ulcer if I had stayed."

Zachary laughed delightedly at the story. "It was self-preservation, of course, Joe. You had no choice but to leave."

"You understand me perfectly. I took as my personal credo that old prayer of 'from your mouth to gay ears.'"

Thomas smiled broadly and said, "I always thought that was 'to *God's* ear,' but I like yours better."

Joe reached up and patted Zachary's shoulder. "We had a little community of brothers with lavender undergarments, if you'll permit the metaphor. I felt it was my sacred duty to keep my sister brothers informed of the doings in the head office. You know, my dear," Joe began seriously, his eyes glinting. "Before this Internet whatnot, there used to be just three ways to spread the gay news." He ticked them off on his fingers. "Telephone. Telegraph. Tell-a-queen."

That made Zachary laugh even harder, and Thomas and Terry as well.

"So what made you leave the order?" Zachary finally asked.

"Well, I'm ashamed to tell you that the bishop caught me

listening in to a phone call with the abbot. When he mentioned replacing Sister Mary-Margaret O'Hurley as the principal of the high school, I gasped. Well, she'd been there since *I* was a boy. The bishop was incensed and the abbot was mortified. It was suggested my true vocation might be as a telephone operator."

Terry put his arm around Joe and kissed the side of his white hair. "I love the image of you sitting at a switchboard, listening in on all the calls."

Joe rolled his eyes. "Darling, I may be a tiny bit older than you—all right, several years older than you—but party lines and switchboards predate even me." He winked at Zachary. "Person-to-person was *quite* the thing in the seventies in Boston, may I tell you."

Terry chuckled. "You see how it is. I wanted to be the comedian in the family, but he turns me into a straight man every time."

"Well, maybe not 'straight' man," Thomas murmured and gave a slight smile. Zachary tried not to notice how soft and generous that smile looked on his lips. He had trouble pulling his eyes away though.

With mock indignation, Terry replied, "Oh sure, Tommy, now you get in on the act too."

As the laughter calmed a bit, Zachary began to feel his second drink easing his nerves. He worked up the courage to ask, "How about you, Thomas? What do you do?"

Thomas crooked his head a bit and smiled at Zachary. "I'm the chief counsel to the Senate Committee on Banking, Housing, and Urban Affairs." At the blank look on Zachary's face, he burst out laughing. "Exactly. Even when I tell them, people have no idea what I do."

Terry said, "He's the *shit*, is what he is. Tommy's involved in major legislation initiatives all around the country. Banking reform, homeland security, you name it, Thomas's office is involved."

"Oh. That sounds like an incredibly important job," Zachary said, immediately hating his lame response.

Joe reached up and put his hands on both of Thomas's cheeks. He said, "It is important. You can't, you simply *can't* imagine all that this lovely man accomplishes with housing for the poor, along with all his other projects. Perhaps he should have taken holy orders."

Thomas looked a bit embarrassed. "Aw, c'mon, Joe. It's a political job, and I'm just another hack," he said. "Nothing like the day-to-day impact you have at the shelter." He leaned down and kissed Joe's forehead, then said to Zachary, "Joe here runs a shelter for homeless LGBT youth. It's called Rainbow Space."

"You're kidding," Zachary exclaimed. "Do you need any volunteers, Joe?"

"Always, dear heart. Would you really be interested?"

"Oh, absolutely. In Ogden I worked at a soup kitchen on weekends, and it broke my heart to see how many kids came in. *Too* many of them had been kicked out because they were gay or transgender."

Sorrow and loss flashed across Thomas's face. They were gone almost immediately, replaced with his brilliant smile as he asked about the soup kitchen. Zachary couldn't help but wonder what brought sadness to those beautiful blue eyes.

Chapter 2

THEY CONTINUED TO talk late into the evening at Mata Hari. Zachary took a moment to send grateful thoughts to Fred, still in Ogden, who had dared him to try a real bar. There he was, as green as could be. But he was talking to an outrageously lovable ex-monk and his sweet and funny husband. Not to mention a man whose good looks, style, obvious smarts, and accomplishments had Zachary crushing on him.

No doubt Thomas could take home anyone he wanted—could and probably had. As a new boy in town with less experience in gay life than a rutabaga, Zachary probably held as much attraction for Thomas as a McDonald's Happy Meal. He refused to let that thought ruin his evening, though. He was having the time of his life.

The sense of transgressing against his parents bothered him but he shrugged it off. He refused to let Jerry and Martha Hall ruin the beginning to his new life, any more than he would let his own self-doubt hold him back.

They don't know where I am or what I'm doing. And they don't need to know.

Joe and Terry moved away to talk with some other friends who had come into the bar. Randy brought another round eventually and then stayed to chat a bit with Thomas and Zachary.

"So welcome to DC," Randy said to Zachary. "How'd you

find my place?"

That was another pleasant surprise. "You own Mata Hari, Randy? It's great." The bartender gave a slight grin—not a full-on smile—but it helped Zachary's confidence. "I went looking around on Yelp, and you're getting great reviews."

"Good to know. I used to be around some crazy press madness, but I'm crap at the online media-presence bullshit, myself. I've been thinking about getting a publicist or something." The bartender looked around the bar and said, "Off to a good start, though."

"You did great, Randy," Thomas said. "I'm really proud of you."

That earned a lopsided grin from Randy. "Well, it was time for a change, and I always wanted to own a bar. Thank God some investor was dumb enough to trust me with his money."

Thomas winced almost imperceptibly, but Zachary caught it. All he said, though, was, "Good crowd, good reviews, great setting. I don't know anything about running a bar, but I'd bet you're going to be a hit."

Randy rapped his knuckles on the bar twice. "Knock on wood," he said, and then he excused himself to serve some new arrivals. That left Zachary alone with Thomas, and suddenly his heart pounded again. He was terrified he would blurt out something idiotic.

"Thank you for talking to me," he indeed blurted out. Then he dropped his head to his chest. "Shit. I just swore to myself that I wouldn't say anything stupid."

Thomas smiled at him but didn't laugh. "Hey, I get it. A strange city, a new bar. It can be intimidating, so I'm glad you took a chance on us. You're fun to hang out with."

Zachary looked up and was surprised to find Thomas staring right back at him. There was interest in that gaze and some heat.

That couldn't be right. What could Thomas see in Zachary? It had to be his imagination. He swallowed and said, "I wish I had Joe's guts to just walk up to a stranger in a bar and start a conversation."

"Hmm. I'm going to guess you don't go to a lot of bars?"

"Honestly? This is the first gay bar I've ever been to."

Thomas was clearly surprised. "Are you a...," he began, but Zachary blushed.

"I'm not a virgin, if that's what you were going to ask." Just in case he hadn't imagined the interest in Thomas's eyes, he didn't want to scare the man off. "I had gay friends in college, and we'd fool around. A couple of us stayed 'friends with benefits' afterward. With the economy and the job market, though, we all ended up moving back in with our parents. There wasn't a lot of opportunity to, umm, benefit. Plus there're really only a few small dive bars in Ogden, and frankly, umm... I didn't...."

"You didn't want to be seen going in there?" Thomas guessed.

Zachary was ashamed for a moment, but Thomas's voice was kind, so he nodded. "Right. My parents are really narrow-minded and controlling. They didn't like my hobbies, my friends.... Telling them I'm gay would have topped the list of my failings. Every time there was news about a Pride rally or gay marriage, they'd rant like it meant the end of civilization. I'm not proud of this, but I was afraid to be open to them. I knew I wouldn't be able to let them spew that shit at me. It was easier to live in the closet until I got away."

He flicked a glance at Thomas, sure he'd find pity or scorn in his face. He was surprised to find sympathy instead. "I guess that's weak sauce, huh?"

"I understand, Zachary. My parents weren't there for me when I really needed them a few years ago. They said some awful things. Luckily I was in a position to move away, but I can guess what it must have been like. Afraid that you'd lose your home."

Zachary nodded. Maybe Thomas wouldn't despise him for his lack of spine. "Exactly. I told you about the soup kitchen where I volunteered. I was so afraid I'd end up there if I came out."

"I have a feeling you're stronger and more capable than you give yourself credit for, Zachary. Look at you. You've just started a new job in a new city and made new friends already." Thomas bumped his glass against Zachary's in a toast. "At least I hope we'll all be friends."

Zachary stood up straight and squared his shoulders, unreasonably happy at Thomas's words. "I hope so too. All of you are so kind, taking in a stray like me tonight." He turned so he and Thomas stood shoulder to shoulder with their backs against the bar, and looked out across the room. Joe and Terry were talking with the piano player.

They stood comfortably silent for a moment. Zachary finally said, "It turns out I should have just left Ogden earlier, rather than try to make the kind of life I want there." He took the last swallow of his drink and set it on the bar. "Anyway, I might be starting late, but at least I'm starting. Is that lame?"

Thomas smiled. "Not at all. Hell, you get the chance to be a kid in the candy store. DC is a great city when you're young. There are lots of fun bars and clubs and things to do and people to meet. A good-looking man like you will do great here."

Good-looking? Me?

Aloud Zachary said, "I'm really going to try to put myself out there. Of course it helps that I've had three drinks, which is way more than I normally drink at parties. With that courage in my veins, can I ask you something that really is undeniably lame?"

"Of course."

"Can I take a picture with you?"

Thomas guffawed but nicely.

"I know it's immature, but my friend Fred back home didn't believe I'd actually go out to a bar alone. The fact that I'm not only in a bar but talking to the most handsome man *in* the bar is something he needs to see. And oh my God, I'm so embarrassed I just said all that out loud."

"Give me your phone," Thomas said and crooked his fingers. When Zachary complied, Thomas waved Randy over. "Randy, would you do us a favor and take our picture?"

Randy gave Thomas the side-eye but shrugged. "Sure. Why not?"

Thomas turned Zachary to face the bar and put his arm around Zachary's waist to pull them together. Randy snapped the photo and handed the phone back to Zachary, who immediately swiped open the picture. There they were—his boring sandy hair and brown eyes leaning toward Thomas's model-gorgeous head as his beautiful smile stretched his full lips in the picture. A few bar patrons and the piano were visible behind them. Zachary immediately messaged it to Fred and typed:

If they could see me now! You owe me ten bucks.

Thomas looked over Zachary's shoulder as he typed, and he chuckled at the message. Zachary was surprised Thomas didn't remove the hand on his waist. He grew even more surprised when Thomas slightly leaned in to him. His body felt strong and warm against Zachary's side and his cologne smelled of spice and citrus. Zachary was uncomfortably aware of his dick thickening up in his underwear. The traitor seemed to remember how long it had been since he'd had sex.

Zachary happened to glance at the watch on Thomas's other

hand, the one not making him nervous and excited as it rested on his waist. He exclaimed, "Is that a Breitling?"

"You're into watches?" Thomas asked. He raised his wrist to let Zachary have a better look at the heavy device.

"Mainly by osmosis. My father has a watch fetish, so he talks about them constantly. His pride and joy is a Citizen Skyhawk he found on eBay and bought himself for his fiftieth birthday." Zachary forced himself to shut up before he said something stupid about his father not being able to afford the kinds of watches he really lusted for. Watches like the gorgeous and expensive timepiece on Thomas's wrist. He focused on the thick wrist under the watch with its dusting of dark hair.

Not helping with the half-chub.

Thomas lowered his arm back to the bar. "Can I get you another drink?" he asked, but Zachary shook his head.

"I'm already saying things I'm going to regret. I can't imagine what I'd do with another seven and seven in me."

"Hmm… then is there anything else you'd like?" A slight smile curved over Thomas's beautiful mouth as he tightened the hand on Zachary's waist farther.

Zachary's eyes went wide. *No WAY.* Then immediately, *Oh God, yes.* He swallowed hard. Trying to sound calm, as though handsome men picked him often, he said, "I can think of something I want very much."

Thomas touched his lips to Zachary's ear. He murmured, "Then how about we say good night to Joe and Terry and get out of here?"

Zachary inhaled sharply. He was letting himself get picked up in a bar by a man he'd just met and agreeing to go off with him.

Does this seem like me? Or the me I want to become?

He imagined what his parents would say if they knew, but he decided that was a matter for some other time. For some reason he trusted Thomas completely. There was something in his manner that made Zachary feel desirable and brave. He decided to let his nerves go and see where the attraction would lead.

Even with that permission to himself, though, he couldn't help but exclaim, "Really, Thomas? You're so far out of my league that we should be in different sports altogether. Or something. Analogies aren't really my forté."

Thomas ran his fingers up and down Zachary's side. "Don't sell yourself short, pretty boy. I can think of many games I'd like to play with you on my team."

Zachary bit his lip, afraid to speak further for fear of sounding so dumb that Thomas might change his mind. Thomas got Joe's attention, and Joe rushed over, arms outstretched, to grab Zachary in a bone-crushing hug.

Joe was obviously feeling the effects of several cocktails. He exclaimed, "Dear heart, I'm delighted we've met and that you are *our* sort of person." Joe pressed a card into Zachary's hand as he stepped back. "Now this is my phone number. I *insist* that you join Terry and me for brunch soon, all right? Please call during the week, and we'll set a place and time." Zachary grinned and nodded. Then he leaned over and kissed Joe on the cheek. Terry shook his hand and hugged Thomas as well.

"Have a good night. Be careful when you leave, though," Terry warned. "You heard about the poor kid, right? He got killed last week just a few blocks away."

Thomas said, "I only heard someone died, but none of the details. Was it a gay bashing?"

Randy had come up behind them at the bar. He said, "The police aren't sure. I've been following the story on some of the local blogs, but there aren't any details, not even a name. It sounded brutal, though."

Zachary shivered, and Thomas put an arm around his waist

again. "There are two of us. We'll be fine," he said.

They caught a cab on P Street, and Thomas held the door open for Zachary. As they settled into the backseat, Thomas asked, "Is my place okay with you?"

Zachary nodded, and Thomas gave the driver an address on H Street. Then he settled back and took Zachary's hand in his. With his other hand, he traced a fingertip over Zachary's wrist and then ran it down the side of his thumb. Zachary inhaled sharply at the gentle, intimate touch and went hard again in an instant. Thomas smiled at him, and his blue eyes smoldered as he leaned in to kiss Zachary for the first time.

The press of his lips was like warm velvet. Zachary yielded instantly as Thomas slipped his tongue inside to caress his. The kiss didn't last long. As Thomas leaned back, inches from Zachary, he murmured, "I've wanted to do that since I first saw you looking at me in the bar."

Zachary put his head on Thomas's shoulder. "I hope I'm not dreaming this in some alcohol-induced stupor."

Thomas chucked quietly. "You're awake, and if I get my way, you'll be awake for a lot longer."

"How far away is your place?" Zachary asked breathlessly.

"Not far. Tell me if you want to slow this down," Thomas said. Then he whispered in Zachary's ear, "But I hope you don't want to go slow."

Zachary ran his hand up the leg of Thomas's jeans, and trembled slightly as he found a thick bulge. Thomas's cock stirred beneath black denim. The hard flesh under his hand gave Zachary the guts to whisper back, "Not the first time, at least. Maybe we'll slow down for the second round." Thomas chuckled and kissed him again, more deeply, until the cab pulled to a stop.

He adjusted himself discreetly as he climbed out of the cab. They had alighted in front of a modern building. Lots of glass and chrome shone in the reflected streetlight. The lowest level of the building seemed to be filled with high-end stores. There were Ferragamo, Louis Vuitton, and other names Zachary didn't recognize. Thomas held open the door to the building, and they stepped into a large, elegant lobby lined in white marble. Thomas nodded to the concierge and led Zachary to an elevator, which took them to a top-floor apartment.

Once inside Thomas pressed a switch. Low lighting filled the space, but Zachary didn't even have time to take in the details. Thomas helped him out of his coat, threw his own on a chair, and led Zachary down a hallway.

Chapter 3

A S THOMAS LED the way to the bedroom, he was surprised at his own eagerness. He'd had no plans to bring anyone home from the bar, but Zachary felt natural and right.

From the moment Thomas caught sight of him at Mata Hari he'd been attracted. Warm, wide-set brown eyes had looked at him from the end of the bar. Wind-tousled, light-colored hair curled around his ears and near his neck. With that beautiful face, wide shoulders, narrow waist, long and surprisingly thick fingers…Thomas was drawn to Zachary. Of course he looked young and inexperienced. When Thomas asked Randy and it turned out he was twenty-seven, Thomas gave himself permission to explore the attraction. It took no more than pointing Joe toward Zachary, where he stood alone by the piano with his drink. Joe was off like a shot to bring him over.

In Thomas's mind Joe was the ultimate litmus test. Anyone too hung up on himself to accept Joe's kindness at face value, or egotistical enough to think Joe was trying to pick him up, wasn't worth knowing. Zachary passed that test with flying colors. He seemed not only happy to have met Joe, but also able to understand how special Joe really was. His good looks jibed with that generosity of spirit, wit, and intelligence. He even threw a bit of sass at Randy, who could be intimidating as hell. Thomas decided Zachary was someone he wanted to know better.

Of course the sex was strictly a one-time thing, but Zachary had the potential to become a friend afterward. Friendship was all Thomas *could* offer, thanks to Charles fucking Rumson. But then, friends were much harder to find than bed partners anyway. Even after just a few hours of talk, he hoped Zachary would be one of those very few to last beyond the sex.

Thomas felt guilty, though, even as he drew Zachary into his bedroom. He'd broken his own rule by bringing a man home without making everything clear. Thomas let no one stay the night, he didn't date, and he didn't fuck anyone twice. It was a point of pride that he always warned his partners for the evening. The rules helped to steer away those who fantasized about something emotional. They also avoided complications after Thomas and his partner found their pleasure together.

Why didn't I warn Zachary?

He wasn't sure, unless…. Could it be he was unwilling to scare Zachary off until they'd had a night together? Perhaps, but if so, that streak of selfishness troubled him. Nevertheless, he decided not to ruin the moment by bringing it up.

In the bedroom Thomas quieted his mind as he turned on the low bedside lamps. He liked just enough light to keep the mood intimate while allowing him to see the body and face of the night's partner. His bedroom shades were open to reveal a stunning view of the Capitol dome, all lit up and glorious. Zachary didn't seem to notice. He had eyes only for Thomas, who unbuttoned Zachary's oxford shirt while they kissed again. Their tongues stroked each other as he spread the shirt open, pushed it off Zachary's shoulders, and let it drop to the floor.

Thomas broke the kiss to admire Zachary's broad shoulders and long, lean muscles. His torso was winter pale and nearly hairless. His nipples showed in relief as wide circles of brown against marvelously smooth skin. Thomas gave in to the tingling sensation in his hands, which ached to stroke over lovely skin. He ran his fingertips lightly along Zachary's neck and his chest and then down to his narrow waist. Zachary's nipples pebbled around the edges as the nubs firmed like small erasers.

"You have a beautiful body, Zachary. Are you a swimmer?" Thomas asked in a low voice.

Zachary nodded. "Yes, for most of my life. I swam competitively in college, but I keep it up now." He licked his lips, and his hands twitched. "Is it all right if I touch you?"

"I'll be very disappointed if you don't."

Thomas pulled his own shirt off and enjoyed Zachary's intake of breath in reaction to his body. Thomas worked out hard and knew the results were good. He was used to compliments, to the point they no longer did anything for him. But there was something in Zachary's expression that went beyond mere admiration and was almost... predatory. He ran his eyes over Thomas's body. That look made his cock thicken in his pants again. He was always the one in charge, the one to set the pace. There was something about that look, though, that made Thomas wonder what it would be like to be the prey instead of the hunter.

But that wouldn't do—not in the short time they'd have together. Zachary leaned forward but hesitated, his desire clearly at war with his caution. Thomas murmured, "Don't be nervous. I want this as much as you do."

He took Zachary's hand and pressed it to his own chest to stroke his nipple with the fingers of that hand. Zachary swallowed hard and then took over. He squeezed tightly and rolled the nipple between his fingers as he came in for another kiss, more passionate than nervous. Thomas opened for Zachary's tongue and felt it slip into his mouth. Zachary's confidence grew and they caressed each other's bodies. He could feel Zachary's erection against his thigh. He was so hard himself that he thought he might injure his dick if he didn't get it freed soon.

He broke the kiss again and stepped back to unfasten Zachary's belt. Zachary kicked his shoes to the side and pulled off his pants. Thomas did the same and then reached one hand into his own black briefs to grasp his throbbing cock.

"What do you want, Zachary?" he asked, letting his eyes smolder. "Tell me. Let me make you feel good." Zachary looked down at Thomas's hand inside his briefs and reached out to tug off Thomas's underwear. He lowered himself slowly to his knees and focused his eyes on Thomas's erection.

"God, that's a perfect dick. Will you put it in my mouth?" Zachary asked as he raised his eyes up to Thomas's face and opened his jaw wide.

Thomas gripped the base of his thick cock, ran the head around Zachary's lips, and left silver threads from the moisture leaking out of the slit. Then he moved his hips forward and slipped into the warm, wet mouth on offer. Zachary kept his gaze on Thomas's face as he sucked gently. He ran his hands up Thomas's thighs while he bobbed his head and took Thomas deeper and deeper into his mouth each time. Zachary swirled his tongue over the head and into the slit. Then he opened his jaw wider and swallowed the entire cock all the way into his throat.

"Shit, you're talented," Thomas swore under his breath. "Suck me. Yeah, like that," he pleaded as he rocked his hips slightly. Not many people could handle Thomas's girth. Yet Zachary just inhaled him, worked his tight throat muscles around the sensitive head, and brought Thomas toward climax too soon. His dick disappeared into Zachary's mouth and then slipped back into sight, all wet and glistening in the low light. Zachary's lips stretched around the thick tube of flesh, and his tongue rasped lightly against its lower side. He moved his head forward and back to take the dick into his throat each time.

It almost killed Thomas, but he gently withdrew from Zachary's mouth and whispered, "No way I'm going to come this soon. I want to see your cock." He tugged Zachary to his feet and slid his hands down Zachary's waist to push his boxer briefs to the ground.

Zachary's long, slim erection was revealed. As Thomas took it in his hand, he said admiringly, "Now that's a prize at the bottom of a Cracker Jack box." He stroked the smooth, velvety flesh.

Zachary grinned and thrust his hips so he moved in Thomas's hand. "I'm glad you like my dick," he murmured. "I like what you're doing with it."

Thomas kissed him again and smiled against Zachary's lips. "Would you like to feel my mouth on this beautiful piece of meat?"

"God yes," Zachary sighed, and Thomas maneuvered them to the bed. He pushed Zachary down so he was stretched across the comforter, then climbed between his thighs to guide his dick into his mouth. Zachary groaned as Thomas tightened his lips below the head and sucked on it. Zachary bucked his hips and shuddered. His muscles tensing, he put one hand on Thomas's shoulder. "I'm so turned on. I'm afraid I'm going to come too fast."

Thomas lifted his head off Zachary's dick but encircled the shaft and ran his hand up and down the warm flesh in a twisting motion. He asked, "Do you want to come this way? Or maybe you'd like to get fucked."

Zachary gasped, and his cock jerked in Thomas's hand. "Holy shit. Just the thought of you inside me—"

"Good. I want that too." He flattened his tongue and licked all around the head of Zachary's dick to clean off the precome that welled up. Then he retrieved a bottle of lube and a condom from the nightstand. Placing the condom in Zachary's hand, he positioned his body to give access to his cock while he returned to licking Zachary like an ice cream cone.

He poured some lube on his hand and rubbed small circles around Zachary's hole. When he took Zachary's big dick back into his mouth, he was guided by the groans he was evoking. Zachary was loud and responsive, which Thomas appreciated in a bed partner.

Zachary's hole spasmed as Thomas slipped one finger inside his ass. He felt Zachary lick up the length of his cock again, then roll a condom over his shaft. Taking the bottle of lube from Thomas, Zachary coated the sheathed erection. Thomas added a second finger in return.

Zachary gasped, "Oh shit, Thomas. You're gonna make me come. Please. I want to feel you slide into me."

Thomas squeezed the base of Zachary's cock tightly to delay his orgasm, He repositioned himself between Zachary's smooth, warm thighs. When Zachary lifted his legs onto Thomas's shoulders, the shaft of his cock slipped along the crease of Zachary's ass. Thomas smiled at the handsome young man sprawled beneath him, all wanton and yearning.

"You're a wonderful surprise, Zachary," he murmured. "I had an intuition that we'd be good together, but I didn't suspect you'd be quite this free." He grasped his gloved shaft and rubbed the head in circles around Zachary's rim. "You really turn me on."

Zachary threw his head back and shut his eyes as he thrust his hips to try to capture Thomas's cock. He moaned, "You're killing me, Thomas. Fuck me. Oh God, just fuck me."

Thomas stopped his tease and positioned the thick head of his cock against Zachary's opening. He applied pressure as he leaned forward, and sighed when the head slid inside smooth as silk. Most men resisted his size, but Zachary was so worked up that he seemed to draw Thomas in.

Zachary groaned again, and then his eyes were open and intent on Thomas's. He said hoarsely, "That feels fucking amazing. You're so damn *thick*. I want it inside me—all of it. Please, Thomas."

"You got it, Zach," Thomas said through clenched teeth. Then he pushed steadily until his balls rested against Zach's upturned ass.

Wait, when did he become Zach to me?

Never mind. He'd think about it later. "God, you feel good," he moaned and pulled back so he could thrust forward again. Zach clenched his muscles to milk Thomas's cock as he withdrew. "Jesus, that's hot." He stretched Zach's thighs farther back so they could kiss as they fucked.

Zach surprised him by using his teeth to capture Thomas's tongue gently. That sent a surge of pleasure all the way down to his cock. The mischief in Zach's eyes was enchanting as he compelled Thomas to keep his head still even as he rocked his hips. Zach's long, hard dick pressed between their bodies, and wetness from the tip smeared his belly.

Zach reached up with one hand to find Thomas's nipple. He squeezed and tugged on it in time with Thomas's thrusts inside him to egg him on to fuck faster and harder. Even though Thomas was on top, Zach seemed to be in charge. He pulled at Thomas as he guided him toward a beautiful orgasm. That was as unexpected as it was new to Thomas, and it spurred him on to greater effort. He flexed his cock as he thrust upward with his hips, delighted to see Zach's eyes roll back.

Zach released the tongue between his teeth to gasp, "Shit, Thomas. I can't hold off. Oh shit, oh shit," and then his cock shot what seemed to be a gallon of come up his chest. It splattered against his chin, the pillows, and even the headboard behind him.

"Fuck," Thomas cursed as his orgasm hit too and he felt his load empty into the rubber. He pressed so deeply inside Zach that he was almost afraid he'd puncture an internal organ. "Ah, Zach, that's too good," he cried out as wave after wave of his orgasm washed over him and out his dick. Zach's eyes were half-closed in ecstasy, and the glow of pleasure on his face warmed Thomas to the core.

Zach wrapped both arms tightly around him and held him until his body stopped trembling and finally stilled. With a groan Thomas shifted positions to allow Zach to lower his legs. Then he held the end of the condom as he slowly withdrew from Zach's body.

Holy shit.

As he rolled onto his back, he pulled off the condom. He tied the end, threw it in the nearby wastebasket, and sagged back down onto the bed, still breathless. Something about the way Zach gave and took pleasure was utterly unique, and Thomas had to squash the thought, *More....*

Zach reached for him and then stopped with a chuckle. "Umm. I'm all sticky here. Do you have a towel?" Thomas gave him a quick kiss and got up to fetch a wet washcloth and a dry hand towel.

Kneeling by the side of the bed, he ran the warm cloth over Zach's body carefully to wipe off the river of come. Thomas stroked Zach's chest, his stomach, and then finally the head of his long cock. He followed up with the dry towel and took care of the lithe body in his bed. He made sure Zach was dry and comfortable.

Thomas's stunned response to the way they fit together alarmed him, and he knew he had to pull his patented dick move. Yet he found himself delaying as he made sure Zach felt good.

He quickly swiped at his own chest and belly. After swabbing at the headboard with a low laugh, he tossed the washcloth and hand towel into the bathroom. When he climbed back into bed, Zach pressed his long, lean body against him. He rested his head on Thomas's shoulder and whispered, "That was amazing. Thank you."

His body fit perfectly, and Thomas held tight for one moment longer. He kissed Zach's brow and told himself it was best to rip off the Band-Aid quickly. In a louder voice than he intended, Thomas turned his head and said, "You're a tiger—I didn't see that coming. I'm glad we had this chance, Zach. You're going to have fun out there."

He felt Zach freeze against his body as he clearly caught the unspoken message. *Out there with other guys. Not here with me.* After a long moment, Zach rolled his face away from Thomas and asked in a quiet tone, "Do you want me to leave?"

His disappointment made Thomas ache. "You're more than welcome to stay the night this one time," he answered. Only then did he realize he had broken another one of his entrenched rules. For the first time in Thomas didn't know how long, he wanted to see more of this surprising young man.

Would it be so bad?

He choked down the thought as well as the regret he felt at pushing Zach away. What if he were wrong again? What if Zach were just putting on an act of normalcy and naïveté? Thomas couldn't take the risk because, even dead, Charles Rumson was still fucking up his life.

"You're a beautiful man, Zach," he said into the silence that lingered between them.

"So you said." Zach climbed out of bed to look for his underwear. If Thomas had hoped to ease the awkwardness, he failed. Silence stretched. Zach's long legs and lean flanks glowed in the dim room. Thomas wanted to reach for him, even though he knew he would merely prolong things.

Zach suddenly whirled to face him, briefs in one hand and shirt clenched in the other. "Did I do something wrong?"

Thomas's resolve disappeared at the sadness he heard in that question. He stood up from the bed and reached out to touch Zach's waist. "No, nothing wrong at all," he said in his most reassuring voice. "This is just how it is with me. I don't date. I don't do repeats. With anyone."

"God, I'm such an idiot," Zach sighed. "I have so much to learn." The disappointment was rapidly turning to hurt. That was par for the course. Normally Thomas would just let it alone, but he didn't want Zach to beat himself up over Thomas's issues.

"I'm sorry, Zach. I should have made it clear before we left the bar that sex is a one-time thing for me. I'd like to be your friend, but I can't do anything more."

Zach looked at him, and a little frown line appeared between his eyes. "Can't? What does that mean?"

Well, shit. The man is quick. I should have left it alone after all.

"Nothing. I'm just an asshole. Okay? Ask Randy. He'll tell you this is absolutely about me and not you. And I know that sounds like a cliché, but it's true. Please don't take it as an insult or a slight. You're a hot man, Zach, and you're going to meet many other hot men. It's what I said earlier—you should be a kid in a candy store and lick every lollipop you can find."

That earned him a little smile. "I was always more partial to pop rocks," Zach said, and the slightest smirk stretched his beautiful mouth.

Thomas relaxed a bit and stroked up and down Zach's side. "How do you feel about Sweet Tarts?"

"Well, you were kind of tasty," Zach teased. "Or are we still talking about candy?"

Relief washed over him. Good. Zach got it. Maybe Thomas would actually manage to keep a friend out of his own fucked-up

situation. He hoped so anyway. Zach had depths worth exploring. As a friend.

*But maybe a little more time together first wouldn't hurt? This
one night?*

Thomas grinned as he said, "I deserved that. Look, Zach, I'm
being honest here. You can leave, which I completely understand.
I'd hope the next time we run into each other at Mata Hari,
you'd still have a drink with me and give friendship a shot. You
could also ignore me, which I would regret, and chalk this up to a
life lesson."

He still had his hand on Zach, and he carefully began to
stroke toward Zach's chest. He didn't quite graze his nipple,
though he could tell it was getting stiff again. "But it's only two
in the morning, and I'm betting you don't have to be up early on
a Sunday. There was big talk earlier about taking the second
round a little more slowly...."

Zach sank down onto the edge of the bed and bit his lower
lip. Thomas sat beside him and looked at him with his best
puppy-dog eyes as he let his hand drift down Zach's firm belly.
His fingertips grazed the wispy hair at the base of Zach's
hardening dick.

"You really are an asshole, aren't you?" Zach observed, but a
smile tugged at the corner of his mouth. "Well, if all I get is one
night with the most handsome man in the world before a walk of
shame in the morning, I'd better make it count."

He fell forward and pushed Thomas onto his back. He
brought his hands up around Thomas's head and tightened his
fingers in his wavy hair.

• • •

ZACHARY WOKE UP in thick, white blankets and looked around
the stark room, confused.

Thomas walked in with two mugs of coffee. "I don't know how you take it, so one is black and one is cream and sugar," he said, holding out both cups.

Zachary ran a hand through his hair and said, "Black is great, thanks." He took the proffered mug and inhaled the strong aroma that wafted out. "That smells great. Thank you."

"My pleasure." Thomas took a sip from his mug, his eyes on Zachary's neck. The silence stretched between them awkwardly. Finally Thomas said, "Help yourself to the shower, if you want. We worked up quite a sweat."

Zachary nodded. "I will. Thanks." He drank deeply from his mug, set it on the nightstand, and climbed out of bed. He hesitated and then said, "I'd better get cleaned up and out of your way."

Fifteen minutes later Zachary buttoned up his overcoat and pushed open the glass door from the lobby. Emerging onto the street, he looked left and right as he tried to get his bearings. Finally he started toward the Capitol. He felt the need to take a long walk while he figured out how he had misjudged the evening so badly.

Of course he had known Thomas was too sexy to find him worth pursuing. But he had felt a connection beyond the physical. Thomas did too. He was almost sure of it.

He tried to let the disappointment go. Maybe Thomas knew what he was talking about. Maybe Zachary needed to grow up, move on, and enjoy the bounty of good-looking men in the city. Be a kid in the candy store indeed.

But it would be hard to forget Thomas's hands on his body or that look of wonder he gave Zachary when he came.

Zachary headed into the chill morning breeze, his head down in thought. He was completely unaware of the man in the silver-framed glasses who trailed after him.

Chapter 4

ZACHARY RELUCTANTLY PRESSED speed dial for his parents' phone in Ogden. His mother picked up. Apparently Caller ID gave him away, because she said, "Oh good. I was going to call you tonight if we didn't hear from you."

He squelched his guilt and just said, "Sorry, Mom. I've been pretty busy settling in to the job and the apartment."

"They aren't working you hard already, are they?" she asked, and Zachary could hear the helicopter-parent edge to her tone.

"I've been to a lot of training classes on how the systems work and how they do things at Treasury. It's fine." He sounded petulant to himself and vowed to work on that. "I really like my boss and the people I work with."

"Well, that's something, at least. I still don't understand why you took that job instead of waiting for the supervisor position to open up here."

"I told you, Mom. This is a great opportunity for me. With Treasury Department experience on my résumé, I can move into higher levels of management."

"But you're so far away in that awful place. It's only a matter of time until the terrorists strike."

Zachary rolled his eyes. "Mom, that could be true anywhere. I'm not going to hide away because of the possibility of an attack."

"Did you find a church to join yet?"

He winced. "Not yet."

"Well, you get on that. The Lord will protect you, but you have to meet Him halfway."

"Yes, ma'am." Desperate to change the subject, he asked about his father and his younger brother. He managed to end the call before his mother could ask if he had met any nice girls yet.

He wished he had the guts to come out to his parents. Every time he reached for the words, though, he pictured scared teenagers holding out bowls in the soup kitchen. What if he told them and then the job at Treasury didn't work out? He might need to go back to Ogden. He couldn't afford to burn that bridge to his childhood. It was just common sense to keep his secret, and his parents really didn't need to know yet anyway.

I'm a fucking coward.

Full of self-recrimination, he listlessly wandered around his one-bedroom rental. He trailed his fingers over the surfaces. The small apartment in Alexandria, Virginia was a short commute from Washington. He liked it well enough. Everything was unpacked. His *Sandman* leather-bound omnibus collection had pride of place among his graphic novels and other books. His DVDs were organized by series and then by year. The *Doctor Who* boxed sets alone took up an entire shelf. Every one of the *Star Trek* and *Star Wars* movies, series, and cartoons were lined up below that.

He'd reluctantly left his comic book collection in Utah, but his books and movies were precious souvenirs. He'd lived childhood as an outsider and a despised nerd. His parents' criticisms every time he came home with a new item they thought was beneath his intelligence had stung. The treasures were proof to him that he had made it through and got out of Utah in one piece.

That night, though, even with the place as homelike as he

could make it, Zachary was unable to settle down. He found he had no patience to sit and watch one of his movies or television shows. He couldn't even concentrate on a book.

What he really needed was to make some friends. Thomas immediately sprang to mind, but he recognized that impulse for a bad idea. The way Thomas had showed him the door Sunday morning was crystal clear. Whatever moment Zachary thought they had shared, whatever pleasure in each other's company and bodies, he must have overstated to himself. Maybe Thomas was sincere about trying to become friends. Zachary knew, though, the sight of Thomas turning his blue eyes to a new partner would flay him to the bone.

On the other hand, Mata Hari was a nice, friendly bar. Joe and Terry were fun. Maybe they'd be around that night. Or he could call the number on Joe's card. In any case Mata Hari seemed like a good place to start meeting new people. It was just a twenty-minute cab ride away. He told himself firmly he was *not* going there to see Thomas. Really.

That turned out to be good, because Thomas wasn't around when he entered the bar. In fact only about fifteen people sat about the main room. Terry was indeed there, talking to a youngish man Zachary hadn't met, but there was no sign of Joe. Zachary took a seat at the bar, and Randy looked up at him as he wiped a glass dry.

"Seven and seven?" he asked.

"Yes, thanks, Randy. Good memory," Zachary said, and Randy grunted. "Quiet night?"

Randy turned to fix his drink but said over his shoulder. "Yeah. Thursdays haven't taken off yet. Thomas won't be in, case you're wondering." He set the glass in front of Zachary, who blushed.

"I wasn't wondering."

"Good."

Randy turned away to rinse some more glasses, and Zachary blurted out, "You guys are friends, right? I mean, he's not just a customer?"

Randy shot him a look that would have made him run a year before. Zachary held his ground, though, and gazed unflinchingly back at Randy. That was part of the reason for the move—to find his balls and finally grow up. He wanted to be far away from the controlling parents who made him feel he had to deny everything true about himself. Next to his parents' constant pressure and disapproval, Randy's glare was nothing. He pushed down the nerves and refused to blink or turn away. After a moment he could have sworn he saw amusement grow in Randy's eyes.

"We're friends," the bartender finally said, grudgingly. "Thomas and I used to work together, sort of, before I retired."

"You look way too young to retire. What did you do before?" Zachary asked.

"I used to be Secret Service," Randy answered as he pulled some bottles out of a box behind the bar.

"No kidding? Was that exciting?" Zachary dared to press since Randy wasn't growling yet.

"Not so you'd notice, most days. But that's kind of the point. When things got exciting, it was usually because they'd turned to shit."

"Oh. Well, that makes sense. I know law enforcement personnel can retire younger than the rest of us, but still, you give up some benefits." Zachary was obviously fishing and Randy gave him a raised eyebrow. He pushed ahead anyway. "Did you have such a burning desire to open a bar that you couldn't wait?"

"That's it, kid. I traded black suits and exotic travel to stock a bar and answer nosy questions." That would have stung, except that Zachary could see an amused glint in Randy's eye.

"Was Thomas in the Secret Service too?"

Randy shot him another look. That one *was* stern enough to make Zachary's testicles run up into his abdomen to hide. "You'd better ask Thomas if there's anything you want to know about him. But I wouldn't bother, kid. He won't answer." Randy turned back to his bottles and continued to check items off an inventory.

Zachary quietly sipped his drink for a minute and looked around the room. He noticed Terry had his hand on the other man's knee, and things between them looked surprisingly intimate. None of his business, he supposed, but Joe was so nice. Zachary hated to think Terry was maybe cheating on him.

Randy apparently noticed where Zachary's attention was focused. He said, "Terry and Joe have an open relationship. Don't judge."

Zachary snapped his eyes back to Randy. "I'm not judging. Honestly. I was worried for Joe's sake, but it sounds like they're fine."

"They are." Randy set down his inventory, picked up a bottle of tequila and two small glasses, and poured them each a shot. "This is for caring about Joe." Zachary grinned and clinked his shot glass against Randy's. They both tossed them back and slammed the glasses on the counter.

Emboldened, Zachary said, "Thomas said I should ask you to confirm he's an asshole."

Randy quirked an eyebrow at him. "Context?"

"He told me he never takes anyone home twice, that it's his issue and nothing to do with me, and that you'd confirm it."

Randy stared at Zachary for a moment. "That's surprising. But yes, all that is true. I've had to sweep up three broken glasses that different people threw at Thomas's head. They didn't believe he was strictly about the fuck-and-chuck."

Zachary winced. "Ouch. I've never even heard that expression before, and I hate myself a bit."

"Like Thomas said, it's his issue, not yours. No repeats, no exceptions. And no more questions."

Randy turned away, clearly done with the conversation. Zachary took the not-too-subtle hint and carried his seven and seven to the piano. The woman playing it glanced up as she moved her hands over the keys.

"The boys here call me Miss Ethel. Anything you'd like to hear, hon?" she asked.

"I love what you're playing now."

She smiled and kept working through her repertoire. When Zachary recognized a Nina Simone song, he began to sing the lyrics quietly.

Miss Ethel nodded encouragingly at him. "That's a nice tenor, hon. Sing out."

The tequila had kicked in, so Zachary began to sing the lyrics with a bit more confidence. Two of the other patrons came over to join him through the verses. When the song ended, one of the men squealed in delight.

"Oooh, that was lovely. You should come sing with the Chorus."

Zachary asked, "Chorus?"

"The Washington Gay Men's Chorus. Auditions are soon, and *you're* front-row material," said one of the men. "I'm Howard, and this is Steve." They chatted, and Miss Ethel obliged Steve's request to play another torch song to which they all knew the lyrics.

*　 ⁂ 　*

RANDY WATCHED ZACHARY out of the corner of his eye. *Nice young man.* He had a spine and a good heart to worry about Joe that way. Randy understood the arrangement Joe had with Terry. Some occasional outside sex was fine if it was with no one they both socialized with and didn't look like dating or an attachment. It wasn't a deal he'd want, but then, relationships didn't seem to take for him in any case. If it worked for Joe and Terry, more power to them.

Zachary clearly meant well, though. Too bad he was the latest in a long line to be hung up on Thomas. Maybe he'd get over the crush and stick around anyway. Thomas could use that.

It surprised Randy that Thomas had told Zachary to ask him for confirmation of his assholery. Not that Randy would hesitate to say it to Thomas's face, but he didn't think his friend had ever bothered before to reassure one of his play partners that the problem was with him. Randy got it, though. That business with Rumson had fucked up his world something awful.

The door to the bar opened. Randy glanced up and immediately stiffened. Twenty-five years in law enforcement let him recognize a cop as soon she walked in, even wearing plain clothes.

Her black hair was pulled into a tight ponytail, and she wore a fitted, gray wool coat paired with dark jeans and boots with thick heels. At a guess she chose the heels to add to her height. She'd be about five foot five in bare feet. A couple of women on one of the sofas discreetly checked her out as she crossed the room to the bar. Randy covered a smile at that.

He thought quickly. No, his liquor license was up to date. His permit for the gun he kept beneath the bar in case of trouble was also current. It must be about something else.

The woman offered a badge as she reached him. "Good evening, sir. I'm Detective Torres, Metropolitan Police Department." Randy glanced at the MPD badge and then back at her. "Do you have a minute for a few questions?" she asked.

"Sure," he said.

Detective Torres pulled a photo out of the inside pocket of her jacket and handed it to him. "Do you recognize this man?"

Randy studied the picture. The face did look familiar—blond hair, hipster beard, and glasses. He was too young and scrawny for Randy's tastes, but fairly nice-looking. "I think he was in here a few times, maybe," Randy said after a minute.

Torres accepted the picture back as she said, "He lived in the neighborhood. We're looking for information on where he liked to hang out, who he knew."

"Knew? Lived?"

"His name is Brian Gallagher. He was murdered in his apartment about ten days ago." Torres watched his face carefully, but Randy didn't fake his surprise.

"I heard someone was killed, but it didn't occur to me it might be someone who came in here."

"The victim talked to a friend the night he was murdered, and he mentioned that he had just left a bar. Do you think it was this one?"

"What night was this?" Randy asked. He tried to think. He was usually good with faces, and a crawling sensation began to climb through his gut as his memory worked.

"Saturday before last. The thirteenth," Torres told him. "His friend said he came to meet a man but left early and went right home. From her phone log, this would have been about ten p.m."

Randy nodded. "Yeah, I remember him now. He came up to the bar to talk to one of my customers and started rubbing up against him. The customer turned him down, and the kid—Brian, you said?—started making a scene and then stormed out."

"Do you know the customer's name?"

Randy sighed to himself but tried to keep his face neutral. "Yes. It's Thomas Scarborough. He's actually an investor in the bar and a friend of mine."

Torres wrote notes on a pad. Without looking up, she asked, "Did Mr. Scarborough follow him out?"

"No. He was at the bar quite a while after Brian left. I can give you some other names to corroborate that."

Torres flashed a glance up at him. "Ex-cop?" she asked.

"I was a Secret Service agent until I retired last year. This is my bar."

Torres looked around and nodded. "Nice place." She focused again on Randy. "Did you see anyone else follow Gallagher out?"

"No, I didn't notice anything like that. Saturdays are pretty busy, and there were plenty of people coming and going."

"I'd like to talk to Mr. Scarborough. Can you give me his phone number?"

"No, but I'll give him your card if you leave one. He's at a conference in Tokyo, I think, but he's due back Sunday."

"You know his travel schedule?" Torres asked, her dark eyebrow arched.

"Like I said, we're friends," Randy explained with a shrug. Torres asked his name, and he gave it. As she continued to scribble notes, he tilted his head toward the photo and said, "Papers called it brutal. Gay bashing?"

Torres considered his question for a moment and then said, "We don't think so. It appears the killer targeted him, but the attack was sexual in nature."

"Shit. Poor kid."

"Yeah. Here's my card," Torres said as she slid the small rectangle across the bar. She held the card down with her manicured nails, which were cut short and carried no nail polish. Randy approved the lack of color. It supported the air of gravity Torres cultivated. "I'd like to hear from Mr. Scarborough Monday morning so I don't need to make another trip over here." Randy nodded. Torres looked around the room one more time, and then her bootheels clicked lightly across the floor of the bar.

As Randy slid the business card into his pocket, Zachary came back to the bar with his two new friends. They bought a round, and Zachary asked, "Did I see that woman flash a badge at you?"

Randy shot him an annoyed look. "You wanna keep it down, kid? Cops are bad for business."

"Sorry. Just nosy. Ignore me."

Randy grunted and started to turn away, but then he said, "Watch yourself when you leave, okay? Someone killed a guy in the neighborhood. The police are investigating, but it makes me nervous."

"Actually Howard and Steve here want to take me to another bar, so we should be fine."

"Good. Stick together until this thing is sorted out." He rapped his knuckles on the bar twice.

•　○　○

THE MAN WATCHED his computer monitors in a darkened room. He had tossed a pair of silver-framed glasses nearby on the desk. The camera hidden beneath the counter along the wall at Mata Hari provided a good view of the bar.

He replayed the recording from a few hours earlier several times. He watched carefully as the woman interviewed the bartender, showed her badge, and offered the photo. From this angle he could make out more of the exchange than he had been able to from inside the bar. It had seemed prudent to remain at a distance from the officer then. Even with no sound capability, the interaction was clear. Someone had connected the bar to that cretin he had punished.

He would have to be more careful. The man drummed his fingers against his desk. He needed to get additional cameras in place, with more lines of sight. Then he could stop taking the reckless action of entering Mata Hari himself, just to be near. It would be difficult to stay away. But he had to do it until he was ready to lay the traces and draw his Beloved to him.

The latest excrescence that had dared to go home with his Beloved had been in the bar as well. He was visible on the tape as he talked to the bartender. The rule was clear. If he stayed away from the Beloved, then there would be no need to chastise him. But the man thought this one, this blond boy, would break the rule. He stayed the night with the Beloved, and now he was back in Mata Hari sniffing around for more.

The man gritted his teeth and thought about different ways to make the creature pay. Then his smile stretched cruelly as he came up with some very pleasant possibilities. If that one did indeed break the rule, then the rule would break him.

Chapter 5

ON MONDAY MORNING Thomas fingered the scrap of paper with the number Randy had read to him over the phone. He felt reluctant to call the police for any reason after the treatment he got during the Rumson mess. But Brian Gallagher was dead. If Thomas could help bring his killer to justice, he would talk to the detective.

He pressed his intercom. "Anne, can you free up twenty minutes or so this afternoon on my schedule? I need to handle something personal."

"Yes, sir," his secretary responded. After a few moments, she called him back to say she had moved a meeting, so he was free at one thirty.

At the designated time, Thomas finished eating a chicken salad sandwich at his desk and threw away the wrapper. After closing his office door, he dialed the number Randy had given him and waited.

"Torres," he heard a woman say in clipped tones.

"Detective, my name is Thomas Scarborough. Randy Vaughan at Mata Hari said you want to talk to me about Brian Gallagher."

He heard a chair squeak as Torres apparently sat down. "Thank you for calling, Mr. Scarborough. I understand you were in Tokyo?" Her tone was polite and friendly.

Ah, we're going to start with pleasantries.

"That's right. I spoke at a conference there. I just got back late last night."

"I appreciate you calling me quickly, then. So as I'm sure Mr. Vaughan told you, I'm investigating the murder on the thirteenth. How well did you know Mr. Gallagher?" she asked.

"Well, I don't really know him. Didn't know…. I mean, I met him at the bar, we hooked up one time, and that was it."

"Is that a common practice for you, to hook up with someone you don't really know?"

Thomas bristled. "I don't see how that's relevant, but yes, I normally keep my sex life separate from my friends."

"No boyfriend?" Torres asked.

Thomas snapped, "Oh, come on. I didn't know I was calling in to a morals lecture."

"Mr. Scarborough, I couldn't care less what you do in bed as long as it had nothing to do with Brian Gallagher's death. But let me rephrase my question. Do you have a boyfriend who might get jealous about your hookups?"

Thomas gritted his teeth. "No. No boyfriend. No lover, husband, wife, significant other, any of that."

"Thank you for that thorough answer." Thomas could hear a pen scratching as she apparently took notes of their conversation. "Now help me with the timeline, please. When exactly did you meet Gallagher?"

"It must have been on the sixth, because I think it was exactly a week before I saw him again. We met at Mata Hari that evening, talked for an hour or so, and then I took him home. He left a few hours later, and the next time I talked to him was on the thirteenth."

"What did you talk about the night you met?"

"Jesus, I don't know. It was bar talk," Thomas said. "He flirted with me, and I was in the mood. We just exchanged the usual banter until we decided to leave together."

"Did he say anything to indicate he was worried? Maybe he was cheating on a boyfriend?"

"No, he didn't tell me anything like that. He seemed fairly relaxed, and I didn't get the sense he was nervous or hiding."

"Okay. Where did you go when you left the bar?"

"My apartment."

"And…?" Torres prompted.

"And." Thomas was exasperated. "We had sex. Is that what you want to know? We had sex. Then he left."

"How many times did you have sex?"

What the fuck?

"How can that be relevant?"

"Humor me, Mr. Scarborough. This is a murder investigation, not a talk show. I'm not asking the details of your life for shits and grins."

Thomas ran a hand back through his hair and snorted. "Two times. We had sex twice. Then I showed him out about one in the morning."

"Impressive. My boyfriend hasn't managed twice in the same night for about two years."

Thomas said drily, "I feel sorry for you, Detective."

She chuckled mirthlessly and continued her questions. "Did you exchange phone numbers or addresses with Gallagher?"

"No. He asked for my number, in fact, and I said that wasn't a good idea."

"Why wasn't it a good idea?"

"I don't hook up with men more than once," Thomas said. "I don't like complications."

"No boyfriend. No repeats. Interesting."

Thomas could hear more scratching of her pen, and it began to bug the shit out of him. He barked into the phone, "Detective

Torres, I only have twenty minutes. Is there anything you'd like to ask me about Brian Gallagher, or are you just going to armchair psychoanalyze me?"

Her tone changed abruptly from friendly to serious. "Did you talk to Gallagher or see him between the time he left your apartment and the evening of the thirteenth?"

"No, as I already said. And I didn't expect to see him on the thirteenth either. I was in Mata Hari having a drink, and he came up to me."

"What did you talk about on the thirteenth?"

"He started rubbing my shoulder, and he whispered that he wanted me to, umm, have sex with him again."

"I'm a cop. You can say 'fuck.' How did you respond?"

"I was talking to someone else, so I shook his hand off my shoulder, and I said that wasn't going to happen."

"By someone else do you mean another hookup?"

"Maybe if you got laid more, you wouldn't be as judgmental about my sex life."

"Maybe if you had talked to Gallagher, he'd still be alive."

Thomas inhaled sharply. "I'm not appreciating the abuse, Detective. I've given you my time, and you chose to waste it on your own personal bullshit. If you have no further relevant questions to ask, then I'm going to hang up now."

Torres ignored his fit of pique and continued to ask questions. "Who were you talking to when Gallagher approached you?"

"A friend. Terry Krasnopoler. We chatted at the bar for about an hour, I think, after Gallagher came and went."

"Mr. Vaughan said he made a scene. Gallagher, I mean."

"Yes. When I told him we weren't going to get together again, he asked me to go out with him for dinner. I said that wasn't going to happen either. He said some unflattering things about the size and firmness of my penis. Then he grabbed my glass from the bar and threw what was left of my scotch in my face. He slammed down the glass and left."

"And what did you do, when he threw the drink in your face?"

"Try not to sound so amused, Detective. It's unprofessional. Randy gave me a bar towel to dry off my face and shirt, and I kept talking to Terry and to Randy."

"All right. When did you leave Mata Hari that night?"

"It was about eleven. I don't know exactly, but I was home by eleven thirty because I noticed the clock when I walked in."

"Who can confirm you were at the bar until eleven?"

"Well, Randy, of course. And Terry was there talking for a while, but he left before me. Oh, and Miss Ethel. That's Ethel Johnson. She plays piano at Mata Hari Tuesday to Saturday. I bought her a drink and chatted with her between sets that evening. I left when she went back to play."

"I'd like those names and their contact information to confirm your recollection of the time."

"All right," Thomas said and read to her Terry and Miss Ethel's full names and phone numbers from the contact app on his phone. "Should I assume I'm a suspect, Detective?" he asked calmly.

"That's a loaded word, Mr. Scarborough," she answered. "You had a public altercation with a man who ended up dead a few hours later. Let's leave it as person of interest for now."

"Let's," Thomas agreed caustically. "I had nothing to do with Brian Gallagher's death. You'll note that I didn't ask for a lawyer to be on the line when we spoke. But I'll leave you to your investigation."

TORRES SAT BACK in her chair after Scarborough disconnected the call. He'd confirmed some of the details from her prior interview of Sandra Yu. She had reported that Scarborough had sex two times with the vic, he didn't give his phone number, and Gallagher approached him without making a prior date. She circled that item in her notes. It meant Scarborough probably didn't know in advance where Gallagher would be that night.

She'd call the contacts he gave but felt little doubt they would also check out. On the other hand, Gallagher was likely killed between midnight and three a.m., so Scarborough's timeline didn't give him an alibi. Another moment's thought, though, and she dismissed the point. Scarborough was clearly intelligent, and her quick research indicated he was a lawyer himself. If he were the killer, he would likely have been cleverer about his cover story.

She deliberately tried to rile him up with the personal questions. Still, his answers didn't set off her bullshit detector. Revenge over a public scene? Unlikely. Scarborough held an important political job. He wouldn't have that with a flaring temper.

Her instincts told her Gallagher making a scene at the bar and then getting killed a few hours later was not a coincidence. Somehow he drew the wrong attention.

She needed to do some more work on Thomas Scarborough.

Chapter 6

ZACHARY WOKE SUNDAY morning to the chirp of his cell phone. Blearily he checked the time—only eight thirty. Ugh.

He didn't recognize the displayed phone number but connected the call anyway. "'Lo," he muttered, his mouth half-buried in his pillow.

"Is this Zachary? I'm sure this was the number you left in your message. Darling, did I wake you?" It took Zachary a moment, but then he recognized the Boston accent.

"Joe, hi. How are you?" Zachary asked with a yawn.

"I did wake you. Oh dear. I'll call back later."

"No, this is fine, Joe. I should get up anyway," Zachary said as he rolled over and stretched in his bed.

"Well, if you're sure. I won't keep you, dear heart. I just want to ask if you're free for brunch today."

"Umm… sure. Why not?"

"Wonderful. Meet us at Mistral about eleven. It's on Fourteenth Street between O and P. Will you remember that, darling, or should I have Terry send a text?"

Zachary chuckled. "No need. I've got it, Joe. Mistral, Fourteenth Street. I'll see you at eleven."

After another ten lazy minutes, Zachary rousted himself out of bed. He pulled on his Speedo and some track pants and a sweatshirt. Stopping only to grab a quick cup of coffee at the corner Starbucks, he headed toward the nearby gym. Its swimming pool was empty that morning. He stashed his street clothes and towel at the side of the room and slipped into the cool water. One hundred lengths of the pool later, he felt vigorous and ready to face the day.

By ten thirty, dressed in nice but casual clothes, he climbed into his car rather than taking the Metro. On a Sunday morning, he figured the drive into DC wouldn't be too bad, and he was right. Traffic was light, and he found the restaurant easily. There was even a parking space less than a block away. All in all it was a positive, upbeat way to spend a Sunday. He practically hummed as he walked into the restaurant.

Then he recalled what a bitch karma really could be. "Ah shit," he muttered.

Thomas sat at a table with Joe and Terry and another man about Zachary's age. They had left an empty chair for him between Thomas and the stranger.

Well, at least it doesn't look like Thomas is here with a date.

Joe spotted him as he entered. He waved effusively while Thomas turned and gave him a friendly yet neutral nod. Zachary bent to kiss Joe on the cheek and then Terry, and slid into the empty chair.

"Zachary, darling, this is Walter," Joe said, and they shook hands. Walter had dark hair, glasses, and wore a sweater vest. He was pleasant-enough looking, if a bit nerdy. But then who was Zachary to make fashion judgments? Pleasant and nerdy was sort of how he saw himself.

"Nice to meet you, Walter," Zachary said. Walter turned red and choked out something polite in response.

Thomas touched his shoulder lightly. "Good to see you again," he said, and Zachary turned to face him. His stomach was in knots. It would have been easier if he didn't catch a moment of heat in Thomas's gaze when their eyes met.

He managed to force out a banal greeting and did his best to match Thomas's light tone. "Good to see you too. I love your shirt." Of course he did—it was beautifully made and tailored to Thomas's muscular body.

Thomas glanced down as if he'd forgotten what he wore and then up at Zachary. He casually leaned back in his chair. "Glad you like it. Coffee?"

"Yes, please." Thomas looked around for the waiter and ordered him black coffee.

He remembered.

Zachary turned away and stifled his disappointment. He would never again see the body under that fitted shirt. Minor regret swelled into a wave that threatened to drown his heart. They had shared one evening in Mata Hari and a few incredible hours alone. It was just long enough for Zachary to glimpse canyons and mountains in Thomas's soul. But from Thomas's reserve, Zachary understood he would never get to explore there.

Joe's voice brought him back to the present company. He said impishly, "Walter, Zachary just moved to Washington recently. It occurred to me that you have a lot in common."

Zachary turned his attention to Walter and tried a smile to help the poor guy relax a bit. "What do you do?" he asked.

"Umm… I'm a financial analyst with the Treasury Department." He said it in a strangled voice and could barely meet Zachary's eye.

"I work for Treasury as well, but I'm in human resources."

"Oh."

Well, that seemed to kill the topic.

Things got a little easier after a pitcher of mimosas arrived, however. Everyone other than Walter relaxed a bit. Joe tried to get Walter to talk to Zachary. Apparently it was an attempted fix-up. Zachary appreciated the thought, but he had his doubts about

Joe's matchmaking skills.

When Walter once again failed to respond with more than a two-word answer, Zachary turned to Joe. "Tell me more about your shelter."

Joe reached across the table to take Zachary's hand and said, "My dear, it's the most important thing I've ever done. We have thirty-five beds, and we try to feed these children one hot meal a day and give them a safe place to sleep. It's never enough, but it's vital to give them *something*. A bit of hope."

Terry smiled fondly at Joe as he removed his wire-framed glasses and tucked them in his shirt pocket. "That's how we met, you know," he said to Zachary. "Joe needed some financial help to set up his foundation and learn how to handle donations."

Joe chortled. "A foundation. As if I were a blue-haired dowager."

"I think you did have blue hair at the time, didn't you?" Terry asked.

"At most it was a blue rinse, just to bring out my eyes."

"Is finding donors difficult?" Zachary asked. "I mean, an LGBT shelter is kind of a charged topic, I would think. Controversial and maybe risky for philanthropists."

Joe answered seriously, "We've been very fortunate on the monetary side." He gave a slight glance in Thomas's direction. "Actually on all fronts. I had no real conception of what I had undertaken. Many, many people gave their time and their talents, as well as their funds, to get the shelter open and then to make it run. We have something of a routine established, and steady financial support. What I find most demanding now is coordination of the day-to-day operations. I insist that the teenagers who stay with us contribute through chores or odd jobs. But just organizing all the volunteers, finding supplies, spreading the word, putting a meal on the table…. Well, I may have taken our

Lord's name in vain more than once."

Zachary and Thomas laughed at that, and Thomas shot him a guilty look, as though embarrassed to share in the joke. That seemed curious to Zachary.

Maybe this isn't as easy for him as he pretends.

Aloud he said, "I'd really like to get involved, Joe. I don't have the money to be any use to you as a donor. I'm super organized, though, and it would mean a lot to me."

"You treasure. Of course I'd love your help," Joe said. "Terry will send you the address, so you just come by one evening after work. I'm there most days until seven."

Their meals arrived, and after a lull, Terry asked Thomas, "What's happening up on the Hill?" Thomas told a funny story about a senator whose name he refused to mention. The guy had fallen asleep on-camera during a committee meeting televised on CSPAN.

"To be fair, we were reviewing the semiannual Monetary Policy Report to Congress. I'm sure the senator had stayed up late the night before reviewing the details," Thomas finished drily. Everyone laughed. Terry commented on the financial reports he reviewed for some clients. That finally got Walter talking a bit as the two of them chatted in the foreign language of accountancy.

With everyone distracted, Thomas leaned in slightly to Zachary. In a low voice, he said, "I'm glad you'll help Joe at Rainbow Space. He tries to do everything but he needs more hands."

Zachary answered, "I'm actually looking forward to it. I have a suspicion that you're the reason his shelter is solid on the financial side, right?"

Thomas glanced at him, obviously surprised he had connected the dots so quickly. Without answering the question, he said drolly, "So. I think Joe has designs for you and Walter."

Zachary shrugged a bit. "He seems nice. Maybe a little quiet."

"Joe wants everyone in the world paired up, so be warned. If it doesn't work with Walter, he'll trot someone else out."

"It's like he's bringing the candy store to me," Zachary said. It was an attempt to be light, but he saw in Thomas's eyes a flash of pain quickly covered with insouciance. "Does Joe try to fix you up too?"

"No. He got that message a while back and finally gave up."

Zachary hadn't intended to say it but found himself confessing, "I did ask Randy, like you told me."

Thomas looked both amused and sad. "I hope he backed me up."

"You mean did he confirm you're an asshole? Yes, he did." Thomas smiled at that. "Even so, you guys seem like good friends."

"We are. I've known him about two years. Ever since I got involved in the political life."

"I'd ask what you used to do before politics. Randy also warned me you don't answer questions about yourself."

"You already know more about me than…. Well, never mind." Thomas looked a bit sheepish, and Zachary had so much he wanted to ask.

He realized he had still hoped that the connection with Thomas might go somewhere, despite all evidence to the contrary.

What a fool.

He had been ignoring the rest of the table. Walter and Terry debated the intricacies of governmental accounting. He was hyperaware of Thomas at his side as he talked with Joe across the table about the shelter. He could even smell Thomas's cologne.

Zachary tightened his shoulders and leaned slightly away. Then he asked Walter about himself. Since Walter had had a second mimosa by then, he finally seemed to relax enough to respond. He turned to talk a bit with Zachary. They didn't have a lot in common despite what Joe said. Yet Walter's gazes grew longer and perhaps a bit warm. At some point he dabbed a crumb off Zachary's mouth with his napkin and smiled shyly.

Zachary felt Thomas stiffen beside him, and he started to get a little angry. Thomas was the one who had said, "No dating, let's just be friends," and all that bullshit. Damned if Zachary would pine after him.

"Walter, would you like to get together for dinner one night this week?" he asked a little more loudly than necessary. "I still haven't been many places, but I really want to get to know Washington." He knew he was being childish, but fuck it. *Fuck* Thomas. If he was a kid in the candy store, then maybe he'd give Walter a lick to see how he tasted.

. . .

THOMAS FOCUSED ON his conversation with Joe, but he felt every movement Zach made. It was like standing with his back to a fireplace on a cold day. Warmth and comfort were there, if he could only make himself turn around and put out his hands. But he'd do no favors to either of them, even though Zach clearly wanted to get to know him better. He had to shut it down.

But why did he not *want* to shut Zach down? He was kind, funny, insightful. How the hell had he guessed so quickly that Thomas was a major source of funding for the shelter? Rainbow Space meant a lot to Thomas, so that Zach wanted to help Joe there pleased him. Thomas was already an adult when his parents turned their backs on him. Still, he thought he understood the pain and terror of those teenagers who found the shelter. Thomas wasn't religious, but he did believe in Joe. If Joe thought he did God's work with Rainbow Space, then Thomas was on God's side for that one.

Somehow he knew Zach would get that. He wouldn't think Thomas was out to impress anyone with his donations. He just honestly tried to help where it would do the most good. Like Zach seemed to want to do as well.

Zach. He had no right even to think of him by a nickname.

Behind him he heard *Zachary* ask Walter out to dinner. He supposed that was for his benefit—a way for Zachary to let him know he wasn't waiting around. Just as Thomas intended.

But hell. Why did it hurt?

Chapter 7

THOMAS HEADED INTO the Senate office building after brunch. He had to prepare for an upcoming negotiation and was surprised when his phone rang. He didn't recognize the number, but it was a DC area code. He connected the call anyway.

"Mr. Scarborough, this is Detective Torres from the MPD. Do you have a few minutes to talk?"

"Of course, Detective. I thought I had answered your questions, though…?"

"You did answer the questions I asked," Torres said drily. "You told me that Brian Gallagher was a one-night stand. You never spoke with him previously. When he came into Mata Hari asking for another date, you turned him down. Three people confirmed seeing you at the bar until eleven."

"Then to what do I owe the pleasure of your call?" Thomas asked.

"You neglected to mention Charles Rumson during our interview."

His gut clenched in reaction to the name. Torres probably heard the sharp intake of breath. He collected himself and then said in what he hoped was a calm voice, "I can't imagine the relevance, Detective. If you know about Rumson, then you also know he's dead."

"Suicide. Yes, I found that. There were quite a few news stories about his death with pictures of you featured prominently. I guess you made for better tabloid covers. I didn't expect you to look like a model, by the way. But it's an odd coincidence, don't you think?" Torres asked.

"I'm not sure I follow you."

"The restraining order *Jason* Scarborough took out on Charles Rumson in Seattle recited that you had a one-night stand with him. He then became obsessed with you to the point of breaking into your home.

"Now, years later, *Thomas* Scarborough has a one-night stand with a man. Someone who broke into that man's apartment murders him, for no apparent reason, after he threw a drink in your face. Whoever did it took nothing. That tends to rule out robbery or even a random or drug-related break-in. My captain expects immediate answers every time a white boy gets murdered. I have to get creative. Maybe bark up a few wrong trees if necessary. Follow me now?" she asked sarcastically, and Thomas sighed.

"Yes, I understand. What do you want to know?"

"Can we meet today? I'd rather go over this in person," Torres said.

"It's Sunday. Don't you have a life?" Thomas responded, annoyed. Then he realized he should get it out of the way before Torres started to interfere with his work. That was not something the chairwoman of his Senate committee would appreciate. "Fine. I have to be at Mata Hari this afternoon to go over some financial matters with Mr. Vaughan. Can we meet there?"

"Three o'clock?"

"I'll see you then."

.   .   .

THOMAS PULLED HIS blue Maserati into the parking lot between Mata Hari and Pyramid. On a Sunday afternoon, it was typically empty except for a few people who parked illegally before heading off for brunch. He was itchy and irritated at the thought of having to relive the story of Charles Rumson. It had derailed Thomas's life. Besides, the Secret Service investigation meant Detective Torres was just wasting everybody's time.

Images flashed through his memory. He saw again tabloid covers with his face staring out, layered over the wreckage of Rumson's car at the bottom of a cliff. He remembered pictures of Rumson's parents being herded into the cemetery. Drumming his fingers angrily on his steering wheel, he stared out at the parking lot. The idea of calling a tow truck on the parked cars briefly tempted him.

"Don't be an asshole, Scarborough," he said aloud. Then he got out, locked his car, and let himself in to Mata Hari. Randy had the house lights on. A barback named Malcolm worked to set new kegs of beer in place for the evening. Thomas pocketed his sunglasses as he called out a greeting.

"Hey, Mr. Scarborough. Randy's in his office," Malcolm said and pointed with his head because his hands were busy.

"Thanks, Mal. Hey, if you're still around in about thirty minutes, I'm expecting a woman. Can you let us know when she gets here?"

"No problem," Malcolm said and then grunted, "C'mon, you mother*fucker*," as he tried to get a keg set.

Thomas made his way back to the office where Randy worked at his computer. He glanced up as Thomas entered and nodded toward a hard copy of a financial statement sitting on his desk.

"Figured it would be easier to have you read paper than look over my shoulder," Randy said. Then he noticed the look on Thomas's face. "Who pissed in your Wheaties?" he asked.

"That detective, Torres. She's coming by at three. She wants to know about Rumson."

Randy's eyes went wide. "What? That piece of shit is two years in the ground. How did his name come up?" When Thomas replayed his short conversation with Torres, Randy grimaced. "She must be desperate for a lead. I ran that investigation on you myself when Grace brought you on board. Ten witnesses saw him drive off the cliff. The car was in Rumson's name, and his family ID'd the body right away. It isn't like there were any loose ends."

"I know. Believe me." The burning in Thomas's gut had turned to worry, and he grew nauseous. "Randy, you don't think it could happen again, do you? Could I have picked up another stalker?"

Randy stood up and came around the desk to grip Thomas's shoulders in his huge hands. "No fuckin' way. That shit is like lightning. It doesn't strike twice. I get that you fucked Gallagher, but I'd seen him around. He was no Boy Scout. The odds of it having any connection to you are minimal."

Thomas nodded, heartened by Randy's assessment. "You're probably right. Look. Since Torres dug up Rumson, she may want to know shit your Secret Service team found. Can we talk to her together, so maybe this whole thing gets put to rest at once?"

Randy said, "Sure, buddy. Let's knock out the cash flow report until she gets here."

*   *   *

DETECTIVE TORRES SETTLED into a chair in Randy's office and crossed her legs. She quirked her head at the bartender. "Do you have something to add to this discussion, Mr. Vaughan?"

"I might," Randy said. "Do you know how I met Thomas?" She shook her head, and Randy said, "Let's get that out of the way first. I used to be the head of the Secret Service detail for Senator Grace Gilbert."

Torres looked puzzled. "I wasn't aware that senators got Service protection."

"They normally don't," Randy agreed. "But since she was also the Senate majority leader at the time, she rated coverage. She decided to hire Thomas for her office, so my team did the background check. This was about a month after Rumson's death, and there obviously had been a shit-ton of publicity. The Senator asked me to be thorough. I was."

Torres scribbled notes. "And...?" she prompted.

"I told Senator Gilbert that Scarborough was the victim and Rumson was dead. I saw no reason to expect that her hiring him would cause any issues. It was over."

Torres didn't look up from her notebook as she said, "I'm not doubting your investigation, Mr. Vaughan. Just doing my job." She pushed her ponytail back out of the way as she looked up again and then said, "All right, Mr. Scarborough. Can you tell me what happened?"

Thomas frowned. "If you agree with Randy, then why do I have to go through this again?"

"Just humor me, please. I've read the Seattle PD file, but I'd like to hear the story from you directly."

Thomas sighed and sat back in his chair. "Fine. Where do you want me to start?"

"How did you meet Charles Rumson?"

"We actually knew each other in a vague way since we were young. His family was rich—richer than mine—and our fathers had done a real estate deal together. Our mothers did some charity committee work too. Anyway, we'd see each other at functions now and again growing up. I never really thought of him as a friend though."

"Then how did the stalking begin?"

"I ran into him one night at a bar. It was completely random.

I wanted sex, and he was there. Charles was just attractive enough to draw my attention that evening, so I took him home. Worst mistake of my life."

"What happened?"

"Well, it went badly pretty fast. He said he'd fantasized about me for years. The fact that we had these family connections made him think we were more to each other than casual friends. It turned out to be his first time with a man—ever. The sex was actually terrible. As soon as I got us both off, I tried to push him out the door. But he was sort of shy and needy, and I foolishly took pity on him. Maybe because I knew him a bit, I felt bad about kicking him out. So I let him stay."

"Do you frequently let strangers stay the night?" Torres tilted her head at him.

"Not usually." *No one but Zach in I don't know how long.* "Look. With Charles I knew he had money, so it wasn't like I worried about him robbing me," Thomas explained. Leaning forward in his chair, he sighed. "That would actually have been so much better, to just get robbed." He looked down at the floor.

"In the morning Charles had been through my kitchen cabinets and made me breakfast. He'd laid out my toothbrush, razor, and shaving cream in the bathroom. It was a bit creepy, but I still wrote it off as him trying too hard. He wasn't the first man I'd brought home who'd never been with a guy before. They tended to be a bit starry-eyed afterward, which is why I usually tried to get them to leave."

"Yeah. You're a real class act. I can tell," she commented, her eyes on her notebook as her pen scratched over the paper.

Randy grunted, and Thomas flushed angrily. "I've never led anyone on, Detective. I always made clear it was just about sex."

"So Rumson, what, missed the memo?" she asked.

"I suppose so. I finally hustled him out the door, and then

twenty minutes later, a bouquet of flowers showed up. When I got home from work that night, he had left a package with the doorman. It had groceries in it to replace what he had used at breakfast. In the box was a note asking to see me again that night and including his phone number."

"What an ogre."

"Detective, I'm trying to get this over with quickly. If you feel the childish need to make a running commentary, you can save us both some trouble. Just go with the file you already have," Thomas said, and heat crept up his neck to his ears.

Randy started to say something, but Torres flashed him a look and he kept his mouth shut. Torres prompted, "So did you call him? Rumson?"

"Of course not," Thomas barked. "I ignored the note. I figured he'd get the hint. At two in the morning, though, my cell phone got a text from him. Now I definitely did not give him my phone number. I always made a point of not giving my number to *anyone* unless I decided I wanted a repeat visit." Thomas flicked a glance at Randy and said to him, "That used to happen in those days, though never anything serious."

He returned his attention to Torres and continued his story. "Anyway, the text said something like, 'I waited at the bar until it closed. Can I come over?' I wrote back something like, 'Sorry, not a good idea,' and shut my phone off. By morning there were fifteen texts and two voice messages from him."

Torres looked up from her notebook. "From the file I gather things escalated after that," she said, and Thomas nodded.

"Texts, e-mails, letters mailed to my apartment or left with the doorman. Charles contacted me everywhere. I left instructions with my building's management that he was *not* a friend, no matter what he might say. They were to tell him nothing about me and never let him in."

"Smart of you, but I'm guessing he didn't take the hint?"

Thomas shook his head. "He showed up at the law firm one day and insisted we had a date for lunch. The receptionist called me. I tried to have him sent away, but it got so bad the firm's managing partner called me in for an explanation."

He cringed internally as he relived the embarrassment of August Drake dragging him onto the carpet. Drake had then actually called his father to complain that *Thomas* was becoming a problem for the law firm.

Focus. Thomas shook his hands in an attempt to release his building tension.

"I changed my phone number and got a new cell. That helped for a bit. But then I'd find love notes tucked under the windshield wiper on my car. I finally tried to talk to Charles. I agreed to meet him for coffee in a very public place, and he brought me an Omega watch."

He felt his pits get damp as he pictured that overcast day. He had picked the outdoor café because it was popular and would be crowded. He saw again the glow in Charles's brown eyes when he presented the watch, and the flash of *something* bad when Thomas rejected the gift. He remembered thinking that Rumson might not be just overeager, but dangerous.

"I refused to take the watch. I told him that there was nothing between us, that it was just a one-time thing, all of that. He got angry for a second, but then it vanished. After that he just had this oddly patient look on his face. He finally said, 'I understand, Jason. I know you're testing me. I want you to know I am worthy of these tests and I will prove my love to you.' Christ."

Thomas ran his clammy hands through his hair in frustration. "I didn't know what to do. I just couldn't get through to him.

"A week later I came home from the office late. I walked into my bedroom to find Charles kneeling on the bed, naked, with all these sex toys spread out. He begged me to show him what he was doing wrong so he could give me what I needed. He, umm…. This is sick."

Torres said with an edge in her voice, "I'm sure I've heard and seen worse than anything you're about to tell me. Please don't protect my delicate ears."

Thomas scrubbed a hand over his face and took a long moment to fight down a tide of nausea. When he was ready, he nodded and said, "Okay. When I brought him home that one time, the night we met in the gay bar, he begged me to fuck him. He acted like he knew what he wanted, so I let him set the pace." Thomas swallowed hard at a memory of Charles getting to his hands and knees. Thin white scars stood out on his buttocks and back.

"He rolled over and… Shit. He asked me to rape him. Those were his words—'Rape me.'

"I hoped he was kidding, but in any case, I wasn't going to fuck him after that. I basically just jerked us both off. So here he was, weeks later, on my bed with some huge dildos lying there. He wanted me to use them on him. He said he'd take them for me to prove how much he loved me." Thomas shivered as he recalled the fear he'd experienced that night. Charles had smiled beatifically at him while surrounded by monstrous toys.

"Well, I turned around, and I ran straight to the front desk. I begged the doorman to call the cops. I never saw Charles leave, but when the police finally showed up and went into the condo, there was no sign of him. I described him to the doorman, and he didn't recall a man who looked like that coming into the building. He swore he hadn't let anyone into my place. That's when I went down to the police station. I filled out a report and got the restraining order."

Thomas's cheeks burned as he recalled the derision from the

duty officer when he filed his complaint. He thought for a while they'd actually refuse to help him. Some officers had chuckled to each other about the fag and his boyfriend having a spat.

He brought himself back to the present and focused on Torres. "Anyway, I had all the locks replaced on my condo. I even changed my phone and cell numbers again."

"Did that work?" she asked.

Thomas sighed. "I thought so at first because things seemed to calm down after that. About two weeks later, though, I came home from a bar with a guy I'd met." At the look in Torres's eye, Thomas turned red again. "Stop judging me. I was still scared, and I needed a distraction.

"Charles must have been watching or something. He walked up to us at a streetlight less than a block from my condo building. He said he was so disappointed, how could our love mean so little to me that I would bring home another man. All kinds of bullshit like that. Of course the man I pulled gave up about ten seconds into this crap and left.

"I just started yelling at Charles that he had to leave me alone and that I felt nothing for him. I was so angry I had to clench my fists to keep from hitting him, but honest to God, I was terrified. I thought that would make it worse. He might actually *like* it and take it as encouragement. The doorman saw the confrontation and called the police. Charles was still there, begging me to love him, when they showed up a few minutes later. They arrested him for violating the restraining order."

Thomas swallowed hard and said in a low voice, "It turned out he had a hunting knife on him. God knows what would have happened if the police hadn't come.

"The papers picked up the story, of course. Since Rumson is a big name in Seattle, it got attention. The law firm let me know that this kind of publicity was very bad for business, and I should move on. I had trouble being alone in my condo. I tried to go home, but my father didn't like how that would look. He had plans to do more deals with Rumson Senior. I had apparently put that at risk by being stupid enough to get involved with Charles. It didn't help that it was just once. Everyone I knew seemed to assume it was my fault. As if I'd somehow invited this insanity into my life. Maybe they were right. *You* clearly think so," he threw at Detective Torres.

Randy rocked forward in his chair and interjected, "Stop it, Thomas. This wasn't your fault. I get how much you blame yourself, even now. But you were an asshat at worst, nothing more. You didn't lead him on or encourage him. You don't deserve what Rumson did to your life."

Thomas grimaced. "Randy, I wish I believed that."

"So the records all show Rumson is dead," Torres said. "How did he die?"

Randy stood up to pace and groaned slightly when his knees creaked. He moved around the office as he answered Torres. "How did he die? Spectacularly. Thomas, tell me if I get this wrong, but about two weeks after the arrest, Rumson was out on bail. He hadn't actually threatened Jason, I mean Thomas. His lawyer convinced a judge that he didn't pose a present threat. The court notified Jason of course.

"Charles didn't go after him again, but a few weeks later, he seemed to crack up entirely. He had this red Porsche Targa with vanity plates—sweet ride, from the pictures I saw. One day he started showing up all over Seattle.

"If you know the town, he hit the big landmarks—first in Pike Place, then at the Needle, then at the zoo. He'd get out of his car and give these rambling declarations of love. People being people, of course, they filmed him on their camera phones. We collected several samples.

"Then he drove to Discovery Park, up where Fort Lawton was, if that means anything to you. He drove his Porsche off the road at Magnolia Bluff and plummeted down the side of a cliff."

Randy finally sat back down as he said, "The coroner retrieved his body. Rumson's mother identified it at the morgue that day, and it was officially declared a suicide."

Thomas said quietly, "I didn't know it was his mother. I can't imagine what that must have done to Nan."

Torres clicked her pen and sat back. "Okay. Those details are all consistent with the report I read, but I do appreciate your help, Mr. Scarborough. How did you come to live in Washington as Thomas instead of Jason?"

"Well, it was clear my legal career in Seattle was ruined. My father had no desire to take me into the family business. I knew Grace Gilbert through family connections. We had supported her three Senate campaigns and had thrown big fundraisers for her over the years. Grace and I had always gotten along well. I reached out to her about any staff positions she might have available. She happened to need someone with real estate and environmental experience. Well, environmental law was my specialty at the firm and I grew up in the real estate development business. Like Randy said, he did the background check for Grace. I came on board and relocated to DC.

"My new position would be somewhat in the public eye, at least with lobbyists and politicos. I loved my grandfather, though, and I wasn't willing to abandon my family name. I decided to go by Thomas instead of Jason. Thomas is my middle name. I filed a bunch of paperwork to change the name under which I practice law. I worked for Grace for about thirteen months, until I got my current position with the Senate committee."

"Does Senator Gilbert know that you're business partners with Mr. Vaughan now?" Torres asked.

Randy's chair creaked under his weight as he leaned forward. His forearms came to rest on the desk as he looked her in the eye. "I don't care for the insinuation you're making, Detective," Randy said. Thomas looked confused. Randy explained, "She's wondering if I covered up something during the investigation and that's why you invested in Mata Hari."

Thomas's eyes went wide and his jaw dropped. "That's ridiculous. Randy and I both worked with Senator Gilbert for over a year, and we became good friends during that time. When he decided to retire early, I encouraged him to follow his dream of owning a bar. I made a loan to Randy to help with some of the start-up costs, plus I invested as a silent partner. This was all disclosed with multiple Congressional offices, and of *course* Senator Gilbert knows. In fact she was at the opening-night party."

"Okay, okay. I'm just doing my job," Torres said and put away her notebook.

Randy growled, "Any more questions, Detective? If not, we need to get back to our business."

"I think that's it. I appreciate your time, gentlemen." As she started to go, Thomas stood up.

"Look, is there anything you can tell us about the investigation?" he asked. "It isn't like we were friends, but Brian seemed like a nice guy. I still can't believe someone murdered him."

Torres slid on her official face. "I'm sorry. I can't comment on an ongoing investigation." He nodded and turned away, though Randy looked speculatively at Detective Torres.

Thomas said, "I'll let you out." He locked the front door to the bar behind Torres, and turned to find Randy at the counter.

"That was fun," Randy murmured sarcastically, pouring them each a shot of whiskey. "You know she was trying to rile you up with her bitchery, right? To see if you'd say something inconsistent?"

Thomas took the glass and tossed it back. He grunted at the burn. "What's there to be inconsistent about? I relive every minute of that nightmare when I hear the prick's name."

"Thomas, you really need to let this shit go and move on. Rumson was just plain fuckin' crazy. You didn't do anything to make him that way, and keeping everyone else in the world at arm's length isn't going to change that."

Thomas slid his shot glass around on the bar top, his eyes down. "Don't you get it, Randy?" he asked in a tight voice. "I am *exactly* the kind of douche bag that creates a monster like that. Charles was the worst, but there were other guys who tried to get close. I pushed them away, and they got hurt and angry. No one else went out-and-out stalker on me, but they could have. I lost my career, my home—even my parents, really. My whole *life*. I can't put it all at risk again. I didn't see Charles for what he was until it was too late. Why would I be any better at spotting the next one?"

I can't take that risk with Zach. More honestly, he amended the thought. *I can't subject Zach to me.*

Randy tossed back his shot. "Buddy, I love ya like a brother. You deserve something more than all these hookups. I mean, good on you for all the ass you get, but I think you want more than that."

Thomas sighed. "What I want and what I can have aren't the same thing."

●   ●   ●

THE MAN WITH the silver-framed glasses rewound his recordings to make sure. The woman who emerged from the offices of Mata Hari was the police detective who had questioned the owner previously. So MPD was still focused on the bar. He swore.

Nothing could sully the Beloved's name. He would have to be extra careful. Or perhaps… leave a trail pointing elsewhere?

Hmm. Something to ponder.

He cued up some music to play as he studied his options. An old song by The Police came on at random, and the man had to smile. He muttered along, "Every move, every breath indeed." It was almost like a love song from him to the Beloved. Perhaps one day soon they would listen to it together. The Beloved would understand how much the man had done for him.

He considered various ideas to protect his grand plan as he sorted through his video recordings of the bar. Then he pulled up the tracking records for the Beloved's Maserati. He studied the images created by overlaying the car's journey on the streets of Washington as though interpreting runes cast by the gods. When inspiration failed to arise, he switched to the view from the cameras trained on the Beloved's hallway, living room, and bedroom.

At least those glimpses into the Beloved's life brought solace as he planned and waited for his moment.

. . .

DETECTIVE TORRES BRIEFED her captain on Monday morning. "I think the Rumson thing is a dead end, sir. Seattle PD and the Secret Service confirmed the perp is dead, identified by his own mother. Rumson never escalated from his declarations of love to violence. Not against Scarborough or any of his sexual partners. Also, Scarborough has banged pretty boys for at least a year, according to the reports I gathered. Gallagher is the only one harmed or killed that we know of."

Captain Nelson pondered that and commented, "It still could be a stalker focused on Scarborough."

"Agreed, sir. That's possible. I'll keep investigating him to look for a connection."

Later one stray thought crossed Torres's mind. She checked her notes to confirm her recollection of the story of Rumson's break-in. He'd had a variety of large dildos and begged Scarborough to use them. Forensics indicated Gallagher was violently sodomized with an object. It could have been a dildo, maybe, except it was covered in sharp protrusions that shredded Gallagher's rectum. That internal mutilation was the likely cause of a terrible death, not the strangulation with his scarf.

It was a stretch. Still, she decided, whatever she'd told her captain, she needed to dig a little more into Charles Rumson.

Chapter 8

"HI, JOE," ZACHARY said when his new friend opened the door to Rainbow Space a few evenings later.

"Darling, I'm so glad to see you. Come in, come in," Joe said as he drew Zachary into the hallway. The shelter was located in an area of DC called Shaw, in a row house sandwiched between commercial operations. A small brass plaque by the front door was the only indication of the building's purpose. The main floor of the row house appeared to consist primarily of one large room with a staircase on the right. The walls were a light yellow, and pieces of mismatched furniture lay scattered throughout.

"This is nice," Zachary said as he looked around, full of curiosity. Joe took his jacket and placed it on a coat tree.

A trio of teenaged boys gathered in front of a TV as they played a video game. "Boys, this is Zachary Hall," Joe called to the gamers. They looked around and nodded quickly but immediately went back to shooting zombies. "Peter and Gideon have been here for some time," Joe commented in a low voice. "Darius just joined us a few days ago. I'm glad they're bonding, even if I could wish for a little more manners."

Zachary grinned. "I'm not offended, Joe. Remind me. How many people does your shelter hold?"

Joe led him across the main room, past a large communal table. They went through a swinging door into a decent-sized kitchen. He explained as he walked, "We have beds for up to thirty-five guests. They're always full, and the actual number we host for a meal fluctuates daily. The dormitories are upstairs, along with an office. The basement unit is for our onsite manager, Vic Wilkins, and the laundry."

Zachary looked around appreciatively as they toured the house. "This is a warm space. Really comfortable. I expected something more industrial, like the soup kitchen where I used to volunteer."

Joe said, "These young people mostly lost their homes when parents or foster families learned they were homosexual or differently gendered. That's why I feel it's so important to try to give them a homelike environment here. I want them to finish growing up. We have rules while they're under our roof. As I mentioned, I insist upon them sharing in chores. They all face tremendous challenges, of course. I hope this stability will give them a sense of normalcy in their chaotic lives."

"Do you take all ages?" Zachary wondered. "Those boys looked really young to me."

"Peter is thirteen, and Gideon and Darius are both fifteen. We've had children as young as ten, though thank the Lord, very few and not very often. I don't let anyone older than seventeen stay in the dorms, though they are welcome for the daily meal. By that age most can handle the burden of finding work and a place to live. I feel I have to free up the beds for the younger ones who are less able to protect themselves. Ah, Jamayqua, dear."

Joe introduced Zachary to a shy, tall youth in baggy jeans and a loose sweatshirt with the Washington Wizards logo. Jamayqua had dark skin and eyes, and her hair was longish. Her bangs had been dyed a bright apple red.

"I like your hair," Zachary said. She blushed and dipped her head bashfully.

"Jamayqua helps with the meal preparation. She's really quite talented in the kitchen," Joe explained. "What are you and Vic making tonight?" he asked.

She answered in a soft, deep voice, "Fried chicken with collards."

Zachary asked, "Is that the same thing as collard greens? I've heard of that dish, but I've never had it."

"Would you like to join the family meal tonight, dear heart? We actually have a few places open."

"Thanks, Joe. I'd like that if I'm not imposing."

"Not at all. Now let's finish the tour and we'll let Jamayqua get back to dinner."

Joe led Zachary down to the basement to introduce him to the manager. A man in his fifties, short and extremely wiry, stood near a commercial-size washer and dryer. He handed clothes to a team of two boys and one girl to fold. Joe introduced him as Vic Wilkins. "Vic has been with me since the beginning," Joe explained and beamed at the man, who was even shorter than Joe.

"Nice ter meechya," Vic said as he shook Zachary's hand. His voice sounded like gravel, and then he coughed thickly and spit into a handkerchief.

"Yuck," one of the helpers said with a giggle, and Vic pretended to swat her behind.

"Manners, Doreen." Joe tried to look stern, but his eyes twinkled.

Doreen said, "Sorry," and Vic shrugged.

"No worries, Dor. My allergies're really bad this year," he added for Zachary's benefit.

Joe introduced the three children helping Vic as Doreen, Michael, and Ty. Ty was quiet, but Michael blurted out, "I saw the last one. It sucked." Zachary's confusion must have shown because Michael pointed at his *Star Wars* T-shirt. "*Revenge of the Sith* was really dumb."

"Oh. I kind of agree with you, Michael," Zachary said. "Have you seen the new *Star Wars* movie?"

"Nah, it's not on Netflix yet. We have to wait," the boy explained. Zachary realized it was unlikely extra money was available to take these kids to a first-run movie in a theater. He felt sort of stupid, so he said, "Do you have a DVD player here? I have all the *Star Wars* movies up to the new one on disc, so maybe we could watch someday."

"Do you have *Beauty and the Beast*?" Doreen asked. "That was my favorite movie before."

Zachary crouched down so his height wouldn't seem intimidating to the pretty little girl. "You know, Doreen, I think I do. I'll bring that one along. What did you like best about that movie?"

She blushed and whispered, "Belle. She was so smart and pretty and brave."

Michael said, "But she was always doing wrong stuff, like when she got attacked by the wolves."

Doreen's face got hot. "She was just scared, and then she saved Beast's life and washed his arm and showed him how to get the birds to eat from his hands."

Ty said quietly, "Paws."

"Yeah, from his paws," Doreen agreed without a break. "And then when Beast was about to die, she saved him. She *saved* him."

Before World War III broke out, Zachary interjected, "She did, but I think they saved each other. They were both really strong."

Somewhat mollified, Doreen backed down and added only "Anyway, she's the prettiest princess."

Zachary looked at the boy whose head tilted toward the floor. "Ty, right? What's your favorite movie?"

Ty couldn't look at him, but he said quietly, "*E.T.*"

Zachary smiled and said, "That's a great one. I haven't seen that in years."

Ty grinned shyly and, without looking up, stuck out one finger. "Home," he croaked in a decent imitation of the alien character.

Zachary touched the tip of his finger to Ty's and smiled. "I'll bring that one too."

Vic said in his rough, stuffed-up voice, "Okay. Movie review is done fer now er we won't finish the laundry in time fer dinner."

Joe led Zachary away as the little team resumed its chores. Doreen called out, "Bye, Mr. Hall. Don't forget *Beauty and the Beast*." He assured her he wouldn't.

As they returned to the main floor, Joe said, "Dear heart, I can see how well you'll fit in here. But don't let them drive you to distraction with their movie demands."

"I won't. It breaks my heart, though. They're so *young*. How could they be so certain that they're gay or transgender that they'd risk everything to tell their families?"

"I've meditated on that often, Zachary," Joe said seriously. "The world has changed so quickly, probably in your lifetime, and certainly over my many decades. Why, I barely even knew the word *gay* until I was in the monastery. I certainly wasn't aware that I knew any men like me. But now these children are exposed to the concept before they have any notion of the consequences. What I try to accomplish with Rainbow Space is to find those sweet children, like Ty, whose only crime was being born into a family that hates. I want to give them a place to feel safe and loved."

Zachary swallowed hard and reached out to grasp Joe's hand. "You're something else, Joe," he said. "I hope when I grow up I can be as good a person as you."

"You'll make me blush, dear heart," Joe said with a smile. "I felt when I left the monastery I discovered my true vocation: to protect as many innocents as I possibly can."

"Do you try to give the residents here religious education?" Zachary asked.

"No, but I don't discourage it in any way either. Some of the children have held closely to their faith. We manage to get them to church or whatever they grew up with. Others have experienced so much wickedness in their young lives that they have no concept of a loving God. I'm not here to change their minds about those big questions, like whether God exists and why He made them different. If, by example, I raise new questions in their mind, I leave that to Providence."

They reached the second floor as they talked, and Joe led Zachary through a series of dormitories. Bunk beds and mismatched cabinets or chests of drawers were crammed into every available inch. Some of the beds held teenagers, sprawling or reading, but most were empty and made up neatly. The third floor similarly held more dorms. Joe chose not to assign dorms by gender, but let the residents group themselves as they felt comfortable.

"Let's talk about how you'd be able to help us, Zachary," he said. "Now I'm grateful for any time at all you can give, and I don't want to be presumptuous. What would *you* like to do here?"

"Well," Zachary started slowly as he thought out loud. "I felt good working in the soup kitchen, so maybe I could help out with the meal preparation. I think I can manage to come by at least two times a week after work."

"That would be lovely," Joe exclaimed. "Vic currently makes sure the meal is ready every day, with a great deal of assistance from Jamayqua. If you could handle that duty a few evenings, Vic could spend more time in the front of the house." He raised his hands together as if in prayer while his blue eyes twinkled at Zachary. "And if you brought a few new recipes into the kitchen, then I'd know that the good Lord truly sent you to us."

Zachary laughed. "I'm no chef, but I do know some good crowd-pleasers that stretch limited food supplies. Chili, Irish stew, things like that."

"Wonderful. I'll show you how we order supplies when we go back downstairs."

"I'd be happy to bring some DVDs and things like that around too. Hang out with the residents on a weekend, maybe?" Zachary offered.

"You'd be welcome. I think you'll find a lot of demand for your attention. The younger ones took to you immediately, and even older boys like Darius would respond well to you. You're closer to their age than Vic or me or Terry. Or even Thomas, for that matter."

Zachary swallowed hard, his throat suddenly tight. "Thomas spends time here?" he asked, aware his voice had climbed an octave. He tried to relax his hands, which unaccountably clenched at his side.

Joe gave him a long, sympathetic look. In a quiet voice, he asked, "Will that be a problem for you, dear heart? Seeing Thomas here?"

Zachary shook his head, afraid to speak. Joe reached out and rested a hand on Zachary's arm.

"Thomas has a powerful impact on men. I understand that. But beneath that beautiful face and troubled soul beats the heart of a saint."

"I don't know that much about him. I just... I wish I did." Zachary found himself unable to meet Joe's kind gaze.

Joe patted his arm again and then dropped his hand. "I don't think anyone really knows him, except perhaps for Randall. I doubt Thomas would welcome it, but I do pray for him to find a companion of the heart instead of just the body." He tilted his head to catch Zachary's eyes and smiled mischievously. "Of course his body is walking sin."

Zachary had to smile. "It's a great body." Suddenly he exclaimed, "Why can't I stop thinking about him, Joe? We only hooked up once and then talked during brunch the other day. I see him look at me sometimes, and I think maybe he feels the same connection I do. But then a wall comes down, and we're strangers again. Just one more man he had in bed and then left behind."

"Ah, my dear. If I had the solution to Thomas, I'd happily share it with you. I wish I could give you hope, but the truth is, I can't. If you'll take an old man's advice, you'll put it in the Lord's hands and move on with your life. Don't wait around and pine for Thomas. Help us here, go out with other men, enjoy your youth and your adventure. If anything would help Thomas see what a treasure you are, it's watching you sparkle and thrive."

"I hear you," Zachary said and impulsively hugged his friend. "Thanks, Joe."

"Please know that you can talk to me at any time, about anything, darling. Now let's see where we are with dinner."

Chapter 9

EVEN KNOWING THE score, even agreeing with Randy's assessment and Joe's advice, Zachary found himself thinking of Thomas far too often. His handsome face, black hair, hard body—sure, Zachary dreamed of those. But besides the spank material, he thought more often about the kindness in Thomas's blue eyes. Thomas's manner with Joe. The hints about using his political position to help the homeless. All of that seemed irreconcilable with the man who so firmly tried to convince Zachary that he was an asshole.

Zachary prided himself on his ability to read people. In fact that was one of the skills that helped him excel at his job in human relations. All of his instincts told him Thomas was a good man worth knowing better. Perhaps less credibly, Thomas had seemed drawn to him. But Zachary knew he must have fundamentally misread the situation.

He was nonetheless pleasantly surprised when he picked up his phone at work one day to hear Thomas's baritone. "Hi, Zachary," he said. "I hope you don't mind me calling. I got your number from Joe."

Zachary's heart began to pound immediately, but he kept his voice as neutral as he could. "Hey, Thomas. No, I don't mind at all. What's up?"

"I have this standard thing with Randy. When I'm in town on a weekend, we like to go to museums on Sunday afternoons.

We maybe grab a late lunch afterward before he heads in to prep the bar. I know you're still trying to learn the city, and it occurred to me that you might like to join us this Sunday."

Zachary felt a moment of blazing hope. Almost immediately, though, he realized that, with Randy there, Thomas wasn't asking him on a date. He answered slowly, "Friends, huh?"

Thomas chuckled a bit. "Exactly. I meant it when I said I hoped we could be friends. You seemed okay with it at brunch the other day."

Zachary swallowed his disappointment and tried to be mature. He really did like being around Thomas, and he wanted more friends in Washington. The idea of a Sunday afternoon at a museum was pleasant. All he'd have to do was control his emotions and his dick.

What could go wrong?

What he said was "Sure, I'd like to join you guys. Thanks for the invitation."

"Great," Thomas exclaimed. "We're planning to meet at the National Gallery of Art. The West Building. Do you know where that one is, or do you want a ride?"

"I think I've seen it when I've gone for a run along the Mall a few times at lunch. It's near the Capitol, right?" Zachary asked.

"That's right. It has a big dome. We're meeting in the main entrance area at noon."

"I'll see you there."

He heard a slight pause as though Thomas wanted to say more. All that came over the line was "See you there."

* * *

SUNDAY MORNING ARRIVED, and Zachary woke supercharged with energy. He crashed halfway through breakfast when he realized it was all due to seeing Thomas again.

He spent some extra time in the pool to get himself ready to face Thomas. The rhythm of his steady motion through the cool water, the pull of his arms, the even breaths, centered him like nothing else on earth. If they were really going to spend time together, Zachary had to accept at face value what he had told him. Friendship was all Thomas had to offer.

Zachary needed a friend too, so he would bury his desire and just do friendly things with Thomas. That became his mantra as he swam his laps. He recited, "To make a friend, be a friend," over and over in his head. It helped as he pushed himself to one hundred fifty lengths.

He rode the Metro to the Smithsonian stop and walked along the Mall until he identified the right museum. He was quite early. The spring weather was beautiful, if chilly, so he wandered up and down the Mall for a while. Across Pennsylvania Avenue the Canadian flag flew over one building. He guessed it must be that country's embassy.

Next to that was a much more modern building, kind of squat and ugly to Zachary's taste. It bore a sign reading *Newseum*. An enormous plaque covered half the facade with the words of the First Amendment to the United States Constitution: *Congress shall make no law respecting an establishment of religion, or prohibiting the free exercise thereof; or abridging the freedom of speech, or of the press; or the right of the people peaceably to assemble, and to petition the Government for a redress of grievances.*

Balconies jutted from the left end of the building. He wondered if there were apartments there as well as a museum. He whistled at the thought of how expensive those would likely be, a few blocks away from the US Capitol, the Supreme Court, and the Library of Congress.

Ah well. It's not like I'd ever get to see the inside of an apartment like that.

He walked a bit more and then returned to the National Gallery with some time left to kill. Sitting in an alcove next to a large fountain, he took a few pictures with his phone's camera. Some were of the Mall, a few of the other museums lining the opposite side, a couple of passersby. One man with shaggy blond hair and glasses caught Zachary's eye. The man seemed to look back a moment too long, but then he turned his gaze forward and hurried on.

Zachary suddenly shivered as though someone had walked over his grave.

"I hate that expression," he muttered to himself as he zipped his jacket. Despite the sunshine it was only March. He was probably just cold.

. . .

SHORTLY BEFORE TWELVE Zachary made his way to the entrance hall. Thomas and Randy conversed by the coat check. Randy had dressed in jeans, boots, and a down vest over a plaid shirt. His rolled-up sleeves showed muscular, hairy forearms. Zachary acknowledged that Randy was dead sexy, but he felt it in a platonic way.

Not like his appraisal of Thomas, who laughed at something Randy had said. Thomas had on tight black jeans that curved around his rear end and showed a prominent bulge in front. Zachary knew what the bulge only hinted at. A knot of desire burned deep in his belly. A sky blue polo with black-and-white piping on the sleeves and collar stretched tightly over his muscles. A few wisps of chest hair poked above the placket. Slight scruff darkened his jaw and made Zachary's palms itch with the desire to stroke his face. Thomas held a light tan jacket in one hand; the other was stuck in his hip pocket.

Zachary tried hard not to stare at Thomas as he walked up.

He called out in the most casual tone he could manage, "Hey, guys."

Randy grinned at him and stuck out his big hand for a shake. "Thomas talked you into joining our outing, huh?"

Thomas started to go in for a hug, but at the last second, clapped a hand on Zachary's shoulder instead. "I may have failed to inform Zachary that you like to show off on these perambulations." His eyes sparkled with amusement. "Randy was an art history major before he switched to criminal justice in college," Thomas explained. "I think he would have been happier as a docent than an agent."

Zachary had to laugh. "Oh Randy. I can just see you guiding tour groups with one hand on the butt of your gun while you *wait* for someone to touch a painting or feel up a statue."

"With this scary mug? They wouldn't dare," Randy growled. "I'd never have to draw."

Zachary looked around the lobby. "Where do we buy tickets?"

Thomas said, "We don't. This is one of the many perks of life in Washington. Most of the museums are free."

Randy threw in, "These works are bought with taxpayer dollars, so they aren't really free."

Thomas rolled his eyes and groused, "Here we go again. Now that Randy is a businessman, he's turning into a Republican."

Randy glanced at Zachary and then said to Thomas, "Let's start in the European paintings galleries. I'll show you the portrait I was talking about."

They bypassed several tour groups in the lobby to climb wide stone steps to the second floor. As they walked upstairs, Zachary asked Randy, "What made you switch from art to the Secret Service?"

"My uncle was a police officer in Portland, Maine. He got

killed in the line of duty while I was in college. Decided I wanted to honor him, so I switched my major."

Thomas bumped his shoulder deliberately into Randy's arm. "C'mon, big guy. Tell him the rest."

Randy glared down at him for a second but then relaxed his frown and shrugged.

"Yeah, okay. My uncle Kevin was gay too. He was the only one in my family who really got me. I think I was closer to him than to my own mother." Randy paused at the top of the stairs and looked up at a large urn topped by a bronze statue. "The Portland Police Department couldn't or wouldn't give Uncle Kev's partner the usual survivor benefits. That pissed me right off. So I got all activist and decided I'd see what I could do to fight the system from the inside."

Zachary asked softly, "Did they get the person who killed your uncle?"

After a moment Randy turned his head toward them. "What? Oh, yeah, they did. Guy flipped out on PCP. He's still behind bars. I check sometimes."

Zachary put his hands in his pockets and studied Randy. "I bet Kevin would have been proud you went into law enforcement for him."

Randy gave him a rueful look. "Actually I think he would have yelled at me for giving up on art. He was the one who took me to museums and plays and things like that when I was a kid. He got me thinking about the relationship between humanity and the arts. So putting down the brush and picking up a gun— Kev might have tried to whip my ass for doing that."

Thomas smiled gently. "You showed me a picture of Kevin once. He probably *could* have whipped you. He was bigger even than you."

"Yeah, but for a big guy, he was a real teddy bear." Randy's eyes glistened a bit. "Tore me up he died so stupidly."

"But you stayed interested in art even while you were in the Secret Service," Zachary observed to shift the mood.

Randy nodded. "Sure. It's always been a passion. There was a fair amount of overseas travel, so I collected shit everywhere I went."

Zachary's eyes widened. "Oh. Then I guess the paintings in Mata Hari are your personal collection."

Thomas grinned. "You're quick, Zachary. I talked Randy out of displaying the really valuable pieces he owns. You never know what's going to happen in a bar, even a piano bar."

"I hear people throw drinks at you, Thomas," Zachary said. "That could definitely mar an oil." He meant it to be funny, but both Thomas and Randy suddenly looked stricken. "What did I say wrong? Randy told me he's cleaned up three broken glasses thrown at you."

Randy cleared his throat and forced a chuckle. "You're right, Zachary. I take it out of his share of the profits." At Thomas's exasperated snort, Randy shrugged. "Kid's smart, like you said. He probably already figured out you're an investor."

Zachary smiled at that. "Actually I had. And anyway, it makes sense since you spend so much time on that bar stool."

"Just don't spread it around, Zachary. Okay?" Thomas pleaded. "I like being a *silent* partner."

"That's no problem. I don't gossip. Hey, Randy, I always wanted to ask—why did you call your place Mata Hari?"

Randy's face, which had been surprisingly open so far, seemed to close down. "I just like that movie," he said in his gruff voice and looked away. Zachary glanced at Thomas and saw his own surprise mirrored there. Thomas shrugged slightly at him, but they dropped the subject.

Randy led them into a series of small galleries displaying

Florentine paintings from the late Renaissance. His steps quickened as they entered. There was eagerness in his voice when he said, "Here we go, Thomas. The painting I was telling you about is in one of these galleries. I want to know if you see it, so I'm not going to point it out."

Randy didn't take them right to a specific work of art. Instead they moved around the walls of each gallery counterclockwise. Randy commented on specific techniques and developments in artistic style as they walked. His passion for the subject made him more talkative than normal.

When they reached a grouping of portraits by Raphael, Zachary studied the works. "I remember that Florence was important in the Renaissance, but I'm not really sure how or why."

"Most historians say the Medici family created an environment for the arts to flourish," Randy explained. Obvious enthusiasm displaced his normal brusque manner. "The Medici were significant patrons. They made it fashionable for others to support art as well. You combine that kind of patronage with the presence of some of the most amazing artistic geniuses ever known, and Florence became an… incubator, I suppose.

"Here. Look at the geometry," he continued. His eyes almost glowed as he indicated Fra Carnevale's *The Annunciation*. "See the way the lines bisect the angel Gabriel from the figure of Mary? The proportions were just perfect. That's one of the aspects Florence brought to the Renaissance. A rebirth of interest in classical measurements and proportions. The relationship of those concepts to the human figure."

Thomas shared a small smile with Zachary and said, "You've done it now. There is no off switch when Randy talks about the Renaissance."

That little smile went straight to Zachary's chest. He started to reach to curl an arm around Thomas's waist to share the moment. Catching himself just in time, he covered the false move by shoving his hand into his pocket. To Randy, he said, "Ignore the critic, because I really am interested. Tell me about this one." They stopped in front of a Madonna and Child. "I get the subject matter, but this seems different from the ones we passed as we entered the gallery."

Randy nodded quickly and said, "Absolutely right. This is by Fra Filippo Lippi. He was technically a monk, but very scandalous."

"Even more so than Joe?" Thomas interjected with a chuckle.

"Well, he lived openly with a nun, and he had a son who also became a well-respected artist. Pretty racy stuff for the fifteenth century. But look what he did to subvert the traditional images. See how the Mary figure looks? How melancholy? It's as if she can see what's going to happen to her son down the road. And look at the Christ child. See the gentle way he's touching her hand, even as he seems to think very adult thoughts? It's like he's comforting her. Fra Lippo brought so much *humanity* to the divine."

Zachary studied the painting with new appreciation and finally said, "I see that. The earlier paintings are more formal and stiff. Posed, I guess. Like idols. This Mary seems to know that she's heading toward a grand tragedy. All she wants to do is protect her son, even though it's Jesus."

Randy said, "That's a good way to look at it. Where earlier artists focused on divinity, Lippo and many Florentine artists were humanists first. They used the religious stories to show the best in mankind."

Zachary looked around the gallery. "It wasn't all religious, was it? There are several portraits here of just, well, people."

Randy agreed. "The Renaissance artists worked for patrons, of course, so many of the subjects were notables or their family members."

They continued to explore the galleries. As they walked, Randy pointed out the unusual position of a hand or a striking use of color. Three quarters of the way around one of the rooms, Thomas stopped in front of a painting of a young man and said, "Oh." His shoulders dropped to a relaxed pose as he shoved his hands in his pockets and smiled at Randy.

Randy nodded at him. "Exactly."

Zachary looked back and forth between the two of them and at the painting on the wall. The tag revealed it was *Portrait of a Young Man*, by Sandro Botticelli. The work showed a handsome—almost transcendent—young man with long, slightly curly hair, wide-set brown eyes, and full lips. The subject wore a red cap and a brown jerkin of some kind. The young man's right hand rested on his breast, and his long fingers pointed toward his left shoulder.

"This is striking," Zachary said as he studied the image.

Randy's lips twitched slightly. "Does it look familiar?"

Zachary tilted his head and looked more closely. "Not really. Should I know this painting?"

Thomas said softly, almost reverently, "It could have been painted of you."

Zachary shot him a glance, certain they were teasing him. "What do you mean? This man is beautiful. He looks nothing like me."

Randy said, "No. Thomas is right. The hair is a little darker than yours and longer, of course, but look at the eyebrows. And the shape of the lips. You could have been the model who posed for this."

Thomas smiled warmly at Zachary. "How about that? The tough-guy bartender thinks you look like a Renaissance painting."

Zachary turned away, overcome with the intensity in Thomas's face. "Ah, you two are just putting me on."

"Nope," Randy said. "I mean it, Zachary. This could be an ancestor, he looks so much like you."

Thomas continued to stare intently at Zachary's face. Despite himself a shiver of desire ran down Zachary's back at the scrutiny.

In a voice grown slightly hoarse, Thomas said, "Even the tilt of your eyes is the same, Zachary. The likeness is remarkable." Their gazes met and held, and warmth bloomed in his heart. Zachary stood a little straighter and tilted up his chin slightly as he met the rapt gaze. The look in Thomas's eyes wasn't sexual. It held passion but not fever. It was… regard. Respect, maybe.

The moment stretched. Thomas wet his lips with the tip of his tongue and prepared to speak.

Before he could, Randy said to Zachary, "I thought of the painting when you came into the bar the first time. I'm not trying to embarrass you. Anyway, I thought you two might get a kick out of seeing this."

Zachary kept his eyes on Thomas, but the moment was gone.

The trio studied the painting a moment longer. Then Randy declared, "Impressionists next," and led them to a different set of galleries.

Zachary could only wonder what had just happened. Most likely he was projecting his own fantasies onto Thomas. But that look he saw in Thomas's eyes stayed with him as they walked, and he wondered at it.

An hour or so later, Randy glanced at his watch. "Shit. I lost track of time. I don't think I can grab lunch before I head in to get the bar ready for opening."

Thomas suddenly looked panicked. Zachary assumed he'd just realized the two of them were about to be left with no buffer to protect Thomas. He might insist he didn't date. Yet an afternoon at the museum—even with Randy in tow—was close enough to make no difference. Lunch, Zachary guessed, would cross the lines Thomas drew.

Unnerved by the glances exchanged near the Botticelli portrait, Zachary wasn't sure what to say to Thomas either. He knew what he wanted to say. *Please take a chance. Have lunch with me. Let's see whether you're as drawn to me as I am to you.* But he couldn't delude himself. Thomas had made it clear he wanted nothing more than friendship from Zachary.

"I need to get going as well," Zachary said. He refused to look at Thomas so he wouldn't see relief in his eyes. Focusing instead on Randy, he said, "This was a lot of fun. You opened my eyes to so many subtleties in the art that I never would have been able to see, Randy. Really, thank you."

Randy clouted him on the shoulder with the side of his fist. "My pleasure. I'm glad you enjoyed it." He glanced over at Thomas and then back at Zachary. "Maybe we'll be able to do it again sometime."

Thomas hesitated and then said slowly, "Yes, Zachary. Come with us again."

Zachary smiled at both of them, though he quickly looked away from Thomas. "Sure. Give me a call whenever you feel like having a third wheel along."

•   •   •

THOMAS WALKED SLOWLY along the Mall in the direction of his condo building, his hands in his trouser pockets. The afternoon with Randy and Zach had been... unsettling. He felt listless as the rest of Sunday stretched before him with nothing special to do and nowhere for him to be.

The sun was out, but a light breeze and low temperature caused him to keep his Burberry jacket buttoned up. After two years he was still learning the seasonal rhythms of DC. Even though it was early spring and the annual Cherry Blossom Festival was weeks away, small knots of tourists already marched along the gravel paths on either side of the Mall. Soon it would be nearly impossible to stroll there as fleets of tour buses discharged their loads of school or travel groups. By the Fourth of July, Thomas would want to be far away from the crowds.

In fact, he mused, he should think about a summer vacation. He would want to get out of the throngs of visitors and away from the humidity. It turned Washington back into the swamp from which large parts of the city had been built.

The best time to vacation would be when the Senate was in summer recess. The demands on his staff would be at their lowest then. But where to go? He considered options as he listened to his feet crunching along the gravel.

Obviously Seattle was out. He hadn't been back there since he left to join Senator Gilbert's staff. His parents had made him feel the entire nightmare with Charles Rumson was his own fault. Well, his father had said it, and his mother dissuaded Thomas from returning to the family home when he really needed a place to regroup. So definitely no to Seattle.

Italy was a thought. It had been years since he spent any time in Rome or Venice. Both places would likely suffer from the same excess of tourists he wanted to escape, though, so maybe not. What about a drive along the Amalfi coast? That was something he'd never done. He recalled an interview with Gore Vidal about Positano or maybe Ravello. Anyway *one* of the towns that dotted the Tyrrhenian Sea. Vidal had talked about a terrace there that he believed provided the finest view on Earth. That was a worthy goal for a vacation—to see for himself the finest view.

As he walked in the Washington, DC spring air, Thomas daydreamed of summer in the warm Italian sun. He imagined himself in a sexy little sports car, top down, racing along winding roads that hugged the steep cliffs. The blue sea would spread out below. They'd pull into a little town for lunch, drink some wine, and maybe laugh about whether it was safe to keep driving. And if the mood was right and the town was beautiful, they'd find a little *pensione* or even a grand hotel. They'd settle in to drink evening cocktails on a terrace overlooking the sea. He could picture turning languidly, setting down his drink to reach for Zachary's hand....

Shit.

Thomas abruptly stopped walking, causing a young couple behind to bump into him. "I'm sorry." He turned to apologize. They laughed it off and kept going, but Thomas didn't move.

I was thinking of Zachary and me on vacation in Italy.

The idea was as stunning as it was alarming. He had been having sex regularly for at least twenty years. He couldn't recall a time he'd fantasized about a vacation with one of his partners. It was always about the sex, and when he'd had someone, he moved on to the next someone. Even when he had occasionally agreed to see a man a few times, he never seriously had the urge to date. Certainly not to take a romantic trip with anyone. Not until Zachary.

It would never happen, he told himself. It *could* never happen. He was a disaster, and the proof was Charles Rumson. Zachary deserved to be with someone who could really appreciate him and take care of him—even cherish him.

Thomas was well aware of how attracted to him Zachary was. The physical aspect was something to which Thomas was accustomed, if not inured. Men came on to him since he was a teenager. But he was also certain that, for Zachary, it was more than that.

Zachary behaved as though he saw something beyond the good looks Thomas had done nothing to earn and beyond the money he had inherited. The look in Zachary's eyes made Thomas feel prouder, smarter, *better*. He wanted to live up to the ideal version of himself that Zachary seemed to see. He longed to wallow in the illusion woven by Zachary's regard. To be wanted for himself, rather than his looks or money.

But it was just a fantasy, of course. Zachary was sharp, quick, charming, and handsome. All too soon he'd see Thomas for the damaged piece of work he really was. Then he'd move on to kinder men who could return his desire honestly and without fear. That being the inevitable conclusion, it was better to keep the distance between them.

Thomas walked on again, resolved to set aside *whatever* it was he felt for Zachary Hall. In order to protect Zachary's innocence, he would quell his own pathetic desire to spend a summer vacation in Italy with a handsome young man who could have been painted by Botticelli.

Chapter 10

WHATEVER FLEETING FANTASIES Zachary created for himself after they spent Sunday at the museum he forced down. Another Sunday arrived and he heard nothing further from either Thomas or Randy. He made up his mind to take Joe's advice. He would set aside thoughts of Thomas and focus on the new life he was building in Washington.

Not that it was a hardship. He liked his job at Treasury and helping Joe at Rainbow Space. The Gay Men's Chorus also turned out to be a wonderful pastime. Rehearsals were filled with men who enjoyed music and singing like he did but who also joked amid the serious work of learning the music.

Zachary found the Chorus to be a riot, and he told Howard so at the end of his second rehearsal. "I'm so glad you got me to audition," Zachary said. "This is tons of fun, and it's a great way to meet people."

Howard giggled delightedly. "I said you'd be front-row material," he exclaimed. "That's where the conductor puts all the best-looking guys for performances. The other second tenors who stand up front are already angling to get you next to them during concerts." Howard paused and then asked, "Would you like to have dinner one night? I mean, umm... go out on a date with me? If you aren't seeing anyone else, that is?"

Although he was slightly surprised, Zachary accepted. Three nights later, they met on P Street for Mexican food. Howard indicated he had parked his car in the lot by Mata Hari. That made Zachary nervous they would end up there after dinner. Sure enough, after two margaritas each, Howard wanted to cap the evening at the piano with Miss Ethel. Thus, despite his intention to stay far away from Thomas until he developed a thicker skin, Zachary found himself walking into Mata Hari again.

The bar was fairly crowded that evening. People stood two deep around the piano and sang along to the score of *Cabaret*. Howard immediately began to chat with several people they both knew from the Gay Men's Chorus. He made a point of announcing that Zachary was there with him on a date. Zachary resisted the urge to roll his eyes at the immediate teasing they received. He said into Howard's ear that he'd get them some drinks from the bar.

Randy and his assistant bartender were both busy, but Joe spotted Zachary as he approached and threw out his arms. "Darling boy," he cried out. "There you are. Now the evening is perfect." Terry stood behind Joe, one elbow resting on the bar. Zachary thought his face looked tight and slightly worried.

The man to Terry's left had his back to them as he talked to a handsome young man. Zachary knew exactly who it was anyway.

Shit, shit, shit. Why did I come in here?

Joe gave him a warm hug, which Zachary returned with a kiss on his cheek. "Hi, Joe, I'm glad to see you. Did Ty like the DVD I left?" He hugged Terry as well and resisted the urge to say something pointed at Thomas's back. Nevertheless, Thomas turned his way. Zachary would have sworn a spark of something warm lit Thomas's eye before he schooled his face to neutrality.

"Zachary, hi. How are you doing?" Thomas asked, slightly aloof. Zachary flicked a glance at the young man who had a hand on Thomas's shoulder, and his stomach sank.

Fine. If that's how you want to play it, you got it.

"Oh, Thomas, good to see you again," he drawled, feigning nonchalance. He stuck his hand out toward the man with Thomas and debated warning him not to expect too much. "I'm Zachary."

"Marcus," the man said, shaking Zachary's hand limply.

Randy freed up. When he met Zachary's eye, he called out, "Seven and seven?"

Zachary nodded and added, "Also a gin and tonic for my date." Catty, he knew, but it was the margaritas talking. "Joe, Terry, can I get you anything?" He pointedly did not offer to buy Thomas and this *Marcus* a drink. He saw Thomas flash a glance at Howard by the piano.

Joe glanced back and forth between Thomas and Zachary, but said, "Well, why not? Randall, this lovely gentleman insists upon another cocktail for us."

Randy nodded. "Vodka rocks, Johnny Walker coming up with your G and T."

Terry asked about his job and his date with Walter while Randy made the drinks. "I hope the two of you got up to some trouble at least," Terry said. "I have a feeling you need help to get a little wild."

Zachary flushed as he recalled how wild he had gotten with Thomas. Of course he didn't share that information with Terry. Instead he laughed a bit and said, "Well, even if that's true, Walter and I didn't really click. We had dinner, but he seemed kind of nervous and distracted all evening. I got the feeling he wanted to be somewhere else. We just shook hands after dinner and called it a night."

Joe exclaimed his disappointment. "I had such hopes for the two of you. Ah well, you're in Mother Joe's hands. I'll have you married off by summer."

Terry grinned slightly but it looked forced. "Now you're in

for it, Zachary. Maybe you should try again with Walter. He was really adorable, I thought." Zachary saw Joe's eye twitch at that remark. Randy arrived with their drinks before he could comment further.

Zachary excused himself with Howard's gin and tonic. As he returned to the piano, Howard—clearly feeling the effects of his earlier booze—gave him a big kiss on the cheek. Zachary childishly hoped Thomas saw it. Not that he was going to sleep with Howard or anything. It was just their first date. In fact, he'd had three first dates already since joining the Chorus, plus the unfortunately boring one with Walter. In spite of himself, he tried to be the kid in the candy store that Thomas urged and Joe seconded in his inimitable way.

But he only took that recommendation so far. Whether because he learned his lesson with Thomas or simply didn't feel the same powerful attraction again, none of his dates ended with more than a kiss. That was plenty for the moment. He'd let himself go with the right man if one came along.

Howard surprised him by asking, "How do you know those people?" His gaze was on Joe, Terry, and Thomas. Zachary felt himself blush.

"I met them when I first came in here, and now I do volunteer work with Joe. He's the one with white hair."

Howard nodded and sipped at his drink. "What about Thomas?"

Zachary frowned in astonishment as the pieces clicked into place. "Oh." Of course. Thomas had slept with Howard. He looked around the bar, vaguely nauseated as he wondered how many other men there had been with Thomas.

"You too, huh?" Howard asked. An edge appeared in his voice as he said, "Well, I hope you know not to get your hopes up. You probably got the same speech as the rest of us, about no sleepovers and no dating or repeats."

Zachary thought he saw a glint of jealousy in Howard's eyes. He decided it was better not to mention that he actually had slept over. He'd even gone on a sort-of date with Thomas. He gave Howard a noncommittal response and then they agreed silently to drop the subject of Thomas Scarborough. They both turned to face the piano and sang several songs with the crowd.

Soon all the alcohol he had consumed produced a definite buzz. Howard was affected too, apparently. He kept touching Zachary, patting his back, and trying to hold his hand. Across the piano Zachary could see the patrons at the bar. He was particularly aware that Thomas still talked with Marcus. Well, at least they hadn't left yet. That would be painful to watch.

Thomas will put a hand on Marcus's back. He'll guide him out of the bar and into a cab that will take them to Thomas's apartment....

"Hey," Howard said into his ear. Then he darted out his tongue to lick Zachary's neck.

Zachary jumped, pulled away, and tried to cover it with a laugh. "Sorry. Ticklish."

"Mmm. Maybe I can find some more ticklish spots later," Howard slurred.

Umm, no.

"Miss Ethel, can you play some more Nina Simone?" Zachary requested.

She winked at him. "Course I can, hon. How 'bout 'I Want a Little Sugar in My Bowl'?"

When the song ended, Zachary made another request, then another. A waiter brought them another round. At the bar Thomas had his back to them. Marcus scanned the crowd as though he no longer had grabbed on to a sure thing.

A bit dazed from the number of drinks he had already consumed, Zachary spun his phone a bit. When Thomas turned his head in profile to say something to Randy, Zachary took a quick picture.

"Wha' was that for?" Howard slurred as he looked at Zachary with suspicion.

"Nothing. Just me being stupid," Zachary told him. A hard glint appeared in Howard's eyes.

Eventually Joe wandered over to say good night, very much in his cups. He hugged Zachary effusively and promised they'd have him over for dinner one night soon. Miss Ethel continued to play as the bar emptied a bit. Howard whispered again about getting out of there. Zachary shook his head and said, "I think I'm fine here."

Howard stood up straight and blinked at him for a minute. His dazed look was replaced with something sharp. He glanced over at Thomas's back and then at Zachary's face. Through the alcohol it seemed to Zachary that Howard had added up the score and realized it left him out.

"Suit yourself. Don't be surprised when he cuts you down if you try to get him away from that guy," Howard said. He pulled himself together and added, a bit tightly, "I guess I'll see you at rehearsal." He left without another word.

Later Zachary leaned on the piano, too many cocktails inside him, alone. His chest ached, but that might have been the liquor. Miss Ethel said quietly, "This is my last set, sugar. You gonna be okay?"

He tried to smile at her. "I'm fine. I swear. Just a wee bit too much to drink tonight. You play like an angel, Miss Ethel." He slipped a twenty into her glass bowl, and she nodded her thanks. Looking around, Zachary realized the place was nearly empty. Randy stood alone behind the bar, drying some glasses.

"I guess Marcus was the lucky boy of the night after all," he muttered to himself. Then he winced. Pain washed through him. He imagined Thomas wrapping his arms around the good-looking Marcus, stroking him off, maybe more.

Unexpectedly dark emotions wove through his heart. He was jealous of a stranger getting to touch Thomas's handsome face and hold his strong body. He was furious at Thomas for denying the simple truth that was right in front of him. He wanted Zachary as much as Zachary wanted him. There was something between them, something more than the physical attraction. At the brunch and at the museum, they had shared something....

He was such a fucking idiot. He pulled on his jacket, wrapped a scarf around his neck, and stepped out into the night.

The parking lot was nearly empty. Sodium lights reflected off the windows of the four or five cars that remained. He could hear club music still pulsing from Pyramid next door. The faint boom-boom-boom sounded like a beating heart.

He stood for a moment in the doorway of Mata Hari and tried to focus on the best place to find a cab. A chill breeze blew across the lot and caused an empty beer bottle to roll over the gravel. He shivered.

After another moment he started to walk toward P Street. The alcohol in his body made him less than steady on his feet. He had to concentrate as he walked—left, right, left, right. Somewhere off to his side, he registered the sound of a car door opening.

"Zachary."

He stopped at the sound of a baritone voice and slowly turned around. Thomas jogged across the parking lot toward him, pulling on a parka as he approached. Zachary heard a car door slam closed and an engine start up. He stood there, confused, until Thomas reached him.

"Zachary, you shouldn't be out here alone. Didn't you hear

about the murder?" Thomas asked.

Zachary ignored the frisson that ran down his back. All he could think to say was "I thought you'd left with Marcus."

Thomas had the grace to look embarrassed. "I was going to, but I decided I wasn't in the mood."

"Oh." Zachary didn't know what else to say, so he just stared at Thomas. He moved his gaze over Thomas's handsome face, his well-shaped mouth, his concerned blue eyes. A lock of wavy hair had fallen forward over his brow. Without thinking, Zachary reached out and pushed it back into place.

"Sorry," he muttered, dropping his hand as he looked at the ground.

"Where's your date?" Thomas asked.

Zachary sighed. "That was a mistake. As was the fourth drink. As was coming to Mata Hari tonight."

Thomas looked at him and then said abruptly, "I'm glad you didn't leave with that guy. You can do better."

"I understand you would know." When Thomas looked away, Zachary chuckled without humor. "Anyway, someone told me to try all the candy in the store. That means I have to expect to get the occasional piece of licorice."

Thomas glanced at him from under his eyebrows. "You don't like licorice?" He gave Zachary the slightest smirk. He had no business looking so handsome doing it.

Zachary turned and began to walk toward P Street again. As Thomas fell into step, Zachary looked at him sideways. "I'm fine, Thomas. Don't put yourself out."

"I told you I'd like to be friends. This is what friends do. They watch out for each other." They walked in silence a bit, and their footsteps rasped on the macadam. Zachary came to a stop on P Street and looked around for a cab.

He was unable to face Thomas as he said, "I'm not sure I'm

strong enough to be your friend." He risked a glance and saw something sad in Thomas's eyes. "I get that it was just one night. I get that you have issues, and who doesn't? The thing is I felt like it could have been more. But obviously I was wrong."

A cab pulled up to the curb, and Zachary opened the door. As he started to climb in, his better manners possessed him. "You need a taxi too, right? We could share this one."

Thomas stared intently at him, his hands in his pockets and his breath steaming in the air. He seemed to struggle with something. Zachary shrugged and got into the cab. "Take care of yourself," he said as he began to close the door.

He was startled when Thomas pulled it open. Sliding into the cab next to Zachary, Thomas called out his address to the driver.

They rode in silence through the quiet streets until Thomas turned to Zachary and took his hand. "Would you come home with me tonight, Zach? I can't give you more than this, but even friends can sometimes make each other feel good."

Zachary tried to think rationally. It was such a bad idea. But Thomas's intense blue eyes on his were gorgeous, his face handsome, and the memories of their night together intoxicating. Zachary never stood a chance. He leaned over and kissed Thomas, ignoring the little grunt of displeasure from the driver.

Chapter 11

NO SOONER HAD Thomas let them into his apartment than Zachary pinned him against the coat closet door. He devoured Thomas's succulent mouth as he shoved his own coat and Thomas's parka to the floor. It might have been Terry's ribbing him earlier or the sense that he would never again see Thomas in this intimate way. Either way, Zachary gave himself permission to go a little wild. In his excitement the haze of alcohol seemed to burn away, but his body felt too hot. He needed to touch cool skin damn quick.

He ran his hands up Thomas's strong neck to his head and clenched his fingers in his dark, wavy locks. Their mouths tangled together. Zachary ran his tongue over Thomas's white, even teeth and bit into his lower lip. Leaning back to tug on it, he made Thomas moan for him.

The apartment was dark except for a dim glow through the windows, but a shaft of light fell across Thomas's blue eyes. Zachary growled, "God damn. You really are the most handsome fucking man in the world. I'll pay for this." A quizzical expression lasted until Zachary grasped the luxurious fabric of his shirt and ripped it open. Buttons flew everywhere and bounced across the hardwood floor.

Thomas drew in a sharp breath and pressed his hands and his back against the closed door. His eyes showed surprise and excitement. Zachary took that as permission to do as he wanted with Thomas's body. He glided lips over the long neck before him, bared his teeth, and scraped them lightly along the jaw. Thomas tilted his head back and exposed his throat. Zachary drifted down with his mouth next, across the silky chest hair and over to one reddened nipple. He snaked his arm possessively around Thomas's waist as he licked and then lightly bit, alternating between nubs. He stopped just at the point both nipples became as hard as little rubies.

Thomas put one hand on the back of Zachary's hair to hold him to his chest. He whispered intently, "Go ahead, Zach. Fucking *bite* me." Zachary did, sharply, and Thomas gasped as he thrust his hips forward to rub his hard cock against Zachary's jeans. "My God," Thomas moaned, "that's so damn hot."

Zachary pulled Thomas's belt loose, then unfastened his jeans and pushed them to the floor. They pooled around Thomas's ankles. Zachary ran his hands over the hard length of flesh still trapped by Thomas's black briefs and stuck his hands inside. With one he curved under to roll Thomas's balls. The other he cupped around the head of his dick, all sticky and wet with precome.

Zachary went to his knees and pulled down Thomas's underwear as he dropped. He stared at the thick and swollen erection for a long moment, as though mesmerized by a cobra ready to strike. A drop of clear liquid pearled at the tip of Thomas's cock. Zachary extended his tongue to lap at it and drew a silver thread back into his own mouth.

Before Thomas could move, Zachary dropped his jaw and lunged to take in his dick. Thomas gasped above him. Zachary swirled his tongue over and around the sensitive head. He flattened it and worked the underside of his shaft while the warm, smooth flesh slid deeper into his mouth. Its thick head pressed toward his throat as Zachary fought and controlled his gag reflex.

He struggled to keep his teeth sheathed as his lips stretched. He tightened his cheeks as he bobbed his head and sucked hard.

The cock in Zachary's mouth grew even more rigid. He grasped Thomas's muscled ass cheeks to pull him forward to swallow him to the root. Thomas cried out as though afraid to blow too soon in the depths of his throat. Zachary's nose tickled against a silky bush of hair. Breathing through his nose to inhale the earthy scent, he worked his throat muscles around the hard dick he serviced.

Thomas moaned to signal his orgasm approached. He dropped one hand to the back of Zachary's head and pulled himself even deeper into the velvet warmth. Before his orgasm became inevitable, though, Zachary pulled off his cock with a gasp. Trails of saliva caught the light as he drew his head back. He spun Thomas around to face the closet door and barked, "Hands on the wall."

THOMAS WAS ALMOST shocked to find himself obeying. It was *so* not who he normally was, but fuck if he knew why. To surrender to Zach's directions felt perfect—welcome, even.

Zach spread his ass with his strong hands. He gasped when Zach ran the tip of his wet tongue up and down his trench. He arched his back, pushed out with his hips, and exposed himself further to Zach's ravening mouth. He whimpered when Zach traced circles around his rim with that warm tongue. Zach reached up between Thomas's legs to grab his sac and tug on it as he stiffened his tongue to push inside. The hand working his balls and the tongue spearing his ass made Thomas squirm and thrust back, desperate for more.

Zach pressed inward and grunted his pleasure as he used his mouth on the tender hole. Thomas felt nerve endings he'd long ignored awaken as he found himself bent almost in half, his ass wide open. He ground up and down against Zach's tongue. The slight stubble on Zach's face scratched against the sensitive skin around Thomas's opening. The tongue that was at least an inch inside him suddenly made him long for the fullness and stretch of a hard cock.

The rim job had Thomas nearly out of his mind with pleasure. He moaned when Zach stopped long enough to say in a husky voice, "I want to fuck you this time." Then he resumed the strokes and thrusts with his talented tongue.

The unspoken question—*Can I?*—echoed in Thomas's head. He hadn't let anyone inside him for years, since even before Rumson nearly ruined his life. He was so aroused by the domination, though, that he realized he would gladly spread his legs—just for Zach.

He licked his lips as he reached back to spread his cheeks for better access. "Do it, Zach. Fuck me."

Zach ran his tongue from Thomas's balls to his taint. He continued to swipe up the crack of his ass and then his back as he rose smoothly to his feet. Wrapping his arms around Thomas's waist, he hugged him from behind. Zach's hard cock, still trapped by his jeans, pressed against Thomas. He thought for a minute Zach might fuck him right there. The mental image made his cock jump, and he worried for a second that he'd come.

Instead Zach stepped back and released him as he said, "Let me see you spread on your bed, Thomas. I want you on your stomach, open and waiting for me."

Oh yes. Even better idea.

He tried to regain some sense of control, as much to prevent himself from spilling there in the hallway as to protect the shreds of his self-image. Pulling up his pants part way, he tried to walk down the hall without tripping.

Once in the bedroom, Thomas quickly stripped off his shoes, socks, pants, and the tatters of his shirt. He retrieved the lube and a box of condoms from the nightstand. When he heard Zach moving toward the bedroom, he climbed onto the thick white comforter. Laying flat on his belly, he aimed his ass toward the door while he spread his legs and tucked his arms.

He heard Zach say, barely above a whisper, "So fucking beautiful." Then he listened as Zach took off his own clothes.

Soon Thomas felt the bed dip. Silky smooth skin slid across his as Zach stretched along his body. His cock rested warm and heavy against Thomas's ass and back as he licked Thomas's neck. Thomas sighed, clutched the comforter under his hands, and ground his dick into the cool fabric.

Zach rolled off and Thomas heard the tear of a foil wrapper. He turned his head to watch Zach unroll a condom down the length of his dick. The sight made his ass clench with anticipation and nerves. He said quietly, "I haven't had anyone or anything inside me in years."

Zach nodded and gave him a devilish grin. "I'll take care of you, Thomas, but I want you to feel this for a week afterward. While you're sitting at your desk, I want you to remember me pounding my cock into you."

Oh God. Thomas ground his hips harder against the bed. Even that threat was sexy, and despite the rough treatment, Thomas felt no fear. He didn't know why he trusted Zach so completely, but he gave himself over to it. Surrendering the last threads of restraint, he begged, "Fuck me. Let me feel your big dick inside my tight ass."

Zach chuckled hoarsely and then pressed his face against Thomas's hole again to lick his rim firmly. He grunted as he nuzzled and worked until Thomas moaned again. Then he popped open the bottle of lube to drizzle liquid down Thomas's crack and along the length of his own sheathed erection. Once he'd returned the bottle to the nightstand, he brought a finger into play. He circled Thomas's opening for a moment, then pressed against the slowly relaxing pucker.

Thomas inhaled sharply as Zach's thick digit breached him and carefully tunneled inside. It burned, but he was so aroused that the slight discomfort faded quickly. Zach slid his long finger in and out and steadily increased the speed and depth as Thomas felt himself go slack. He murmured, "I can take more," and clenched his jaw before he could add "sir."

What the fuck am I doing?

When Zach pressed two fingers into his ass, Thomas thrust back onto Zach's hand. He raised his hips so he could draw his knees up to his chest and rest his forehead on his hands. He whimpered and cried out as Zach turned his hand and crooked his fingers to graze Thomas's prostate. "Holy shit," he gasped. "Oh, Zach. That feels incredible. Can you please fuck me now?"

"Not just yet, stud," Zach said in a low, steady voice. "You're still so tight you'd cut the circulation off on my cock, and I'm going to need it to fuck you deep and long."

Zach kept torturing him as he worked his fingers in and out and occasionally pressed against his gland. Thomas felt precome drip from his cock onto the bed.

"You're beautiful like this," Zach murmured. "You're all spread out for me and you feel smooth and warm inside." Thomas moaned at the praise and squeezed his muscles to try to trap Zach's hand inside him. "I can't wait to slide into you. Do you know how hard you make me?" he purred. "Reach back and grab my cock now. I want you to think about how much of me you're going to feel inside your ass soon."

Thomas reached out as instructed. He almost sobbed in excitement as he wrapped his fingers around Zach's gloved and lubed erection. In return Zach added a third finger to his ass. It brought only the briefest discomfort as he spread Thomas's hole farther than it ever had been before.

"So good, Zach. It feels so good," Thomas moaned and pressed back against Zach's hand. Then he moved his own fist up and down over Zach's long, sheathed cock. He squeezed it tightly and gasped, "I want to feel this dick inside me."

"I love that you call me Zach. No one else does." He kissed the back of Thomas's neck again, and then he withdrew his fingers. The absence left Thomas's hole empty and lonely for a moment until Zach moved into position behind him. The latex-encased head pressed against his opening.

"I want you to clench hard for me now until I tell you to release it," Zach said in a voice that brooked no argument. Thomas did as he was told and squeezed his hole as tightly as he possibly could. When Zach said, "Now," he relaxed and then gasped as Zach pressed into him. The head of his dick sank in, bigger even than the three fingers Thomas had rocked against.

"Ah, you're perfect," Zach sighed. Thomas relaxed into the penetration, shivering when Zach pushed more and more of his long cock inside.

It should have hurt, but the sensation of being filled, of being *taken*, brought a warm glow of peace and completion. Moments into the invasion, Thomas felt intimations that he was perhaps a fraud. All those years he had maintained a careful distance and control. He had *always* taken charge as he found his pleasure in the bodies of countless men. Yet Zach had taught him something new about his own body and his own desires that he never before recognized.

Zach pressed farther into his ass as he demanded access. Thomas was surprised to feel tears prickle at the corners of his eyes. A thought flickered through his mind—a wish that he could have more than just that night. He pushed the idea away to deal with another time. This night he wanted to give himself. He found it surprisingly easy to surrender into pure physical pleasure as Zach began to fuck him in earnest.

The strokes were long and deep. Thomas stretched his legs out again until he was flat on his belly so Zach could pound him into the mattress. He heard himself utter encouragements to go hard, go deeper as Zach used his body. He lost himself until he was aware of nothing more than a cock moving inside his rectum. His mind was free and drifting, and he thought he could lose himself in sensation. At the same time, he didn't want to miss a precious stroke. He needed an anchor, so he grabbed one of Zach's arms to pull around himself as he gave everything he was capable of giving.

Zach rested his forehead against Thomas's neck as he thrust faster. Thomas felt the cock inside his ass grow even harder. "Tear me up, Zach," he gasped. "You promised I'd feel it for a week."

Zach absolutely *roared* and pressed his full length so deeply inside that Thomas cried out, and then he could feel Zach spasm. He tightened his arms and lifted Thomas's chest off the bed until Thomas's thighs rested on Zach's as he shuddered. "Aaah, Zach...," Thomas moaned.

Zach rubbed his still-hard dick against Thomas's prostate and murmured against his neck, "Come for me now." Suddenly Thomas's own orgasm took him. Zach fucked him through it, cock buried inside his ass, arms wrapped around his chest. Thomas thrashed and twitched and shot ropes of come all over the comforter.

When it finally ended, Thomas collapsed forward on the bed and luxuriated in the weight on top of him. Zach nuzzled the back of his head and his neck and moved his softening dick idly inside his body.

Thomas's heart rate gradually slowed. Slightly embarrassed at his own behavior, but still in the flush of a great orgasm, Thomas asked, "Where did that come from?"

Zach chuckled slightly against his back. "I have no idea. I've never done anything like that before. I just suddenly knew that if this was the last time we could ever be together, I wanted everything from you. So I took it." He put one hand on Thomas's hip and gripped it tightly. "I took *you*."

"Zach…."

"No, don't. You've been completely honest with me. I knew the score before I came home with you again. This night with you was a gift I'll remember for the rest of my life."

Zach reached down to hold on to the condom as he withdrew from Thomas's body. Then he climbed out of bed to remove and tie it off.

As he stood by the bed, he reached down to stroke Thomas's back. Softly, he said, "I'll keep trying the friendship thing with you, Thomas. But truthfully I don't have much hope for that. It's going to kill me when I see you go off with another man, knowing he gets to have what I want. But I *will* try."

Thomas said, "Hold on. I'll get you a towel." He rolled off the bed to grab a couple from the bathroom. They faced each other as Thomas wiped and dried Zach's semihard dick. Dabbing at the bedspread, he murmured with a smile, "I wonder if these stains will come out of a Frette duvet cover."

"You could add it to my bill along with the shirt I destroyed," Zach said with what looked like a grimace.

Thomas answered, "The shirt gave its life for a worthy cause, so I can't let you pay me for it. That was… astonishing, Zach. I never even imagined I'd like being handled the way you did me."

Zach kissed him and then reached for his clothes, no longer able to meet Thomas's eyes at all. "I'm going to go. Thank you for this."

"You don't want to stay the night?"

"I can't. It'll hurt worse in the morning."

"I'm sorry." Thomas hung his head for a second, but Zach was right—it was probably better that way. He put his arms around Zach and sighed.

Suddenly Zach struggled out of the hug in which Thomas had wrapped him. "No," he declared. "You don't get to be the victim here."

Thomas leaned back and dropped his arms to his side in surprise. "What are you talking about?"

"That sigh you just gave. Like I'm abandoning you."

"I wasn't...."

"Yes, you were, Thomas. I said you've been honest, so don't suddenly turn this into a scene."

"Zachary, I don't know what you're talking about." Panic twinges started to run up and down Thomas's spine.

"You are way too smart to get away with that bullshit, Thomas. You know the effect you have on men. I think you *use* that so you can preserve this illusion that you're just a, I don't know, a player who only wants sex and is too worldly for a relationship." Zach's voice was becoming strident, but Thomas let him bare his frustration. He deserved the chance to have his say, even if Thomas really did not want to hear an indictment.

"I'm listening," he said gently.

Zach growled, anxiety rolling off him in waves. "This does me no good, but maybe, just maybe, it will help you with the next guy you bring home who would give a shit about you if you would permit it."

"Picture it from my perspective. I'm new in town, inexperienced, excited. I meet a man in a bar who is devastatingly handsome—don't you dare smirk—and for some reason seems interested in me. He brings me home, and we have the most incredible sex of my life. Twice, in fact. Then he kicks me out the door the next morning. He says I should go have fun with other men and forget about him.

"Except he flirts with me at brunch. He invites me to the museum. Everywhere I look is this extraordinary man, and I'm told to accept being nothing more than his friend."

Zach began to pace around the room. "But wait. I come to a bar one night with a date, and there he is again. I leave alone, and he follows me. He brings me back to his apartment. The frustration and the lust and the—okay, goddammit—the overwhelming, impossible desire to have this man for my own just consumes me. Again we have the most explosive sex I ever dreamed of. Richter scale. And then it's over again. And I'm supposed to be his friend. Again."

Guilt roiled Thomas's stomach. It was all true. He had pushed Zach away and then pulled him back in when he felt lonely. He had known he could count on Zach's obvious feelings for him. God, he really was a bastard.

Zach came to a stop in front of Thomas, his eyes wide. He asked incredulously, "Be your friend? I get it, Thomas, honestly. Sex is easy for you, but I think it's a *friend* you really need. I want to be your friend, so much, because you're one of the most astonishing people I've ever known. But Jesus Christ, how can I? Am I a bad person because I can't be around you without thinking how good we could be together? Am I a loser because I wish you'd just cut the crap and let yourself get to know me? Am I a failure because I can't pretend you mean nothing more to me than a buddy?"

Thomas shook his head urgently. "Of course you aren't a loser or any of those terrible things you said, Zach. Please believe me. I'm the broken one. I know that already."

"But *why*, Thomas? It's so easy to hide behind these dramatic statements and give me nothing of substance to explain it. Why are you broken, and why won't you take a chance to see if maybe I could actually help you heal?"

"I just… I can't, Zach." He pleaded with his eyes for Zach to believe him, to understand there was nothing here for him. After the havoc Rumson wrought in his life, Thomas was sure he was beyond repair.

Zach searched his face, and his eyes darted back and forth as he looked for some reason to hope. Thomas schooled his features carefully to give nothing away. It would be cruel to give Zach any reason to hang on. After a minute Zach dropped his chin and turned away, defeated. He sat on the bed to tie his shoes, clearly unable to look Thomas in the face any longer.

"Let me call you a cab, at least. There's still a maniac out there somewhere," Thomas said. Zach nodded but kept his gaze on the ground.

At the apartment door, before Zach left, Thomas took him in his arms, forced him to turn around, and hugged him hard. "Good night, Zach. Be well."

Zach hugged him back and rested his face against Thomas's neck for a moment before he pulled away. "You too, Thomas." And then he was gone.

Thomas closed the front door and sagged against it for a moment. He leaned his forehead against the painted wood. His ass ached in a way that reminded him of how he had been filled for a brief time, and then of his solitude.

His heart hurt from the things Zach had said and the painful questions he asked. In minutes Zach stripped away Thomas's self-deceptions that he was just someone who liked sex with lots of different men. He exposed instead a manipulative asshole who used his looks to draw in an endless stream of casual partners to fill an emptiness he hadn't acknowledged. But Zach wasn't trying to be cruel. Thomas doubted he even had that capacity. No. Zach cared about him despite the whipsawing and wanted Thomas to let someone get close to him. To be a friend.

Thomas whispered into the dark, empty apartment, "If I could let anyone in, Zach, it would be you."

*   *   *

THE MAN IN the silver-framed glasses stabbed at the replay button over and over. His blood pounded in his ears, louder with each repetition. His hands shook as he worked his equipment. The camera angle showed nothing but the darkened apartment. Yet he heard clearly his Beloved say, "If I could let anyone in, Zach, it would be you."

He had been so close to snatching the creature earlier in the parking lot, risky as he knew it was with the police sniffing around. Then his Beloved came out of the bar and they went off together in a cab. To hear his Beloved give those words to his latest *toy*—words He had denied to all others—was more than anyone could bear. Zachary Hall deserved a very special punishment for his... violation.

Opening the box that had arrived in the mail that day, he removed a large and thick rubber phallus. It was fifteen inches in length and nine inches around. He admired its thickness. He contemplated the protests and cries of anguish he would hear as he forced it inside the creature. Cries that would turn into ecstasy as he made his lesson clear.

He heard a low roar come out of his own chest as he began to hammer nails all around the head.

Chapter 12

"MR. SCARBOROUGH, CAN you meet me today?" Torres said with no preliminaries. Her voice on Thomas's cell phone was deadly serious. Thomas felt his testicles shrivel as fear crawled in his stomach. "I need to show you some pictures."

"Is it another killing?" he gasped. *Not someone else I knew, please. Not Zach....*

"I'm afraid so," Torres answered. "MO appears to be consistent, along with some other similarities. I need to know if the victim had a connection to you or to Mata Hari. I'm going to see Mr. Vaughan this afternoon as well. Perhaps you can join us?"

He couldn't wait that long to know. "Please, can you tell me his name?" Thomas could hear the tremor in his own voice, the slight begging.

Torres sounded apologetic. "I can't do that until my department is ready to make a statement. But I can show you the pictures...."

"Where do I find you?" he asked immediately.

"It takes too long to get through security and into any of the Senate office buildings. Can you meet me at the fountain in front of the Capitol? I can be there in ten minutes."

"Anne, I'm running an errand," Thomas called to his secretary. He grabbed his coat and then hurried as fast as he could to meet Torres. It was a cold, cloudy day with a threat of snow, but that wasn't why his hands trembled. It had been two weeks since he'd seen or heard from Zach. It couldn't be him.

Please....

He hurried across the plaza to where the detective waited, dressed in a gray wool coat. With no greeting she handed him a manila envelope.

"They aren't crime scene photos. They're recent pictures of the victim that we got from his mother. I need to know if you recognize him."

Thomas nearly dropped the envelope, but he managed to slide the photos out and stare at the array. He almost sagged in relief. It wasn't Zachary or anyone else he recognized.

Torres watched him closely, though. He shuffled again through the four photos of a nice-looking young man, probably college age, sporting a trendy haircut. "I don't believe I've ever seen him before," Thomas said at last as he glanced at the detective. "You think it's the same killer, though?"

"You're sure you don't know him?" Torres asked. "Please take another look."

He went through the array again but then shook his head. "I'm sure I've never talked to this kid, and I definitely didn't take him home. I think that's really what you're asking." Thomas slid the photos back into the envelope. "Is there a connection to Mata Hari, like with Brian Gallagher?"

Torres hesitated but then said, "Actually not that we've found yet. I'll ask Mr. Vaughan to look at the pictures too, but the night this man was killed, he had been at a dance club in Southeast DC."

"And you won't tell me why you think it's the same killer?"

"I can't release that kind of detail. Let's just say there was a particularly brutal element here. It mirrors what was done to Gallagher and makes a coincidence unlikely."

"I'd like to say I'm sorry I couldn't help you, Detective, but the truth is I'm relieved," Thomas admitted. "Whatever is going on, it doesn't seem to have anything to do with me after all."

. . .

TORRES GOT BACK to the station later that afternoon, frustrated as she reported to her captain. "Neither Scarborough nor Vaughan recognized the victim, Daniel Owen."

She ticked off the points from her notes. "He was found in his own apartment, front door unlocked but no sign of forcible entry. Nothing stolen, as far as his mother can tell. The perp strangled him and forced a foreign object into his rectum. The cause of death was something that shredded his colon and bowels from the inside. All of those details are highly similar to the Gallagher case. Yet so far I've turned up no connection to Mata Hari, to Scarborough, or to the neighborhood where Gallagher bought it. Maybe that will change when we've gone over the footage from the security cameras at the dance club... umm...." She checked her notes. "Horizons."

Captain Nelson looked at the scene photos from Forensics and fought back a wince. "I agree this isn't a coincidence, even though the murders are almost two months apart. We may have a serial killer going after young, white, gay men after they leave bars alone." He tapped the end of a pen against the photos as he thought. Then he sighed and closed the case file. "Maybe it's one of those moon things where the bastard kills under a certain phase each time."

Torres said, "Already checked. Two nights ago, when Owen was killed, was a first-quarter moon, whatever the hell that means. Gallagher's murder was just past the new moon. Plus we don't know of anyone he killed in March, so he'd be skipping a cycle."

"Okay. That doesn't sound like the right track." Nelson frowned as he continued tapping his pen against the closed folder and finally tossed it aside. "Shit. We have to go public, but the reaction is going to be bad." He sighed. "Let me get the LGBT Liaison Unit involved with a press conference. Those guys can make the rounds of the bars to spread a warning."

"Yes, sir. That makes sense. I'll prepare a list of talking points."

"I need something solid, Torres." Nelson scowled and said, "If we really do have a serial killer...."

"I know, sir, and I'm working on it. Maybe something on the security tapes will help or we'll turn up a connection to Scarborough. If the perp strikes again, well, maybe the details from a third murder will reveal more of a pattern."

"Torres, I don't want there to be a third victim," Captain Nelson stated in his most withering voice. "Get this wrapped. Now."

* * *

"HERE YA GO, Maria. Just arrived." A secretary handed Torres a thick manila envelope that afternoon. She paused from writing out the press notes Nelson wanted. The envelope was from the general manager of Horizons. It contained security footage for the night Daniel Owen had been murdered.

She looked at the discs stacked on her desk and sighed. Three cameras in the club to check, and she needed to go over at least an hour on either side of Owen's exit—maybe more. His friends reported he had been with them at the club until about eleven thirty. He said he was tired and wanted to head home. They never saw him alive again.

She grabbed more coffee and picked up her cell. "Ramon, hey. I won't be there in time for dinner. I've gotta shit-ton of work to do." She rolled her eyes as her boyfriend bitched. "Don't be that way, baby. It's work. I told you.... Well, then, go see a movie with your brother or something…. Baby, I need to go. I gotta get started watching footage." She disconnected the call while Ramon was still complaining.

Torres wasn't sure why she even kept him around. He wanted a girl who made dinner for him and was waiting when he got home from his job. That was not her. No way, no how. Full of dark thoughts and grumblings, not to mention bad coffee from the precinct machine, Torres cued up the first CD.

Two hours later she sat up straight in her chair. She backed up the footage and replayed the sequence again. Someone was there that she would not have expected. The image quality wasn't that good, but she had talked to that man not too long ago. The day she checked Scarborough's alibi.

She picked up her phone and called Captain Nelson. "Sir, you wanted to know anything I found. This may be just a coincidence, but I have a connection between Horizon and Mata Hari. It's a guy named Terry Krasnopoler."

. . .

THAT EVENING THOMAS slid onto his usual stool at Mata Hari. Randy poured them each a shot without asking. "Helluva business," he said, obviously referring to the second dead man. "The police put out his picture this afternoon and asked for information. Kid's name was Daniel Owen."

Thomas tossed back the contents of his glass. When he had set it on the counter, he said quietly, "I nearly shit my pants when Torres called. I thought it was going to be someone else I had fucked around with."

Randy filled his shot glass again. "I know, buddy. But now I think it really was just a coincidence that you took Gallagher home."

"What do you suppose is the common element she's talking

about to connect the murders?" Thomas asked.

Randy shrugged. "It could be anything, though Torres said it's sexual. Maybe he marks 'em or something. Frankly this is why I went Secret Service. I don't think I'd have the stomach to investigate these kinds of crimes."

Looking over Thomas's shoulder, Randy's expression changed. He murmured, "She's back already." He straightened up as Torres approached the bar. "Evenin', Detective. More questions or more bad news?"

"Questions, Mr. Vaughan," she said and nodded politely toward Thomas. "Mr. Scarborough."

"More questions for me?" Thomas asked, ready to be annoyed, but she shook her head no.

"Well, maybe," she amended and added, "But I'd like to talk to you alone, Mr. Vaughan, if possible."

Randy gestured for his assistant to keep an eye on the bar and signaled Torres to follow him to his office. Thomas stayed on his stool, burning with curiosity. He knew Randy would tell him everything she said anyway.

He looked around the room out of habit. Many of the faces he saw were regulars. Good for Randy for building a steady clientele already. He met the eyes of someone he was pretty sure he had fucked a few months before. Turning his head away, he prayed the man wouldn't come over. He saw some new faces too.

One man stood alone by the piano, and another leaned against a wall. That one was a good height, lean, and wore his hair long. He was probably in his early twenties. Maybe a college kid from Georgetown or George Washington University. His tight jeans showed narrow hips and quite a package. He looked back at Thomas, and his lips curved into a slight smile. Yes, he was interested. Thomas could have him in the back of a cab in ten minutes and stretched out on his bed in twenty.

But the hair wasn't quite the right color. His eyes were too dark, shoulders too narrow, and Thomas abruptly realized he was doing it again. He was comparing the stranger to Zachary, and he found the stranger wanting.

He sighed and turned back to the bar. As he lifted his drink, he heard a low voice at his elbow.

"Hey, sexy. Remember me?" He turned, and the guy he had fucked previously stood at his side. Thomas had no idea of his name.

"Hey, you," he said carefully. "How've you been?"

The man licked his lips. "Well, much better since I saw you sitting here. I still think about that time."

Glenn? Ken? Thomas tried desperately to recall a name. He didn't know why he should bother. Suddenly he didn't want to be the asshole who fucked guys and forgot them. "Sure. That was fun," he said. He had a vague recollection that the guy was really flexible.

The man reached out his hand and lightly brushed his fingers over Thomas's forearm. "So much fun," he agreed. "You had me twisted up like a pretzel."

Thomas turned his body slightly as he moved his arm away and said, "Well, it's nice you stopped by."

The man—*Denny?*—didn't take the hint. He leaned closer to Thomas and cooed, "I could really go for a rematch tonight. The things you did with my body were just amazing."

Thomas felt his stomach tighten and sweat dampened his palms. He kept a light voice as he said, "I'm flattered, but I'm sure I told you I don't do repeats."

"Hmm... what if we change it up a bit?" the man pressed again. "The hot number by the door I saw you eye-fucking. I bet he'd be up for a little three-way with you and me. That wouldn't exactly be a repeat."

Thomas started to get annoyed. "Then you should go talk to him, but leave me out of your plans. I'm not interested."

The man stepped back and gave a snort of disgust. "Fine. You're too old for me anyway. I was just going to throw a pity fuck your way." He turned and left, thankfully without throwing a glass at Thomas's head.

Thomas sighed and took a sip of his drink. He heard Torres say, "For all this game you supposedly have, you sure do piss off people."

Thomas whirled, ready to snipe back, but Torres had a look on her face that was more amused than condescending. Randy was behind the bar again, his face slightly white and his jaw set. Thomas asked a question with his eyes, and Randy mouthed the word *Later*.

He forced himself to relax. Turning back to Torres, he said with a shrug, "Like I told you. Everyone gets the memo, but some forget."

"It must be lonely, though," she said, looking Thomas in the eye. "Do you ever want to break your own rule?"

I already did with Zach.

"Are we continuing the interrogation now, Detective?" Thomas asked, though he tried to keep his tone light.

She glanced around. No one other than Randy was near the two of them at the moment. She asked in a soft voice, "What is your relationship with Terry Krasnopoler?"

Thomas nearly reeled back in surprise. "With Terry? What are you talking about? We're just friends."

Randy said nearby, "Maybe you want to talk in one of the other rooms where it's quieter. Or use my office. I don't care."

Torres stepped back and checked to see if Thomas was following. She led the way to Randy's office, for all the world like it was her own.

In Randy's office Torres closed the door behind them and sat in one of Randy's visitor chairs. Thomas took the other one. "What's this about Terry, Detective?"

"Let me ask you, Mr. Scarborough. Have you ever had sex with Terry Krasnopoler?"

"No, of course not. He's just a friend. Him and his husband Joe."

"How long have he and"—she glanced at her notes—"Joe Mulholland been together?"

"Well, I don't know for sure. I think five or six years, though I recall they just got married last year."

"Is their relationship close?"

Thomas squirmed a bit. It wasn't for him to discuss their arrangement with a police detective, not without a very good reason. "I would say so, but you'll have to ask them about that," he said.

"I will. Have you ever sensed that Mr. Krasnopoler might think of you as more than a friend?"

Thomas almost laughed. "Honestly no. You've already made up your mind I'm a complete egotist, Detective. When I tell you that Terry has never shown the slightest interest in me that way, you should believe I know what I'm talking about."

"Fair enough. It's just an angle I need to explore," Torres said. Then she changed topics. "The night that Brian Gallagher was murdered, you spoke at the bar with Mr. Krasnopoler." Thomas nodded. "You told me that Mr. Krasnopoler left the bar before you did, correct?"

"That's right. He left, and I stayed a bit longer to talk to Ethel."

"Which she confirmed." The detective looked at her notes and knit her dark eyebrows together. The hesitation on her face indicated to Thomas that she wasn't sure whether to go with her next question. Finally she asked, "Did you ever see Mr. Krasnopoler in the company of Daniel Owen or Brian Gallagher?"

Thomas sat up straight in his chair, suddenly alarmed. "What? Terry and the victims?"

Torres nodded. "You told me that you didn't recognize Daniel Owen when I showed you his pictures. I'd like you to think about it again for a minute and tell me if you ever saw him, perhaps with Mr. Krasnopoler."

Thomas was definitive. "No. I'm quite sure I never saw that man before in my life. With Terry or anyone else."

"How about Gallagher?"

Thomas frowned and squinted as he thought. "Nothing comes to mind. I don't recall noticing Brian before the evening we hooked up. And then I saw him just the one additional time, the night…."

Torres nodded sympathetically, which surprised him. "I'm reasonably sure Mr. Vaughan will tell you this the minute I leave anyway, so I may as well mention that he saw Gallagher and Mr. Krasnopoler having a drink together about a week before you picked up Gallagher."

Thomas blinked. "That's… surprising. But okay, Brian and Terry had a drink."

"They left together afterward. Mr. Krasnopoler was also at Horizons the night that Daniel Owen died."

Thomas's jaw dropped. "The dance club? That doesn't seem like a place Terry would go. Are you sure?"

"Yes, I'm sure."

Thomas thought rapidly and concluded, "But you must not have anything connecting Terry directly with Owen."

Torres narrowed her dark eyes at him. "Why do you say that?" she asked.

"You mentioned that Randy saw Terry with Brian, but you

didn't say anything about Terry with Owen. If Randy had seen him with both men, you would have said that. Also you asked me if *I'd* seen Owen and Terry together. If you had something that linked them together specifically, I think you would have shown me a picture. It sounds like you're fishing for a connection."

She closed her notebook and stood. "I appreciate your time, Mr. Scarborough."

"You're going to talk to Terry, I take it?" Thomas asked.

Torres made a noncommittal grunt and left. Thomas remained in his chair, stunned, but he wasn't surprised at all when Randy joined him a minute later.

The bartender closed the office door behind him and sat heavily in his own chair. It squeaked as he leaned forward. "What do you think?" he asked Thomas.

Thomas answered with a question. "Did you really see Brian Gallagher with Terry?"

Randy nodded. "Yeah, maybe a week before you guys hooked up. Terry put the moves on him, Gallagher seemed to like the attention, and they left together. I told you Gallagher was no Boy Scout. Not that it means he deserved what happened to him. Terry's picked up other guys before. You know that."

"I know but... well, it's weird that we apparently had sex with the same guy."

Randy shrugged it away. "What would Terry be doing at Horizons, though? He just never struck me as the type to hang out at a dance club."

"Maybe he was there with someone else?"

"Maybe," Randy agreed. "Helluva coincidence, though."

"This is going to hurt Joe. I don't care what kind of arrangement they've got. Something like this will get out and embarrass them both."

"I thought that too. I considered calling Joe or Terry, but I don't want to interfere with a police investigation."

Thomas looked sharply at him. "Randy, are you suggesting that maybe *I* should call one of them?"

Randy's hesitation showed he had indeed thought about it, but he shook his head. "No, don't. It will just make it look like we think there's something to it. And Torres would find out eventually, one way or another. I say we keep our mouths shut and see what happens."

Thomas nodded. "Agreed. But I'm with you, Randy. No fucking way is Terry involved in two murders."

Chapter 13

THAT SAME DAY, in the kitchen of Rainbow Space, Zachary cranked the burner under the oversized stockpot to make chili. Jamayqua rapidly chopped onions on a cutting board beside him as he poured vegetable oil into the pot.

The smooth tap-tap-tap of the knife helped Zachary leave behind a tough day at work. He even welcomed the acrid scent of onions in his nose and the slight burn in his eyes. As the oil heated in his stockpot, Zachary worked to get his head away from the office and into the kitchen. He was also brooding a bit over the last few chorus rehearsals where Howard had been cold to him. Zachary had few enough friends in DC. The way Howard glowered at him across the rehearsal space when they caught each other's eye distressed him.

He tried to push his concerns into a corner of his mind while he watched Jamayqua work. After a few minutes, he commented to her, "You've got mad knife skills. Where'd you pick those up?"

The shy girl wouldn't look up at him but answered quietly, "My dad ran a little diner over in Anacostia. I used to help him." She passed him the cutting board full of neatly chopped onions, and he added them to the pot.

"Would you keep an eye on these while I get the beans and tomatoes?" Zachary asked, and Jamayqua took the long wooden spoon from him without another word. Almost as tall as Zachary, she had trouble finding women's clothes to cover her long legs among the donated goods. She wasn't wearing a hair net, which was a problem. Zachary suddenly guessed that she kept her bright-red hair long and hanging forward to disguise her Adam's apple.

He retrieved two industrial-sized cans of crushed tomatoes and a vat of beans Vic had left to soak for him. At the same time he snagged a net and a long kitchen towel. Bringing his ingredients to the counter, he said, "Hey, Jamayqua, look at me a minute." She tilted her head up but kept stirring the onions. "C'mon, face me. It's just us."

She rested the wooden spoon in the pot and stood up straight, though her warm-brown eyes stayed on the ground. Zachary tossed the end of the kitchen towel around her shoulders. He tied it like a scarf and turned the knot so it rested fashionably on her shoulder. Then he handed her the hair net. "I know you hate it, J, but you gotta wear this. You never know when we'll get inspected."

Jamayqua grimaced but took the net, put it on, and tucked her apple-red hair into place. She fingered the scarf Zachary had made her, flashed him the barest smile, and whispered, "Thanks." It looked to Zachary like a million-watt grin, though, and it lightened his heart as he prepared the chili.

Terry popped his head into the kitchen. "Hey, Zachary. Hi, Jamayqua. Joe's sending me to the hardware store. Do you need anything?"

"Actually yes," Zachary said. "Could you pick up some plastic sheeting? The bathroom window on the second floor is broken. I thought we could tack some plastic down until we can get it replaced." Terry gave him a salute and left, only to be replaced by his husband.

"Jamayqua, that's a fetching scarf," Joe said. He eyed the chili ingredients Zachary had assembled. "I'd say we'll have enough chili for, oh, thirty tonight. Dear hearts, would you mind making some trays of cornbread as well? We're short on fresh greens, but we need something to keep these bellies full."

Jamayqua surprised them both by saying, "I'll make the cornbread, Zachary. These onions are ready for you to take over."

"Thanks, honey," Zachary said as he added beans and tomatoes to the pot. "How are you, Joe? I feel I haven't gotten to spend much time with you lately."

"And I miss you, darling boy. Not just here at the shelter. I haven't seen you out and about in a few weeks now."

"I'm sorry I haven't been by as much lately," Zachary said. "I was at a work conference for several days, and then I had a lot of catching up to do when I got back."

"Please, no apologies. We're grateful for the time you can spare, but your life has to come first." Joe patted him on the arm as he said, "Though Terry and I do miss running into you at Mata Hari."

Zachary focused on the chili. "Well, you know, I've been trying to get around to some of the other places in town too," he said, unwilling to meet Joe's eyes. "I've been here over two months already, and there's so much of DC still to explore. I haven't even made it up the Washington Monument yet."

Joe laughed. "Heavens, that's no crime. I've lived here twenty years, and I've never done that either."

Zachary grinned at him as he looked up. "We should go sometime. Maybe a double date?"

Joe's eyes went wide as he asked, "Oh, are you seeing someone now, dear heart?"

"Just recently. We actually met at that work conference I went to in New Orleans. Sam's an IT consultant, and he was there for the trade show part, but he lives here in Washington."

Joe regarded him for a moment, clearly thinking of Thomas.

Then he almost visibly pushed that thought aside. "How wonderful, Zachary. The more love we make, the more love there is to share around." Jamayqua giggled behind them. Zachary had forgotten she was there.

"Well, we're not there yet, so you and Terry are going to have to make up my share."

Joe murmured, "Well, Terry is certainly sharing." When Zachary shot him a surprised look, Joe continued in a brighter voice. "Dear boy, I must have all the details. Tell us about your new beau."

Zachary did, happily. Sam had caught his eye as they both circulated at the cocktail party that kicked off the first day of the convention. He was good-looking, but in a normal way, not the Thomas way that was too much to bear. Zachary spotted him at the bar, and Sam looked back with a friendly grin. Zachary thought about what Joe would do, and he started to go over. But a former colleague from Utah approached him, so he stayed to catch up. When Zachary looked again, he was gone.

Fifteen minutes later he appeared at Zachary's side and introduced himself as Sam Ryder. He was several inches shorter, but Zachary looked into his brown eyes and liked the frank interest he saw there. They started talking, and Sam made a comment about *The Walking Dead*. That sent them off on a discussion of their mutual love for the show and the original comic books. Sam invited him to dinner after the cocktail party ended to keep the conversation going.

Sam had traveled quite a bit and his stories were fascinating. Zachary found himself confessing how boring he felt he was and how much he wanted to push to be more. They flirted, but it was light and easy—a touch on the wrist by Sam, a little nudge with a foot by Zachary. He wasn't sure how far he wanted to take it at a work conference. Aside from his intention not to have sex again too quickly, he worried about someone seeing him slip out of a stranger's room.

Sam got it, though, and was a complete gentleman. He walked Zachary to his hotel room. Once he made sure no one was around, he gave Zachary a lovely good night kiss. It might not have made his heart race the way Thomas's kisses did, but it was sweet and held promise. Sam said in a low, warm voice that he'd really like the chance for them to get to know each other better back in Washington. He gave Zachary his phone number and Zachary went into his own room alone.

"Since I got back last Wednesday, we've been out three times already, Joe," he explained. "Sam just *gets* me. We like the same books, the same TV shows. He's a nerd like me, but he does interesting things for work and travel."

"Darling, I'm hearing you sell yourself short," Joe protested. "You are endlessly fascinating and kind."

"Aw, thanks. I'm not knocking myself. I'm just realistic. I'm still basically a kid from Utah who's never been anywhere or done anything interesting. But I'm really trying to break out of that shell. I think Sam's going to be fun to do that with."

"Well, if he makes you happy, then I'd love to meet him, dear heart," Joe enthused. "Why not bring him by Mata Hari tonight?"

"Umm… I don't think that's a good idea. I'd like to get to know him better before, well…."

"Before he meets the whole gaggle of us clucking queens. Of course," Joe said with a laugh. "Well, then, let's think about a night you can come for dinner—just the four of us. I'll talk to Terry, and you check with your new beau."

"Thanks, Joe," Zachary said, more for not mentioning Thomas specifically than for the invitation. Joe patted his arm and went back to his office while Zachary and Jamayqua finished dinner prep.

Chapter 14

A S ZACHARY CLIMBED into bed a few nights later with a book, his phone chimed with a text message from Sam:

Just want to say good night and ask if you're free for dinner tomorrow.

Zachary smiled as he typed.

I'm rereading Dune *because your comments about parallels to current terrorist tactics piqued my interest. I'd love to talk to you about it over dinner tomorrow.*

Perfect. Let's go to Corduroy. Great food and a nice quiet place to talk over a bottle of wine.

Done, but I'm buying this time. Text me address and time.

Will do. Sleep tight. XOX

• • •

ZACHARY SET THE phone on his nightstand and picked up his book again. Sam had taken him to some great restaurants already, so it was definitely his turn to pay. He just hoped Corduroy wasn't too expensive. Either way, though, it'd be worth it.

It was a pleasure to spend time with someone whose company he enjoyed. Sam shared his interests, pushed his intellectual curiosity, and—most importantly—didn't seem terrified of a relationship. He was glad to take the physical side of things slowly. Falling into bed with Thomas the night they met was completely unlike Zachary. He wouldn't have done it except for the alcohol and the dare from his friend Fred.

Plus the fact that I wanted Thomas the moment I set eyes on him.

Zachary brushed away the stupid voice in his head. That had been an aberration, a mistake. Or, more charitably, a nice memory he'd be able to dust off in the future. He'd recall that once—okay, twice—he'd been with a man that smart, that accomplished, and that gorgeous.

Sam was much more his speed. Maybe tomorrow—or soon, anyway—he'd be ready to make a move. Ramp things up a bit to show Sam his interest in exploring a relationship.

Will I throw him against a wall? Lick his ass and fuck him into submission?

Zachary shivered at the memories of his second encounter with Thomas and felt himself get hard. Finding that streak of dominance inside himself was a surprise. Not unwelcome, but unsuspected until then. He had loved the way Thomas respond-ed, and he was frankly proud at how good the sex was.

He'd had a decent amount of experience in college, once he found a few gay guys to hang with. Since most of his small circle—like him—were afraid of being seen going into a gay bar. Instead, they all practiced on each other like fiends.

Nearly everything he knew about sucking and fucking came from those dorm-room encounters. They had traded partners and switched up positions. After college, he, Fred, and their buddy Frank all returned to their childhood homes in Ogden. They continued to rely on each other for relief, but it was hard to find discreet places to get together. The situation wasn't exactly conducive to learning new moves or techniques.

But someone like Thomas knew how good-looking he was and took it for granted that men would fall all over themselves to sleep with him. He no doubt had hundreds of sex partners. Surprising him had felt special. Zachary alone discovered some button to push that Thomas had never even noticed about himself.

He groaned as he recalled the way Thomas shivered when Zachary *claimed* him. Reaching into his sleep pants to grasp his hard dick, he stroked it as he thought of that night with Thomas. He worked his flesh and tortured himself with vivid images of Thomas undone beneath him, calling him "Zach" as he came. Zachary shuddered and shot his load into his sleep pants.

After a minute he climbed out of bed to clean himself up and change into a pair of boxer briefs. Then he threw the sticky pants into his laundry basket. No more, he told himself. If he wanted a chance of making something work out with Sam, he had to stop thinking of Thomas.

SAM WAITED AT a table in Corduroy when Zachary arrived. He looked nice in a blue shirt and sports coat, with his slightly long, auburn hair brushed back casually. He stood to kiss Zachary on the cheek when he reached the table.

As they both sat down, Sam said, "I hope you don't mind, but I ordered some martinis already. Dry with olive *and* a twist, right?"

Zachary chuckled. "You really pay attention. I haven't had a martini since that first dinner in New Orleans, and you still remember."

"Of course I do," Sam said with a grin. "I got up the nerve to ask out a handsome man like you. You can bet I remember every detail."

The waiter brought their cocktails, and they touched glasses and chatted easily for a bit. When they opened their menus, Sam asked, "Have you seen the new *Captain America* movie yet?" as they looked over the options.

"What kind of nerd would I be if I hadn't waited in line for the first midnight showing of *Civil War*?" Zachary said, and he smiled. "I'd like to see it again, though, if you're interested."

"That would be great. Better yet, can we do a marathon of *First Avenger* and *The Winter Soldier* before going to the new one?" Sam asked.

"Sebastian Stan is so hot, right?"

"I know. I keep hoping they'll ramp up the bromance and have Cap and Bucky get it on."

That was how the conversation ran all night, and Zachary was in heaven to let his geek flag fly. He wanted to make a profession-al name for himself, advance a career, find a new identity as an out-and-proud gay man in DC. Yet he didn't want to let go completely of the things he had loved through high school and college. Things like comic books and superhero movies.

"Movie marathon. Roger," Zachary said. "How about Satur-day? Oh, wait, I can't. I'm working at Rainbow Space that day. Sunday?"

"I can do Sunday. No problem," Sam answered as he took another sip of his martini. "Is this the LGBT shelter you told me about?"

"Yes. I'm going to do some work with Joe. He's the guy I mentioned who runs the place. I'm going to get his donor database updated, and then we'll be making dinner for the kids. Hey, what about making our Marvel-movie marathon a group thing? We could invite any nerdy teenager who wants to participate."

Sam tilted his head. "Is it awful of me if I say I'd really like to spend the time with just you this Sunday? Maybe we could do a group thing the following weekend. Maybe some *Star Trek*?"

"It isn't awful at all. I get it. I'll talk to Joe about a viewing party next week."

"I really admire that you do so much for these teenagers. I might have some time to help too, if you wouldn't feel like I was crowding you. This is your thing, and I don't want you to feel you have to share it."

Zachary sat up straight and said, "Are you serious? I'd love it if you got involved. God, there're so many things that always need to be done. Even with the chores that Joe requires the kids do in return for their bed and meal. There are a couple of computers at the shelter, but they run like molasses, and the software is way out of date. Maybe you could help us get them at least into the twenty-first century?"

"Sure. That shouldn't be hard," Sam assured him. "I'll take a look when we have the marathon next week."

The food at Corduroy was arranged artistically on their plates. It tasted rich and exotic to Zachary's untrained palate. He was nervous about his cauliflower soup with parmesan, but the creamy texture quickly had him scraping the bottom of his bowl. Sam offered him a taste of lobster carpaccio, but that was a little more than Zachary felt ready to handle. On the other hand, his lamb loin with spinach was delicious and satisfying, and Sam's flounder was delicate. After the elaborate presentation, Zachary felt relieved when the check wasn't astronomical. He placed his credit card in the black folio.

Sam said, "Thank you for dinner. You didn't have to do that."

"I know, but I wanted to. I may not be a fancy consultant, but I'm hardly struggling."

"I didn't mean to imply that," Sam said. He bit his lip and

looked concerned. "I just enjoy doing things like this with you."

"Me too. Hey, what about having a night cap somewhere?" Zachary asked. Mata Hari crossed his mind, but he wasn't ready to take Sam there, not until things were more established between them. He didn't want to risk facing Thomas yet. Once he was more secure in a new relationship, it wouldn't hurt so much to see Thomas hook up with some other guy.

Yeah, right.

Sam smiled shyly. "How would you feel about coming back to my apartment for that night cap? No pressure, but I think it would be nice to spend some quiet time together."

Zachary took his hand across the table. "I'd like that."

* * *

SAM'S APARTMENT WAS in the Penn Quarter, in the residences attached to the Newseum, on the top floor. As they entered, Zachary looked across hardwood floors and a large Persian carpet. A wall of windows faced south across a balcony. The view was of the National Gallery, lit up and magnificent. Beyond that, several of the Smithsonian buildings lined the far side of the Mall.

As soon as Sam took his coat, Zachary walked to the windows and didn't hide how impressed he was. He tried hard not to think about his trip to the National Gallery with Thomas and Randy. He called out over his shoulder, "Sam, this is incredible. What a view. I noticed this building once when I was walking on the Mall, and I never dreamed I'd see the inside of it one day."

"I've only lived here a few months, but I really like it. Now can I get you that drink? What would you like?"

"Surprise me," Zachary said. A few minutes later, Sam brought him a glass filled with a creamy liquid.

"This is my version of a Nutty Irishman. It's Bailey's, Frange-lico, and fresh mint over crushed ice," Sam explained.

Zachary took a sip and murmured appreciatively. "That's delicious. Like dessert in a glass."

"Come sit with me." Sam held out his hand and led Zachary to a sleek, upholstered sofa that faced the wall of windows.

He picked up a remote and pressed a button. The lights in the apartment dimmed so they could better enjoy the view spread out before them. He pressed another button and a hidden sound system began to play the orchestral score to *The Lord of the Rings*. Zachary chuckled and leaned back and into Sam, who put an arm around Zachary's shoulder. They sat contentedly and sipped their drinks as they enjoyed the view. Finally Sam took both of their empty glasses, set them on the cocktail table, and leaned in to kiss Zachary.

It was a sweet kiss, friendly and warm, and Zachary enjoyed it. He put his arms around Sam, pulled him closer, and opened his lips slightly to invite Sam's tongue inside. Sam felt nice in his arms, and his body was lean and wiry.

I could get used to this.

He relaxed, and Sam made him feel good. Little was happening for him below the waist, but so what? It was new, and they were just getting to know each other. There was no rush.

Sam seemed to feel the same way because he leaned back from the kiss and said softly, "I really like you, Zachary. I don't mean to be presumptuous, but I need to say that this is enough for me tonight. Making out, I mean. I hope that doesn't pose a problem."

Zachary smiled and ran a fingertip along Sam's jaw. "Believe me, that's fine. I like taking it slow too. You feel great, and I like kissing you. This is really good for me for now."

Sam kissed him again and said, "I'm glad. You make me feel safe and protected, and I like that." He pulled Zachary closer to him, and they snuggled together on the sofa contentedly. Then he murmured against Zachary's head, "I heard that 'for now,' by the way. Believe me, I see a 'now' when I'm nowhere near as uptight with you."

"Ditto," Zachary said, and he tried hard not to think about the last time he let down his guard and rained passion upon....

Stop it. Sam is perfect for me. Don't fuck this up.

Chapter 15

MORE THAN A week after Torres came by the bar to ask about Terry, Thomas stared at the scotch Randy had poured for him. He resisted the temptation to down it; he didn't need to get buzzed. There was a big committee meeting scheduled for the morning. In fact he shouldn't have stopped in at all, but it had been weeks since he'd run into Zachary. Thomas thought maybe he'd be in the bar. He wanted to know if Zach was doing well after the way they left things that night at his apartment. That was all.

Disgusted at his own lies, Thomas left the glass on the bar and rotated his stool to look at the crowd. Not that he was on the prowl or anything. He just wanted to distract himself by taking a look at his investment. He was very happy for Randy—he had found a new direction. It turned out being a bar owner suited Randy perfectly.

Thomas was surprised to see Terry on one of the couches, next to—was that the guy from the brunch with Zach back in March? *Walter. Holy shit.* Thomas was in no position to judge, but after Torres's questions, that felt a little wrong. Maybe too close to home. Terry spotted him and looked sheepish as he sat a little straighter and removed his hand from Walter's knee. Thomas nodded at him and then turned away to avoid any further awkwardness.

Randy said behind him, "Yeah. I don't feel right about it

either. Terry's been in a couple of times now with that guy, but never with Joe around."

Thomas asked quietly, "Have you heard anything more from Torres?"

"No," Randy said. "I think we would have heard if she'd made any connections to Terry."

"Well, in any case, this is just more proof that relationships aren't worth the effort." Thomas subtly tipped his head toward Terry and Walter on the couch.

Randy scoffed at him. "First, don't jump to conclusions. Second, I call bullshit."

Thomas's eyes widened. "What bullshit?"

"*Your* bullshit, brother. I haven't seen you pull so much as a phone number in weeks."

"So what? All this shit with Gallagher and then Daniel Owen had me freaked out."

"Right. Nothing to do with Zachary Hall?" Randy asked as he nudged a full glass of scotch toward Thomas.

"He's just a nice guy. Nothing more," Thomas said, but he sipped his liquor as an excuse to look away.

Randy gave a wolfish grin. "If you weren't part owner here, I might have to kick your ass for lyin' to me."

"Randy, don't push. Please. Zach is just a friend now."

"Zach, huh?" Thomas refused to respond, so Randy finally rapped on the bar twice and left him in peace.

In peace. That was a joke. Fuck if he didn't think about Zach all the time. He had thrown up a mirror to Thomas about his shitty behavior. Even so, Thomas longed to be with the man who actually *saw* him and let him get away with nothing. The moment in the parking lot when Zach had called him on fucking that guy Howard, but let it go, stirred something. It wasn't shame—exactly—for his sleeping around. He just wished he had less of a past. Dammit, he wished he could be a better man.

Thomas could admit it to himself, but to no one else, not even his closest friend, Randy. Zach fascinated him. He wanted nothing more than to spend a week with him somewhere warm and far away from the prying eyes of DC. The Italy fantasy refused to die, and he let himself draw out the dream when he lay alone in bed at night. He imagined how he'd surprise Zach with plane tickets. What Zach would look like on a hillside with the sun setting behind him over the sea.

Zach was a glorious mass of contradictions. He was shy and self-deprecating, yet the way he ordered Thomas around indicated a confident, capable man. He needed only a little encouragement to step out into the light. His versatility in bed said he was almost preternaturally secure in his sexuality. Yet he feared coming out to his parents. He was generous of spirit and absolutely serious about helping Joe in his work at the shelter. Still, he had a naïveté about him. That suggested he had never been through the kind of pain that produced the teens who needed his help.

Thomas's traitorous mind had tormented him during the lonely nights since he brought Zach home the second time. What if Thomas wasn't as toxic as he believed? What if there was a way to tell Zach about Charles Rumson, to explain his fears, and what if Zach understood?

He was so lost in thought that evening that he almost didn't hear Randy say, "Uh-oh." He looked around to see Joe standing at the door of Mata Hari, staring in misery at Terry and Walter. Terry turned bright red and jumped to his feet as Joe rushed to the bar.

"Randall, please," Joe begged. "It can't be here."

Randy nodded and held open the bar pass. "Down the hall to the right. My office is unlocked." Joe gripped his arm in gratitude and then disappeared. Terry was right behind, but Randy lowered the bar pass in front of him.

"Terry, I think Joe needs a minute," Randy said, and a growl edged his voice.

"Goddammit, Randy, I just need to talk to him," Terry pleaded. He looked up at Randy, who was using his height and mass to refuse passage.

"Sorry, Terry. Not here. Give Joe some space and talk at home." Randy flicked his eyes to Walter, who was rapidly pulling on his coat and clearly preparing to run. "Or don't. You're going to have to choose."

Terry looked over his shoulder at Walter and back at Randy, his jaw set. "There's no choice to make. Joe is my husband."

Thomas got up and put an arm around Terry's shoulder. "C'mon. Let's sit over here a bit until things calm down. Randy, can you send Mal over with some Perrier? I don't think either of us needs another drink right now."

Terry let Thomas pull him into one of the small rooms off the main bar, and they sank into facing chairs. Terry leaned forward and put his face in his hands. "God, I think I really fucked up," he moaned.

"Do you want to talk about it, Terry? I'm not here to judge anything."

Terry sighed and dropped his hands to his knees. "I know you won't judge, Tommy. I just got… carried away. Walter is young and sexy, and I feel young and sexy with him."

"So what happened?" Thomas prompted.

"I don't *know*. When we had that brunch all those weeks ago, he slipped me his number. I was flattered, sure, and I thought he was sexy as fuck, but I wasn't intending to do anything about it. Then Zachary said the two of them didn't hit it off, so I figured, what the hell? Joe never cared before about my little adventures.

It's always been with strangers, though, not with someone we both knew. And never more than once. Walter and I got together, but I didn't tell Joe. It seemed like there was no need to worry about being found out. So we got together again, and then… well, shit. I realized that I was playing with fire, but Walter just turned me on."

"Terry, even *I* get that there's a difference between one quick hookup with a stranger and intimacy with someone you both know."

"I know that, Tommy. I do. It was just so exciting to see myself through Walter's eyes. For whatever reason, he actually seems into me. Maybe it's just a daddy fantasy or something for him, but it made me feel like I was hot shit. I did stupid things. *Young* things. I even went with Walter to that dance club, Horizons."

Thomas said, "Oh," in a surprised tone, and Terry's head shot up.

"That detective talked to you, didn't she?" Terry asked sharply.

There was no point in dissembling, so Thomas said, "Yes, she did. We figured it was better not to say anything to you. She'd find out and it would look like Randy and I warned you. Like we thought you had something to do with it."

"You and Randy both, huh? Well, it turns out it's possible to feel even worse than I did two minutes ago."

"Terry, don't. Neither Randy nor I have the slightest doubt that you're not involved."

"Thank you. I appreciate that. Honestly."

"Does Joe know Torres was asking questions?" Thomas asked hesitantly.

Terry shook his head. "No, but I'm going to have to add that to the list too." He looked up at Thomas. "I might as well tell you. I was at Horizons with Walter, and we left together. We were at his apartment for hours afterward. He talked to Torres as well and confirmed that already."

"That's good," Thomas said. "I mean, that it's clear you had nothing to do with Daniel Owen's murder."

Terry grimaced. "It's so sad. I guess you know I fucked around with Brian Gallagher too."

Thomas nodded. "It's kind of odd, but it's not like we keep tabs of each other's hookups. There might be dozens of other guys we've both slept with."

Terry scoffed. "Yeah, right. Look at you, Tommy. Who's going to want an aging, boring-ass accountant after they've had you?"

Thomas looked at him sympathetically. "Is that what this is about, the fling with Walter? That you're getting older?"

Terry ran a hand through his hair and sighed. "I suppose so. Finding someone that young who actually wanted me made me stupid. I thought—"

"You thought you'd get away with it. Then you got sloppy and brought him here," Thomas kindly finished for him, and Terry nodded miserably. "Do you love Walter?" he asked. "Would you leave Joe for him?"

Terry raised his head sharply. "God no. I love Joe. This thing with Walter was, I guess...."

"An infatuation."

"Yes, infatuation. A fucking crush," Terry moaned and hung his head. "I didn't mean to hurt Joe. I was just another middle-aged idiot with a hard-on."

"I understand. I think Joe will too, when he's calmer. For what it's worth, my suggestion is that you head home and wait for Joe. Talk to him like you talked to me and be honest. Let him see it was your dick driving the bus, not your heart."

Terry nodded. "That's good. That makes sense." He reached for his wallet, but Thomas waved him away.

"Tab is covered. Don't worry about it." Terry got up and left the bar without another word. Thomas downed his Perrier and headed to Randy's office to see what Joe needed. An absurd thought crossed his mind—*I don't want an open relationship. I would never share Zach*—but he stomped on it and tried to focus on his friend in pain.

Chapter 16

ON SATURDAY ZACHARY arrived at the shelter a bit early. He was surprised to find that Joe wasn't around. Other volunteers had stepped up to keep the operation on the rails. One of them—Lamar something—told Zachary that Joe said he needed a little breather from everything. "He runs himself ragged here, so I'm glad he's taking some me time," Lamar observed, and Zachary agreed.

Vic let him into Joe's office, and Zachary settled down to work on the donor records. He spent an hour updating information about the contributors and their donations. After printing a series of thank-you letters, he organized them for Joe to add a personal, handwritten note and signature. He was alone, and suddenly curiosity overwhelmed him. The office door was open, but the computer screen faced away from the door. No one would see what he looked up. He quickly ran a search on Thomas Scarborough.

"Holy crap," Zachary whispered at the list of large cash contributions Thomas had made over the last two years. It had to be more than a million dollars.

"Zachary, hi," he heard and looked up to find Thomas himself standing in the doorway. He knew his face had turned red as he worked the keyboard quickly to close down the computer program. He prayed Thomas would write it off to surprise. They hadn't been in the same room in weeks—not since that night in

Thomas's apartment. His blush could easily be attributed to that rather than his snooping.

Or to the longing he still felt at the sight of Thomas's face.

Zachary stood up. "Hey, Thomas. How have you been?" His voice was stiff and formal, and Thomas clearly heard the edge. Zachary felt a surge of remorse and guilt when he compared his reaction to Thomas to how he felt around Sam.

God, what is wrong with me?

"I've been good," Thomas answered cautiously. "Busy, though. The Senate is taking a recess soon, so many pieces of legislation are getting pushed before everyone leaves town."

"Does that mean you get a break too?" Zachary asked as he tried to think of a polite way to escape Joe's office and bring the encounter to an end.

"Not really, though my phone won't ring as much with a daily crisis. Well, it looks like you were busy. I won't keep you." Zachary was relieved when Thomas turned and started to leave, but then he hesitated and looked back. "I miss running into you at Mata Hari," Thomas said in a softer voice.

"Yeah, I just needed a break," Zachary answered. He forced himself to look at Thomas directly. "I've started seeing someone."

Pain immediately flashed through Thomas's eyes. "Oh, that's great. I hope it works out for you," Thomas said, his voice a bit raw as he looked away from Zachary. "I'll let you get back to it," he muttered.

．　．　．

THOMAS STALKED DOWN to the kitchen. He intended to run an inventory on pantry supplies so he could restock what was running low. Visions of Italy splintered and broke apart in his mind's eye, and his chest hurt. He hadn't realized how much hope he'd poured into his dream of Zach on a terrace overlooking the sea. Until the dream was gone.

Goddammit. It's your own fucking fault.

But he wanted to yell anyway. At Charles. At his parents. At himself.

He slammed open the kitchen door and became aware of wide eyes on the tall, thin teen working at the kitchen counter. "Sorry, J," he muttered and took a deep breath. "I'm just in a pissy mood. Ignore me."

Jamayqua looked down at the vegetables she was chopping, but said nothing. Thomas stepped into the pantry and worked through the preprinted lists Joe used to determine what goods were needed. By the time he finished, he was back in control.

He returned to the kitchen and said calmly, "Jamayqua, I'm heading to the store soon. Is there anything special you want me to pick up, besides what's on Joe's checklist?"

She looked up under her bright-red bangs, barely met his eyes, and asked in her soft, deep voice, "Is everything okay with Joe?"

Thomas tried to look reassuring. "He's fine, really. He's just going through a bit of personal stuff, and he needed to recharge the batteries. He'll be back soon. But in the meantime, you know if you need anything, you can ask me or Vic."

Jamayqua nodded and kept chopping. Thomas started to go, but she called out, "Could you maybe pick up some cumin seed and coriander? I have some ideas for a couple of dinners, but we don't have much in the way of spices."

"Of course. I'm happy to do that. If you send me a list of spices you'd like in a text, I'll pick them up this evening."

"Thanks, Thomas," she said, nearly in a whisper.

As he walked back to his car, Thomas thought about Jamayqua's question. He pulled out his phone and dialed.

"Joe Mulholland," he heard over the line, but the voice was

unusually subdued.

"Hi, Joe. It's Thomas. How are you?"

"I've been better, darling. We've decided Terry should stay elsewhere for a little while, until we see if we can work this through. He's moved in with David James and his partner Brandon. I'm not sure whether you know them."

"Oh, Joe. I'm so sorry," Thomas murmured. "Would you like to have dinner with me tonight, to talk or not as you please? I'm running to the store for the shelter, but I'll be wrapped up by eight."

"You're a dear man, but I don't want you to feel you have to get in the middle of this," Joe said. "Terry is your friend too."

"I can listen without taking sides. I'm good at that. And honestly you'd be doing me a favor. I'm feeling down myself, so maybe we can cheer each other up." It was a bit manipulative of him to hint that he needed Joe's company, but it was also true. Alone he'd do nothing but think about Zachary moving on.

Joe chucked drily, "We'll either perk each other up or drag ourselves down together. But I choose to take the offer at face value. Why don't you pick me up when you finish the grocery run? We'll try that new Indian restaurant in Cleveland Park."

"Great. I'd love some chicken tikka masala. I'll call you when I'm on my way."

By the time Thomas reached the wholesale market, Jamayqua texted him a variety of spices. There wasn't room in the shelter's food budget for those items, so he'd just pay for them separately. Jamayqua really had an interest in cooking. He knew some chefs around town who might be willing to take her on, maybe give her some experience and direction.

And speaking of Jamayqua… he thought about the troubles she encountered with the restrooms in her school. Someone needed to address the controversy that certain factions were

drumming up over whether students could use only the bathroom of their birth gender. A few states handled the matter
directly, but there were many cries for federal involvement on
both sides of the issue. There was an opportunity there, Thomas
thought. He needed to talk to his committee chairwoman about
pursuing some research.

It felt good to focus on something positive instead of hating
himself for his uselessness over Zachary.

Chapter 17

"CORIANDER, TURMERIC, ALLSPICE...."

The man with the silver-rimmed glasses reviewed the text message. It came from someone whose phone number registered as Dwayne Horton but whom his Beloved had stored in his phone as Jamayqua. The ghosting program he'd finally managed to install on his Beloved's phone worked perfectly. He'd found a Trojan virus he could attach to a spam e-mail. It had taken him weeks to break the encryption protocols installed on the government-issued cell phone. Finally, though, he was in. He felt so much calmer, so much closer to his goals.

He scanned the list of e-mail messages and the phone log. There appeared to be no recent contact with the Zachary creature. Nor did he find signs of anyone new. That was hardly surprising, given the Beloved's resistance to providing contact information to playthings.

On the other hand, he was almost disappointed. He wanted to try his new machine out, give it a practice run before he put his endgame into motion. He considered the one who had bothered his Beloved recently at Mata Hari. Though his video feed lacked sound, he'd had a clear view of the cretin's lips. He'd made out the words "You're too old for me anyway."

The slight infuriated him, quite aside from its ridiculousness. His Beloved was ripe and mature like the best wine. He was a paragon among men. Yes, that churl might be just the candidate.

He tilted his head as he considered the implications of The Rule. Had the boy irritated the Beloved enough? Had he been marked out for punishment for daring to speak again to the Beloved? He studied the recording of the Beloved seated on his bar stool. There was no clear guidance in his actions before the police detective stepped into the image to speak with him. He concluded the woman's interruption was all that prevented the signal from being given. He should indeed chastise the irritant.

His little trick with the boy from the dance club seemed to have turned attention away from the Beloved, as intended. If it was what the Beloved wanted, he could risk taking that insulting young fool. He made a note to himself to follow up. He just needed to remain careful and find ways to throw off the police. They had announced they were looking for a possible serial killer. He chuckled to himself at the absurdity of the term.

Of course, even with the police watching for patterns, he refused to change the central theme in his chastisements. With each punishment he learned so much. His pulse began to throb as he turned away from his array of computer monitors. He got up to check again that he had assembled the new device correctly.

The padded bench was solid. He shook the apparatus with all his weight, and it barely moved. The leather cuffs for wrists and ankles attached to the bench with extra bolts. With their thick buckles and their hooks to keep the legs elevated, no one was getting out of those.

And as for the heart of the machine, well, it took his breath away. The large Lucite rectangle on its heavy steel pedestal gleamed and caught the late afternoon light. It prismatically shed rainbows on the leather bench. Inside the box, shiny gears and pistons were intentionally left visible around the engine he had chosen. The design specifications called for less horsepower and torque. For what he had in mind, those safety concerns were irrelevant. The steel rod he had used was three quarters of an inch in diameter. It extended from the mechanism by two feet—again, more improvements on the designs he had purchased over the Internet. Nestled inside its Lucite coffin, the machine was heart-stoppingly elegant and sleekly dangerous.

To complete his tests, he positioned clamps on either side of the bench. He was careful to protect the leather as he used the clamps to secure an inch-thick block of plywood. The rod glinted about a foot away from the surface.

He activated the small remote control device he had made, and the gears began to turn on low. They caused the rod to extend and retract, extend and retract. He shivered. The movement was as smooth as ice. The end of the rod merely tapped the wood each time. It left slight dents but no more damage than that. On low.

His heart beat faster, and he let the tension build with each stroke of the piston. He grew hard inside his pants.

Tap—tap—tap.

The steady back-and-forth motion of the rod, the clean turning of the gears, and the shimmer of light were almost unbearably exciting. He was close to coming without even touching himself.

Tap—tap—tap.

When he could hold off no longer, he pressed firmly on the button for high power and the machine gained speed and force.

Tap—tap—TAP.

The end of the steel rod punched cleanly through the plywood, and sawdust burst into the room from the neat hole left by the rod. With each further stroke, the rod plunged in and out of the same hole, and the man pictured someone in place of the plywood. Some creature like Zachary Hall, subjected to his glorious machine....

He squeezed his eyes shut as he hunched over and ejaculated into his pants at the image he had created. Ah God, he was almost ready.

Chapter 18

ZACHARY'S E-READER DROPPED to his lap. Once again he had lost the thread and momentarily nodded off. Truth to tell, he was bored in his apartment.

The last two weeks, he and Sam had gotten together for dinner and a little fooling around almost every evening Zachary wasn't at Rainbow Space. The *Star Trek* marathon Sam had suggested was a hit, though Sam had to beg off at the last minute for a business trip. When he returned to town, though, the absence seemed to have prepared him to go a little further. Their make-out sessions got hotter, even if they were still fully clothed. Zachary thought he might want to push the envelope a bit. Maybe try to get Sam horizontal so he could explore that nice, lean body he felt under the expensive shirts and trousers.

Not that night, though. Sam was on another business trip for a few days to help a client with something IT related. Zachary didn't know if Sam sold them software or set up systems for them or something else techy. Whatever. When Sam was in DC, the job gave him a lot of flexibility. From the looks of his apartment, it was quite lucrative too.

Zachary was enjoying Sam's company. It surprised him, though, that left to himself for a few nights, he wasn't able to keep himself busy. He called Vic about stopping by the shelter, but Vic said there was nothing going on that needed Zachary's help. He should go out and enjoy the early May weather.

So Zachary tried but failed yet again to get into a book he had downloaded onto his Kindle. He finally tossed it aside in disgust. Flipping channels on the TV, he paused no longer than a few seconds on each. Soon the remote joined his discarded Kindle. He had already memorized his sheet music for the Gay Men's Chorus. Besides, he didn't want to think about the chorus. It reminded him of how cold Howard had been since the night of the bad date all those weeks ago. He also didn't want to call his parents. He'd just face yet another grilling on whether he had met any nice girls at the fictitious church he told them he attended.

At eight o'clock Zachary gave up on trying to amuse himself. He headed for the Metro into DC, just to be around people. It had been several weeks since he'd been to Mata Hari. He was ready to risk facing Thomas.

I hope.

At the bar he scanned the good-sized crowd as he removed his light jacket and stored it with the coat check. No sign of Thomas, which made him feel simultaneously relieved and disappointed. No Joe, no Terry, but Miss Ethel was at the piano.

Randy gave a slight grin when he spotted Zachary at the bar. Without asking he poured a seven and seven and slid it toward Zachary. "Hey, kid. Haven't seen you around much in a while," he said.

"Ah, you know. I've been trying to get the feel of the city," Zachary said as he took a sip. "But this is still my favorite bar. I missed hearing Miss Ethel play."

"Yeah, she was a good hire. Thomas was right about that one." Randy rapped his knuckles twice and started to turn away. Zachary couldn't help himself from taking the door Randy had opened.

"He's not around tonight, huh?" he asked, knowing he was transparent as all hell. "I haven't seen him for a few weeks. How's he been?"

Randy stared at him for a minute. "Good, I think. He hasn't been in much these last few weeks either."

Zachary couldn't let it go. "Oh? I thought this was his main hangout."

Randy shrugged. "Used to be. Probably still is. He just needed a change. Anyway, he's in Geneva this week for a conference on some environmental shit. He won't be around till the weekend, I figure."

Zachary sipped his drink. Randy apparently decided the conversation was over. When he moved on to tend some customers, Zachary took himself to the piano to enjoy Miss Ethel's playing.

"Hey, sugar," she said. "I thought you forgot about me."

"No way," Zachary said with a smile. "I've been a little busy, but no one does Nina Simone like you. I needed a fix."

She chuckled a bit. "Do you play, sugar?" she asked.

"A little. Nothing like you, but I've studied some."

"Any four-handers?" Zachary named some Debussy and Fauré pieces, and she nodded.

"I know the Fauré. Come sit by me, sugar. Let's give it a try."

"Randy won't mind? It's a bit more, uh, formal than you usually play."

"Let's give these gents some class. What d'you say?" she prompted, and Zachary slid onto the piano bench next to her.

It took him a minute to warm up, but soon their hands glided through a few movements from the *Dolly* suite. When they finished they received some nice applause. A few people came to the piano to add to Miss Ethel's tip bowl.

"That was real nice, hon. I think I'm going to take my break now," she said.

"Can I buy you a drink?" Zachary asked.

"Well, why not?"

Ethel and Zachary made their way to the bar. "That was impressive, kid," Randy murmured as he served them. "I had no idea you could play."

"Thanks. Miss Ethel covered up my mistakes, though. She made me sound much better than I actually am." Zachary clinked glasses with her as she laughed.

They talked for a bit about the four different regular gigs Miss Ethel worked. When she returned to the piano for another set, Zachary turned to listen to her play.

He started when Randy said behind him, "Too bad Thomas wasn't here for your performance. He's really into music. On the board of a performing arts center in Maryland, stuff like that. It'd impress him."

Zachary turned to face him. He was surprised not only about the information regarding Thomas, but that it came from Randy. "That's really interesting. I didn't know he was a music lover. But then, I don't know much about Thomas personally."

"Not many people do. He's a good friend, but you can see why he has trouble making new ones."

Zachary's heart beat staccato as he looked at his drink. "I said I'd try to be his friend," he confessed, "but I don't think I can really do that."

He sensed Randy nodding. "I hear ya, Zachary," he sighed. "Thomas is complicated. He's got a bunch of issues, and they're not for me to explain."

Zachary was annoyed to feel his eyes burn, and he couldn't help lashing out a bit as he looked up. "After the second time we got together, I hoped I'd hear from him. Even knowing about these mysterious issues and rules." *Even after hearing I was a fuck-and-chuck.* "What was I going to do, though, when he didn't call? Stalk him?"

Randy reeled back a bit, clearly surprised at the word. Zachary wasn't sure why. It was just something people said.

"Anyway I'm seeing someone else now," he continued. "We've been going out for about a month. He actually talks to me."

"Why haven't you brought him in yet?" Randy's mouth twisted into a wry grin. "Oh. Because of Thomas."

"Sort of. I didn't think I could handle watching Thomas leave with a man," Zachary confessed. "So I wanted to make sure I was in a good space before subjecting myself to that."

"I hear ya. Anyway, good for you. Who's the new guy?"

"Sam? He's an IT consultant, whatever that means. He's a bit nerdy, like me. He likes *Star Wars* and superhero movies."

"Looker?"

"Well, I think so. Here. I have a picture from when we went to see *Civil War* a few weeks ago." Zachary pulled out his cell phone and opened up his photo app. He flicked through, paused, and then flicked in the other direction.

"That's odd." He frowned. "I remember taking the selfie when we were standing in line, and I showed it to Sam later."

Randy shrugged. "Technology and I aren't exactly friends either. Maybe it's lost in the clouds, whatever the fuck that means." He turned to serve a customer.

Zachary swiped through his photo album as he muttered, "I admit I'm no techie, but really, this makes no sense. Here're the pics from the following week, when I ran a bunch of *Star Trek* movies for kids at the shelter." He smiled at a pic of Jamayqua and Joe laughing together as they ate popcorn out of a huge bowl. "And here's an older one…."

The picture he had swiped up was more than a month old. It showed Thomas alone at the bar the night Zachary came in drunk with Howard and ended up back in Thomas's bed. He had forgotten he had that picture. It felt like betraying Sam to even be looking at it because the image evoked a churn in his gut.

He swiped again a few times, angry at himself, and came across the pic Randy had taken of Thomas and Zachary together at the bar. It was from the very first time Zachary wandered in, the night he went home with Thomas all excited about possibilities.

The picture was a good one. It showed Thomas's handsome face, intelligent eyes, and white smile. Zachary admitted privately that he looked pretty cute too with his head tilted toward Thomas. In the background he could see the piano and a bit of Miss Ethel's shoulder. The pic also revealed a man with shaggy blond hair wearing what appeared to be wire-framed glasses. The man in the background was looking right at their backs, so the camera flash had reflected off his lenses.

Huh, that was funny.

Zachary swiped back to the pic of Thomas alone at the bar some weeks later. He used his fingers to enlarge the picture slightly, and there it was again—the glint of camera flash off glasses. The same man with blond shaggy hair stood against the wall. He looked directly past Thomas at Zachary's camera.

"Hey, Randy," Zachary called out. "Does this strike you as peculiar?"

Randy came back and leaned over the counter as Zachary showed him the two pictures on his phone. "Look, these were taken more than a month apart. Both times this guy happened to be right in the camera sight and looking straight at me. Do you know who he is?"

Randy frowned as he took the phone out of Zachary's hands. He enlarged each photo as much as the image allowed and squinted his eyes. "It couldn't be," Randy muttered to himself. "Could it?" He looked up to see Zachary watching him closely, and he said, "I don't know who it is, kid. I think I remember him because of that bad haircut. Came in a few times, starting around the time that Gallagher—" He stood straight. "Can you forward those to me, Zachary?"

"Sure, but why?" Zachary opened a message and typed in the e-mail address Randy gave him.

"I'm probably crazy. I just think I'm going to show these to someone I know. See if—well, never mind."

Zachary didn't buy the way Randy tried to brush him off. Something was up, but getting it out of him was beyond Zachary's abilities.

"Another drink?" Randy asked.

Zachary put away his phone and stood up. "No, thanks. I'd better get home. It's a work night."

*　*　*

AS SOON AS the bar closed down, Randy went to his office. He called up the message Zachary had sent to him with the two pictures attached. Opening the browser on his computer monitor, he did what he could to maximize the images and focus on the man in the background. He could tell the glasses had silver-colored frames. The flash that reflected off the lenses obscured enough of the face that he couldn't see the features clearly. But what he *could* see worried him. His instincts told him it was important.

Years in federal law enforcement had produced a certain snobbery about the MPD's capabilities. But it was Torres's investigation. She needed to be told, even if he was completely wrong. It was after two thirty in the morning, though. When he found her card in his desk drawer, he just fired off a text.

This is Randy Vaughan at Mata Hari. Possible lead I'd like to discuss with you.

His phone rang seconds later and startled him into nearly dropping it. He connected and said, "I didn't expect to get you tonight, Detective."

Torres sounded exhausted. "I have a case review with my captain tomorrow. Shit, today. What do you have for me?"

Randy explained about the two photos. "Look, this may be nothing. I do have a lot of regulars, so it's not that surprising two pictures would show the same person in the background. But in both cases, he was near Thomas, and in both he was looking right at the camera. That tells me he was looking *at* Thomas."

"Or at the other customer, this Zachary Hall," she commented. Randy's blood ran cold. "Tell me what you're thinking, Mr. Vaughan. I get that this may be nothing, but you have more years of experience than I do. I'd like to hear from you."

"Thank you for making me feel old," he growled. "Okay. This is crazy, but there's something about the face in these pictures that reminds me of Charles Rumson."

Chapter 19

RANDY HEARD HEAVY silence over the phone. When Torres finally spoke, her voice was flat. "They remind you of Charles Rumson. The Charles Rumson you assured me died two years ago."

"I stand by our investigation. Every fact we had available at the time showed an open-and-shut suicide. Still there's something familiar in the face, at least what I can see of it. Maybe a brother?"

"Okay. Forward the photos to me, and I'll see what we can do. Maybe the forensics team can enhance the image. Anything else, Mr. Vaughan?"

"No, that's it. I'll send 'em as soon as we hang up." He did so, and then he debated whether to mention anything to Thomas. But he didn't want to stir that particular shit pot unless he had a good reason.

. . .

THREE DAYS LATER Torres took the question of whether to talk to Thomas out of Randy's hands. She came into the bar at seven thirty on Sunday when Thomas happened to be in. Randy tensed when he saw her approach the bar holding a large envelope.

"Mal, can you cover for fifteen?" he asked his bar back.

"Sure, boss. It's slow so far," Malcolm answered.

"Thomas, I have a feeling you might want to be part of this," he said as he nodded in Torres's direction. He signaled her to come to his office, and Thomas joined them, mystified.

When Randy had closed his office door, he crossed his arms and let Torres speak. "Our forensics people did what they could with the images. Since they were taken with an older model cell phone camera in poor lighting conditions, there wasn't much they could do. But see if you recognize him." She pulled two eight-by-ten pictures out of the envelope.

"What's going on, Randy?" Thomas asked. "Who took the pictures?"

As he handled the photos, Randy grunted, "Zachary Hall. These were on his phone, and I asked Detective Torres to see if she could make them clearer." He looked at the two images, one in each hand, and offered them to Thomas. "Here. See what you think."

Thomas accepted the pictures. In each he could see part of his own face. The images were centered on a man with shaggy blond hair and glasses. Because of the magnification, the man's face and features were blurry. The light that reflected off his lenses obscured his eyes. The fact that Torres and Randy were both staring at Thomas clued him in, though. His heart began to pound. He looked from the photos up to Randy's face.

"You think this is Charles Rumson?"

"Question is, what do *you* think, Thomas?" Randy answered. "I never met the guy. I only saw file photos and blurry videos."

Thomas looked again and tried to superimpose the hated memory on what he saw printed in his hands. He slowly shook his head, and Torres exhaled heavily. Thomas glanced at her. "I see what Randy is talking about, but it just doesn't seem quite right. The hair is wrong, and I remember Charles with a thinner nose, kind of sharp and pointed. He was, I'd say, gaunt. This person has a rounder face. It's been two years, though, so…

maybe?"

Randy asked, "Did Charles have a brother?"

"No. He was an only child, like me."

Torres took the photos back, and her shoulders slumped. "Damn. That was looking to be the first real lead we've turned up."

Randy said to her, "Set aside for a minute whether this is Rumson back from the grave. Something is off about this guy staring at Thomas... or at Zachary."

"Wait. Do you think this guy was involved with what happened to Brian Gallagher?" Thomas asked, and his jaw dropped at the implications.

"I remember noticing this guy not long before Gallagher got killed. The hair, mainly. From these pictures he was in the bar at least twice after that too."

"The time-stamp on the second picture is about three weeks before the Daniel Owen murder," Torres observed. "But you say you don't recall seeing this man in here since around then?"

Randy nodded.

"I thought there was no connection to me or to Mata Hari," Thomas directed at Torres.

"No connection we know of besides you and Mr. Krasnopoler having sex with Gallagher," Torres said. "The second vic has no ties here that we can find. But we don't have enough information to rule out that the killer started here."

Randy added, "Or could come back."

"Do you think Zachary is in danger?" Thomas heard the raw fear in his own voice.

"I don't see how that could be." Randy considered carefully. "Zachary took the second picture, what? Seven weeks ago? And I haven't seen this guy around in a long time. Maybe since that night, even."

"We have to tell him," Thomas said. "If there's the slightest chance—shit."

"Do you have his number? I should interview Mr. Hall," Torres observed.

Thomas nodded and reached for his phone. As he read the digits to Torres, his hands started to tremble. "Randy, I can't have another stalker. I just can't. And Charles is dead."

"Buddy, what can I tell ya? The odds are astronomically against it, but my instincts tell me this guy"—Randy tapped the photos—"is *wrong*. Now it could be a complete coincidence he shows up in two photos of you, weeks apart."

"Or it could mean something," Torres finished. "Mr. Scarborough, can you give me anything to work with here? I can arrange for a police escort or a protective detail if you have *anything* that supports Mr. Vaughan's concerns."

Thomas sank into a desk chair. "Honestly nothing. After I heard about Daniel Owen, I convinced myself that it really didn't have anything to do with me. So maybe I haven't been as careful or observant as I should be. But I can't think of anything out of the ordinary that's happened." He looked up at Randy. "How could it possibly be Charles? I thought the investigation was conclusive."

Randy frowned. "We reviewed all available evidence at the time, and the case was neat. It's just that seeing these images put a funny thought in my head—that maybe it was *too* neat. Detective, you said you've read the Rumson file from Seattle PD, right? Did anything strike you as odd?"

Torres shrugged. "I reviewed it, and I assume it was the same file you saw." She reached into her shoulder bag and pulled out a thick folder. "Since you mentioned Rumson when we talked, I brought this along. My captain would have my ass, but if I get it back tomorrow, he doesn't need to know, does he?"

Randy took the file. "That's good, Detective. I'll review this tonight and see if I spot anything that could be useful. I can return it in the morning."

She nodded. "I'm taking a big risk here, but one sick fucker is still out there. I don't want him to strike again—not if there's anything we can do to prevent that."

Thomas asked Randy, "Is there anything I can do?" He clenched his gut and asked, "Should I look at the file too?"

Randy shook his head. "I don't think that's necessary. Let me go through it and see if I have any questions you might be able to help with. Why don't you focus on talking to Zachary to make sure he keeps his guard up?"

"Good. Yes. Call Zach. I can do that." Thomas tried to hide his relief at not facing Charles, even on paper, but he knew the other two weren't fooled.

"I've got to get back to the bar. I'll look this over later," Randy said, and he slid the folder into his desk and locked it. "Thomas, you can stay in here to call, if you want." He left to guide Torres back to the front of the house.

Thomas tapped his phone nervously. He hadn't called Zach since he invited him to the museum, which seemed long ago. He'd fooled himself into thinking they could be friends. Then he fucked up even that by breaking his own rule and bringing Zach home with him a second time. He couldn't be sorry about it, though.

That night with Zach was one of the most exciting, satisfying experiences of his life. Zach got under his skin like no one else and made Thomas long to set aside the armor. To *really* take a chance on getting to know him. That was probably no longer possible. Zach had moved on, and Thomas had no one but himself to blame.

But reaching out that way, calling him out of the blue... he was afraid of having his words thrown back at him. He was afraid of rejection.

"Fuck you," Thomas muttered to himself. "This isn't about your ego. Be his friend." He dialed Zach's number before he could change his mind.

It connected on the third ring. "Hello," he heard Zach say cautiously.

"Zachary, it's Thomas Scarborough." Silence at the other end. "I hope I'm not catching you at a bad time, but I just need to talk to you for a minute."

"Umm… this is fine. What can I do for you?" His voice was guarded, a bit distant.

"Look. Randy showed me those two pictures from your phone. This is going to sound odd, and I don't mean to be an alarmist. You know about the two gay men who were murdered in the past couple of months? Well, there's a very small chance that the man in your pictures is involved."

"What?" Zachary's shock was palpable, even over the phone. "You think the murderer was in Mata Hari?"

"It's just something the police are checking into, okay? I don't want you to panic or do anything about it. I just want you to be careful."

Silence again for a beat, and then Zachary asked, "Why do I need to be careful?"

Thomas tapped a finger on the desk. "The guy in your pictures seemed strangely focused on you and me. Remember, this is probably nothing at all. But you should know—the first man who was killed, Brian Gallagher? Well, I brought him home with me about a week before he died." Silence again, and he could just imagine the look on Zachary's face.

Shit.

"It was before I ever met you. And I didn't know the second

guy at all, I swear. It's just a coincidence that I met Gallagher, and it was just one time."

"Well, one and done. That's the rule, right?" Zachary said in a voice grown rough.

"It *was* the rule...."

"Don't you dare," Zachary barked out. "Don't you dare say anything about that second night or make a joke out of it."

"I wasn't going to. I just wanted you to know I never saw Gallagher before that one night, and it never happened again. I didn't know Owen, the second victim, at all. There is every reason to think this is just a coincidence. The man in the pictures you took probably has no connection to any of it. I just thought you deserved to know so you can be vigilant."

"Vigilant." Zachary sounded disgusted. "It's like you're calling to tell me you might have given me an STD. Except that instead of Chlamydia, I may be in the crosshairs of a killer. Because we had sex."

"Oh my God. That's not what I meant at all." But he knew that, as harsh as Zachary's judgment sounded, that was exactly what he was saying.

"Zach, I'm sorry. I didn't call to upset you or to make you afraid. I wanted to call you before, so many times. I'd pick up the phone and then just stare at it. I didn't want to crowd you, and I know you've started seeing someone. But you needed to know this. Shit, I should have had Randy call."

"Yeah. I think that would have been a good idea," Zachary said, but his voice was less harsh. He was silent for a moment and then spoke in a softer voice. "Do you know how many times I hoped I'd hear from you, Thomas? How many times I went to Mata Hari, or specifically *avoided* it, just because you were on my mind? And then to have you finally call about *this* shit...." Thomas squeezed his eyes shut at the anguish he heard. "Fuck,

Thomas. Just—fuck."

"I know." Thomas paused. "Zach, I'm damaged. I wish I had explained to you why I am the way I am, but there's no point now. You're better off with someone who understands how special you are. Even if it isn't possible for us to be friends—and I'd completely get that—I want you to be happy."

"I can't do this anymore tonight. I'm sorry," Zach said. "Can you have Randy call me if there's anything else I should know?"

"I will," Thomas said softly, and Zach hung up without saying good-bye. Thomas stared at Randy's desk for a long time. He tried to reconcile himself to the understanding that he would probably never see Zachary again.

* * *

THE MAN WITH the silver-framed glasses seethed at the call logs. The Beloved had called that creature Hall—that *cretin*—again. Weeks of no contact, and now an infuriating development. He hadn't managed a way to hack the calls themselves. The e-mail records from his Beloved's phone contained no insight into what was discussed. He was in the dark. But his Beloved had initiated the phone call, had reached out. Why?

He checked the video footage of Mata Hari to search for guidance. He watched the police detective head into the back with the bartender and the Beloved. She emerged twenty minutes later with just the bartender. With no audio and no way to install a camera in the bartender's office, he was just speculating. Perhaps he had not been as successful as he had hoped at laying the false trail?

The boy he'd killed across town, the one the papers named Daniel Owen, was a mere means to an end. He helped lead attention away from the Beloved. There was the added bonus of getting to work with his special toys and the satisfaction of work well done. Yet he took no special enjoyment in killing that boy.

Not like the slow, careful pleasure he would take in chastising Zachary Hall.

Chapter 20

ZACHARY SPENT A sleepless night thrashing in his sheets. *Fuck* Thomas Scarborough and his beautiful face and his perfect body.

He drove his fist into the down pillow and then turned it over, looking for a cool spot. He burned with anger and frustration. Maybe Thomas owed him no explanations, but this was huge. The times they had spent together, both in and out of the bedroom, the moments of intimacy real or imagined… Thomas hadn't so much as hinted he might be putting Zachary in harm's way. Who did that? Maybe Thomas the Asshole wasn't as much of an act as Zachary had convinced himself.

Despite his anger Zachary couldn't believe himself to be in any danger, not really. Learning Thomas had sex with that poor man, Gallagher, before he died was painful at a level Zachary never even imagined. But even worse was to recall those halting phrases from Thomas. His concern. His suggestions that he had wanted something more.

Goddammit. Zachary was seeing Sam. Even if it was going slower than he might have liked, they had a good time together. Sam was kind and sweet and not afraid to show his feelings. He was *perfect* for Zachary.

So why was he awake at three a.m.? Why was he remembering Thomas's body under him as he drove his cock inside and made Thomas moan and come apart? He found no answers, or at least none he could live with.

Zachary did finally manage a few hours of sleep. He woke to a text message from Sam, which immediately made him feel guilty for his nighttime struggles.

> *Hey, Z. Got back on red-eye. I missed you. Can we have dinner?*

Yes. That was what he needed—to spend some time with Sam and get fucking Thomas out of his head and out of his heart.

> *Great. Where and when?*

He figured Sam was probably asleep after his late-night flight home from wherever. By the time he got out of the shower, though, Sam had invited him to his apartment that evening for dinner in and a movie. Zachary confirmed, and during his commute to work, he thought about pushing the relationship to a more physical one. Frankly he was horny after all that reminiscing about Thomas. He and Sam were ready for the next step.

·   ·   ·

RANDY WAS AWAKE at what was—for him, since his retirement—an ungodly hour. He had carried the file on Rumson home from the bar after closing and spread it on his dining room table. It took him hours to go through the materials and check the details against his recollection from when his team vetted Thomas. After all that, only one item puzzled him. He wanted to talk to his former deputy at the Secret Service to discuss it. That was why he was up again at eight to call his buddy. He hoped to catch her on her way to DC before the day got crazy.

Lily Woods picked up right away. "Randy. This is a surprise. How's the bar doing?"

Randy chuckled, "Off to a good start. No bar fights, no crazy agents to corral. I shoulda done this a long time ago."

"Don't bullshit me, RV. You're bored, aren't you?" she asked. Randy smiled at the old nickname. It was based on his initials and a memorable training exercise involving a Winnebago at the Federal Law Enforcement Training Center a few years earlier.

"No way. Being a bar owner may not come with the thrills of tailing a protectee, but I don't have to wear a black suit every day. That's gotta count for something."

"If you say so. Don was just asking about you yesterday. We should all get together for lunch soon."

"That'd be good. Or you can all come by the bar. Drinks on me." As soon as he said it, Randy knew it was a bad idea. Secret Service agents in his gay piano bar. Yeah, no. It was their discovery he was gay and kept that secret for years that drove the final spike into his career. *And let's not forget Trevor and his contribution to my early retirement.* Randy shook to clear his head. *Another day.*

Lily laughed nervously and changed the subject. "Why are you calling so early, RV? I figured retirement at least meant sleeping in."

"Do you remember about two years back, when we vetted Jason Scarborough for Senator Gilbert's staff?" he asked.

"The good-looking guy with the stalker? Sure, I remember."

"Do you recall anything odd about that investigation? Anything that didn't add up?" he asked.

"What's this about, Randy?" Lily asked, and he could picture her frown.

"I'm not asking about anything classified. Something has come up. It's nothing to do with Service business. I had a reason to look back at the Seattle PD file on the stalker, Charles Rumson."

"And you want to know if we missed anything?" Lily prompted.

"Not exactly. Well, maybe. If you think I'm out of line, I'll drop it, Lily. It's just... I saw a picture recently of a guy who reminds me too much of Rumson. I need to know if there's a possibility he faked his death."

Shit. There it was, out in the open. Lily might refuse to answer him. She might even report that he was nosing around old files and draw attention he didn't care to have anymore.

The silence stretched, and Lily finally said, "There was one thing that bothered me. Rumson's mother... she came to the morgue alone to identify the body a few hours after it was brought in. I had given birth to Kirstin a few months earlier. I was only just back from maternity leave when this happened. I remember thinking, if that were my child, I could never deal with it by myself, or so efficiently."

"Huh. I never thought about it that way," Randy said. "The guy was all over the news before the actual crash, so I just assumed that was why she was there so quickly."

"That may be right. We interviewed her, of course, and I think she said something like that. Once Mrs. Rumson ID'd her son, the family refused to authorize an autopsy. They had the body out of the morgue and to the funeral home that same day. Nothing improper about that, of course. It just struck me as unusually cold."

"Do you recall anything about Rumson's finances?" Randy asked.

"Hmm. No, nothing special comes to mind. He was rich, I recall. A trust-fund guy. But that's it. What have you got?"

"The Seattle PD file contains a note about the First Washington Bank trust department calling to report a financial red flag after Rumson's death. Then there's a follow-up note less than two hours later that says the issue was resolved with the family. No specific details."

Lily apparently thought about it and then said, "That doesn't ring a bell at all. Not saying I would have done anything more with it if the family reported no issue. But I would have remembered that. When was this?"

Randy checked the case file. "June first."

"We wrapped our report in May. I think May twentieth." She always remembered dates, so Randy took her recollection at face value.

"So this was something that turned up after we vetted Scarborough. It wasn't significant enough for anyone to bring it to our attention," Randy summarized.

"Sounds right to me," Lily said. "Before you ask, RV, I don't think I could call Seattle for more information without getting an official go-ahead. Is that something you want?"

"No, Lily. Thanks. I'll let the local police decide if they want to take this further."

They chatted for a few minutes more. Unfortunately, the gulf between a retired and active agent meant they had little of substance they were able to discuss. The call ended with a promise by Lily to stay in touch.

Randy called Detective Torres next and explained what he had found. "Look, it's not much, I know, and I don't mean to distract you by pointing at a ghost."

"I understand, Mr. Vaughan."

"Randy."

"Okay. Randy. And if I had anything else to go on, this would get pushed back. But I don't have another angle. I'll call Seattle and see if I can find out anything more about the financial issue. A serial killer rarely stops at two. There is no doubt in my mind that's what we're dealing with—a serial killer preying on gay men. I hear a ticking clock in my head."

Chapter 21

ZACHARY ARRIVED AT Sam's apartment that evening with a bit of a headache. After his sleepless night, he couldn't get the call with Thomas out of his mind. Was it really possible a killer had been that close to them in Mata Hari? And Thomas's words—what had all that meant? About his being damaged?

When Thomas called him "Zach," he felt it in his chest. That recollection of a few nights of intimacy that would never be repeated. It was shitty for him to even think about Thomas and how he had pined for something that could never be.

His guilt persuaded him not to mention to Sam anything about his conversation with Thomas. Even the most innocuous comment about the killer would lead to a discussion Zachary wasn't ready for. He wanted to focus on Sam and not get bogged down in something that had gotten up his hopes, once upon a time.

Sam kissed him hello at the apartment door. He held on a little longer than usual as he tightened his hands a bit around Zachary's waist. Despite Zachary's resolve to move things forward, at a flash of nerves he broke the kiss to press a bottle of wine into Sam's hands.

"Oh, thanks. I missed you," Sam said, and Zachary felt bad all over again. "You look tired. Bad day at the office?"

"Yeah. Just some tough personnel issues I'm working through with one of the field offices." Zachary hung his jacket in Sam's coat closet and said, "Sorry. I'll shake it off in a few minutes."

"Don't worry about it. Fix yourself a drink and have a seat while I work on dinner."

Zachary smiled wanly at Sam. "Thanks for the free pass. You're a prince among men."

Sam laughed. "No, I'm selfish. I want you to have a chance to unwind so we can enjoy our evening together." He pushed Zachary toward the living room and said again, "Have a drink, and I'll join you in a few."

Zachary poured himself a vodka tonic from the mirrored bar cart at the side of the living room. He sank onto the sofa to enjoy the view. The National Gallery was gorgeous in the twilight. It glowed in its uplights against the backdrop of a sapphire-and-amethyst sky. Sam bustled around in the kitchen. The sound of him chopping vegetables on a cutting board helped Zachary relax as he nursed his drink.

         o   o   o

AT MATA HARI, Randy's cell buzzed in his pocket. He signaled for Malcolm to take some customers. Then he turned around as he retrieved the phone and saw Torres's number flash up. "Evening, Detective," he answered. "Any information?"

"Just Torres is fine. Yeah, I have some intel," she said. "I got off the phone with the Seattle police officer who annotated the Rumson file. His best recollection is that First Washington identified a large transfer of funds from Rumson's account. This was *after* his date of death. But when he called Rumson's mother, she told him it was just part of dealing with his estate and not to worry about it. He wouldn't have remembered, except we're talking about more than six million dollars."

Randy whistled. "I'd remember that too. But why would First Washington contact the police? An executor transferring funds would have to use letters testamentary, which would be registered first with the bank."

"Good point. I may not get anywhere with the bank, but I'll give it a try tomorrow."

"It's three hours earlier in Seattle," Randy commented wryly, and Torres grunted.

"You sound like my captain, Randy. Okay. I'll give it a shot now. Hey, one other thing came up. The officer I talked to pulled up his own notes to help me out with Rumson. He was the one who called Mrs. Rumson because he had met her when she came to the morgue to claim Charles's body. She had been almost panicked, he said, when she came to the station. She swung around her husband's name like a club. That got the body released and out of there as quickly as possible. The commissioner was a personal friend, so things happened a lot faster than was usual. Rumson's body was cremated before the day was out."

"I suppose, at the time, it would have just seemed like grief."

"Agreed, so what stood out to this officer was that, when he got hold of Mrs. Rumson to ask about the money, he was all prepared for a big emotional scene again. Instead she was calm and matter-of-fact about the whole thing, like it was just a business transaction. This is less than six weeks after Rumson's death, remember, which seems like a short time to get over the suicide of your child."

Randy asked flatly, "Do you think there was a cover-up?"

"I'm not sure exactly what I'm thinking, Randy," Torres confessed. "We have a man obsessed on Scarborough to the point he broke into his home and contacted him relentlessly at work. This same stalker violated a restraining order but apparently never attempted to harm or threaten Scarborough. We have a very public series of attention-grabbing displays before Rumson's car plunges off a cliff. We have a mother who sweeps in and pulls strings. She arranges the immediate release and cremation of her son's body before an autopsy can be performed. And then we have six million dollars that apparently moved after Rumson's death. His mother waves that off calmly as no big deal.

"And then, two years later, we have a sadistic killer torturing young gay men. One of them had sex with Scarborough. We have two photos of a man who has some resemblance to Rumson but Scarborough can't rule him in or out. I'm not saying I'm not suspicious. There's just not enough here to take to my captain, let alone to a DA. And even if I did, what would I be asking for?"

"I hear you, Torres. You need something from the bank or from the mother to connect the dots better."

"Exactly. I'll try the bank now, but I have to brief my captain before I reach out to the family."

"Let me know if you want to talk more. Maybe bounce ideas off," Randy said.

"I appreciate that. I'll let you know what I find out."

Randy stewed about it all evening. Part of it was professional. His team had reviewed that file and told Senator Gilbert the case was pristine. The bigger part of it was personal. Thomas was his friend. He had made up his mind when he saw Thomas walk through the door and into Mata Hari. Thomas needed to know what they had found, as little as it was.

*   *   *

ZACHARY DIDN'T SAY much through the dinner Sam had prepared for him, except to compliment him on the perfectly done pork chops. They made light conversation. His head ached with the strain Thomas had dropped on him and the lack of sleep, but Sam seemed okay with the low-key evening. They sat side by side at Sam's glass dining room table, both facing the wall of windows and the evening sky.

"I'm really sorry, Sam," Zachary said. "I don't mean to be moody and quiet. It's just work and stress are getting to me today."

And guilt.

Sam took his hand and kissed the back of it. "Relax. I'm enjoying your company. We don't have to sit and gab every evening. Honestly I like just being with you this way too."

"You're so sweet," Zachary said.

"Speaking of sweet, I got you something on my trip. Don't get nervous. It's just a little present. I'll save the big flashy gifts for when we've known each other longer." Sam waggled his eyebrows and grinned. "Or maybe biblically."

Zachary laughed as Sam got up and retrieved a silver-foil box wrapped in a blue ribbon. "It's some really good Swiss chocolate. I picked it up in Geneva before I came back to the States last night."

It was on the tip of Zachary's tongue to comment on the coincidence of Thomas and Sam both being in Geneva at the same time. He caught himself just in time. Sam didn't know Thomas, and Zachary certainly didn't want to explain why he knew where Thomas traveled. That would open the door to a lengthy conversation Zachary wasn't prepared for.

"I love chocolate," he exclaimed instead. "When I was swimming in college, it was always a struggle with my coach. I'd say I was burning enough calories to eat a box at a time, and he'd call me lard ass. We were very close." He pulled off the bow, opened the box, and helped himself to one of the chocolates inside. "Oh, that's so good," he moaned. The treat melted in his mouth, and he offered the box to Sam.

"I'm glad you like it," Sam said, but he declined any chocolate. "Do you feel like some coffee? I can put on a pot while I do the dishes."

"I should clean up since you cooked for me," Zachary protested, but Sam shushed him.

"I can tell you're exhausted and you've had a bad day. Let me take care of you tonight. It really won't take long to load the washer."

"My grandmother would spank me for my bad manners, but I'll just say thank you," Zachary murmured.

"You go sit on the sofa. I'll put some John Williams on for you, and then I'll come join you when the coffee is ready." He kissed Zachary on the top of his head and collected their plates and silverware.

Zachary did as instructed and leaned back into the luxurious sofa to watch traffic move along the Mall. He bit his lip as he considered Thomas's warning again. It was ridiculous to think he could be a target. He was nobody.

Except that he had had sex with Thomas, and so had one of the two victims. Well, by that measure, probably *hundreds* of men were targets, and he wished that didn't still bother him. Thomas was clear from the beginning about his own promiscuity, at least. What he wasn't clear about was how he was damaged and why. And the mixed messages he sent about his feelings for Zachary. It was like he wanted to share something important but couldn't lower his guard enough.

Dammit.

Zachary's thoughts drifted back to his conversation with Randy. To his odd reaction when Zachary had used the word "stalker." Could Thomas have been the victim of a stalker? That fit the current situation, maybe. Was it recent? No, that didn't make sense, since Thomas's one-and-done rule seemed to have been in place for a long time.

He could hear Sam bustling around the kitchen as he loaded the dishwasher. He shouldn't be thinking about Thomas. He should focus on Sam. Sam just *got* him, and he liked the same music, the same books, and the same movies.

Zachary frowned. It really was remarkable how much Sam and he had in common. He couldn't have asked for a man with so many of the same interests. Sam was always ready to do exactly what Zachary wanted.

Except show up at the shelter. He canceled at the last minute before their *Star Trek* marathon. He had an excuse why he couldn't come any other time Zachary asked.

Then Zachary thought about the one missing photo from his phone—the selfie he took with Sam when they stood in line for a movie. It was almost like someone deleted that single picture from his phone. Who?

No. Why?

Maybe because that person didn't want to risk it being seen by someone. But who would know Sam, that he'd even worry about that? He was just a nice, quiet consultant who brought Zachary chocolate. He was *Sam*, who'd just come back from Geneva.

Thomas had been in Geneva.

Chapter 22

THOMAS'S FOREHEAD GLISTENED with a sheen of sweat when Randy finished explaining what he and Detective Torres had learned. He tossed back the scotch that Randy had pressed into his hand right before he dragged Thomas into his office.

The terror of those weeks in Seattle, when Charles was absolutely everywhere, poured through him. The helplessness he felt when no one would listen or, even worse, blamed him for somehow leading Charles on. The panic when he found Charles naked in his bedroom. In his own *bedroom*, goddammit.

Thomas turned and hurled his glass against the wall of Randy's office. "Jesus *Christ*, Randy. How can this be happening to me again?"

Randy held up his hands as he tried to calm Thomas down. "Look. I'm telling you what we're investigating. I'm not telling you it's Rumson for sure or even that you're somehow connected to the murders. I just think you need to know. That glass is coming out of your profits, by the way."

Thomas glared at him. "Don't make jokes, Randy. You're trying to handle me, and that isn't what I need."

"What do you need?" Randy asked gently.

"I—I don't know." Thomas ran his hands through his hair and then tugged until his scalp hurt. "No, that's not true. I need to know Charles Rumson is burning in hell now, not going after people just because I fucked them."

"Is there any chance that his mother would tell you the truth or that you'd believe her if she said Charles was dead?" Randy asked.

Thomas looked at him, wide-eyed. "I... doubt it. I never had any contact with her or Charles's father after he killed himself. Not much before either. They were acquaintances of my parents—business or country club associates at best."

"Well, what about your father? Could he press the issue?"

Thomas grimaced and clenched his jaw. Mason Scarborough had done everything he could to drive his son out of Seattle and away from lucrative development deals with Rumson Global. "No. He won't so much as make a call about this if I ask him."

"Okay. We'll have to leave that to Torres and see what she can do through official channels." Randy called up the two images of the shaggy-haired man on his computer and positioned them side by side. "I dunno, Thomas. This was my idea, but if this is Rumson, why has it been so long since he did anything violent?"

"Oh God. Zach was right," Thomas moaned.

"About what?"

"I called him yesterday to let him know. Just about the possibility that this had to do with someone targeting people around me. He said it was like I'd given him an STD and made him a victim because he slept with me." Thomas turned green and swallowed hard. "I think I'm going to be sick."

Randy pushed him into his small private bathroom just in time. Thomas heaved up the scotch and everything he'd eaten that day. Randy rubbed his shoulder awkwardly until the retching stopped. Thomas dropped to the bathroom floor and leaned against the wall. Randy handed him some paper towels and a cup of water, then flushed the mess away.

When Thomas had calmed a bit, Randy stepped back. "Look,

I don't know what's going on with you and Zachary. It's different than anything you've had since I met you. I already know that you slept together more than once, but it's not even just that. The look in your eyes when his name comes up. The fact that you haven't pulled any playmates since you met him…. You've got it bad for him."

Thomas didn't try to deny it, but he hung his head. "It doesn't matter. I waited too long, and Zachary moved on. And he's right. I may have put him in danger as surely as if I'd given him a disease."

"I've seen the way he looks at you, Thomas. Yeah, he's seeing someone—this guy named Sam I guess, but he's got it as bad as you do. Talk to him, Thomas. Help him be safe, at least. We'll talk to Torres if we get confirmation of any of this shit, and we'll arrange a protective watch for him. Just in case Rumson knows who he is and is following him."

. . .

ZACHARY'S HEART POUNDED. He tried to calm down and tell himself he was being an idiot. "Hey, Sam," he called out.

"Yeah?" he heard from the kitchen.

"Can I grab some aspirin or something? This headache still won't go away."

"Sure. You know where the bathroom is. There should be a bottle of Advil in the medicine cabinet." Zachary heard Sam close up the dishwasher. He made his way down the hall, arguing with himself.

This is ridiculous. Sam had nothing to do with two murders or what's going on with Thomas. It's just a stupid coincidence, both of them being in Geneva at the same time.

Although he'd been to Sam's apartment four or five times, they'd never really moved beyond the living room. He hadn't been shown around, except for a quick trip to point him to the hall bath. So he didn't know which door led to Sam's bedroom, how many rooms the place had—nothing.

He ignored the hall bathroom and tried the next door he came to. It was locked.

Why would you lock a door inside your apartment?

He listened and could still hear Sam in the kitchen as he ground coffee beans. His heart was in his throat, but he moved down the hallway to the next door. It seemed to be on the same side of the hallway as the living room. He carefully turned the knob.

That one opened into a large bedroom. It had to be Sam's, he figured, because of the king-size bed and the row of windows facing the National Gallery. A low lamp burned on the bedside table. He could see a bathroom, and he headed that way. If Sam came in, he could always say he was searching for aspirin and thought this was the bathroom Sam meant.

He slipped across the room quickly, but he had no idea what he was looking for. What would show him he was wrong? The chest of drawers along one wall called to him.

He listened again. A cabinet door closed, and he heard the clink of china. Sam was still preparing the coffee. He began pulling drawers open quickly and shutting them again as quietly as he could. Underwear, socks, T-shirts, polos.... He paused and listened. He heard no sound from the kitchen.

Shit.

He hurriedly slid open a final drawer on the bottom right of the dresser, and he gasped. A blond wig lay nestled on top of a pair of glasses with silver frames. And was that a prosthetic nose?

The man from the bar had hair and glasses exactly like those in his pictures. But even more than that....

He remembered sitting outside the National Gallery of Art

weeks earlier. A man had passed by and looked at him too long. A man with the same hair and glasses.

It was Sam. It had always been Sam.

Zachary was on his knees, stunned, and he sat back on his heels. Behind him he heard, "Well, shit. Time for Plan B."

Before he could turn, something smashed into his head, and everything went black.

Chapter 23

THOMAS PACED AROUND Randy's office. He'd been there for an hour while Randy returned to the front to take care of his bar. He couldn't make sense of the mess, and that wasn't like him. He *made* himself focus.

If Charles was alive, if he was truly back to burn down Thomas's new life, then Thomas had to make a plan. He had to figure out how to handle it differently this time. Thomas had an important staff position with the United States Senate. Surely there were resources that could help him. Or he could leave. He could use his money and position and try to draw Charles after him and away from the people he knew.

He didn't want to go, but he had to consider it.

All of his life, he had been sure and confident—the lucky one, gifted. Even when he was a child called Jason, he knew he was good-looking. People went out of their way to do things for him, just to be around him. He grew up in the luxury provided by his grandfather's success in business and his father's acumen. He accepted the luxury as though it were an accomplishment—his birthright.

He was smart too, his intelligence honed at the best schools his parents' money could provide. When he was fourteen, he had sex for the first time, with one of his younger teachers. Jason had set his sights on Mr. Creed, sure that was the right man to educate him—not in trigonometry, but in how to exchange pleasure. Creed was shocked at his approach, but he caved within a week. Jason learned what he needed to know and moved on to his classmates.

It was delightful. It was a game. He was careful in his selections, and he tried to be kind. The captain of the football team had never even considered sex with another boy. That is, until Jason seduced him over a weekend study session. When it was over the football player was overcome with the beginnings of guilt. Jason soothed it away and assured him it was just an exploration. Nothing to worry about or regret. And it worked. Jason was the coolest kid in school, so if he said it was all right, the football player could accept that.

Dozens of others followed, all eager to be with Jason. When he decided to find out whether he was bisexual, girls were just as easy to get into bed. In college and then law school, it was the same—anyone he wanted came to him. A few bed partners got close, and he permitted it for a time. Just to try out the shape of a relationship, to see if that was a coat he might like to wear. It never was, though. Within a few days or a week at most, he would disentangle himself as gently as he could. He'd try to convey regret as he showed the man to the door.

He was rich, handsome, and smart. The world opened itself up to his explorations.

And then Charles Rumson happened. A whim, like so many others Jason had indulged, but with terrible unforeseen consequences. He could still remember when he spotted Charles in that bar in downtown Seattle, standing by himself against the wall. He was thin, dark, and yearning.

Seeing Charles in a gay bar didn't exactly surprise Jason. They had met in passing over the years at the country club or various events that warranted the presence of their respective parents' offspring. He had seen Charles's hungry looks at him, but those were so common that Jason accepted them as tribute. He always had other shiny things to distract him and never considered a tumble with the shy, awkward Charles.

But that one time, he hadn't settled on a partner for the night and looked over the crowd. Seeing Charles alone and lonely stirred a bit of feeling in Jason. He felt an urge to be kind, to help out a childhood acquaintance, to perhaps ease him into the world of gay life. He caught Charles's eye and beckoned him over. He still remembered the flash of relief and pleasure that crossed Charles's face when he realized Jason Scarborough wanted him to come closer.

After two drinks the look changed to adoration.

Even if that made Jason a bit wary, he pushed his concerns aside. It was too late that evening to go after anyone better suited for some fun. Charles was nice-looking even if he was a bit thin for Jason's taste. He remembered leaning down to whisper in Charles's ear, "Do you want to get out of here? Maybe go play around at my apartment?" The look in Charles's eyes—burning excitement, so close to fervor—should have warned him. He was thinking with his dick by that time, but he specifically recalled saying to Charles, "It's just this one time. You get that, right?"

Charles nodded, but the fire in his eyes was undiminished.

He followed in his own car to Jason's building. As soon as they were in the bedroom, he threw himself at Jason like a drowning man. He practically choked Jason with tight arms around his neck as he kissed him with a tightly closed mouth. Right away Jason knew the sex would be a disaster, but he still tried. Charles was aggressive but unsure—limp like a fish one moment, then trying to force Jason's cock up his ass the next. Jason finally calmed him down a bit, got him to stretch out on the bed, and held him as they jerked off together. Charles rolled his head into Jason's shoulder and cried as soon as he came, while

Jason awkwardly patted his back.

Charles whispered through his tears, "I wanted to do more for you, Jason. I'm so pathetic."

Jason did his best to soothe him. He whispered in return, "It's just nerves, Charles. Everyone's first time is a bit awkward. You'll see. The next guy you're with will be so much easier and better."

Charles craned his head back, his eyes wide as he met Jason's gaze. "You're so kind, Jason. So beautiful. Even my mother wants you. I heard her talking to one of her friends at that museum gala. I can't believe I get to have you."

That was the first real sense of alarm Jason felt. "Charles, this was fun, but remember, I told you it was just a one-time thing. Okay? And you really can't talk to your mother about it. You know that, right?"

Charles just put his head back on Jason's shoulder and wrapped one arm tightly around Jason's waist. Jason lay on his back and tried to think of the easiest way to clean Charles up and get him out the door. When he nudged Charles, though, he had fallen asleep. Against his better judgment, Jason let him stay the night.

That was the beginning of the end of his life as Jason Scarborough. All of his accomplishments, his education, his good fortune deserted him. No matter what he did, he couldn't get rid of Charles. The harder he pushed, the more he strove to be an asshole and drive him away, the tighter Charles clung.

After the scene at his law firm, he received a summons from his father. They met in Mason Scarborough's office with its floor-to-ceiling views of Puget Sound. He could still hear the disgust in his father's voice.

"I could give two shits who you sleep with, Jason, but this is unseemly, and it reflects poorly on our family. I've had a call from Augie. He's worried about your future with the firm."

"Why is August Drake calling *you*?"

"Don't be naïve. You were hired because of your name. When you soil that name, you do harm not only to your own prospects, but the rest of us as well."

"I thought I was hired because I'm a good lawyer," Jason muttered, but his father waved it away.

"Your legal skills are irrelevant to this discussion. When you lie with dogs, you wake with fleas." Mason's voice rose steadily, and there was an angry glint in his eye. "You have made a mess of this in every way possible. Rumson Global is an important part of my plans. You will not be permitted to ruin that because you let your dick make your decisions." Mason slapped his palm on his desk hard enough to make a family photo fall over.

"What do you want me to do, Father?" Jason demanded. "I've tried the police, and they tell me there's nothing they can do."

"The police? Good God. What are you thinking?" Mason raged at him, and Jason felt his own temper rise.

"I'm thinking I need to get this little shit out of my life and make him leave me alone."

"We're just months away from completing the baseball stadium project with Rumson Global. I need that to go smoothly so Nathaniel Rumson will continue to partner with us. I expect you to handle this quietly and keep the police and the press far away. If this boy wants you to fuck him, then by God, fuck him."

Jason stared at his father, speechless. Mason pressed the button on his intercom. "Donna, we're done in here. What's next on the calendar?" Dismissed, Jason got up and left the office.

The constant notes and deliveries of flowers and messages on his car, and the knowledge that his father wanted him to play the whore to keep his business deals alive, left Jason drained and exhausted. In a moment of weakness, he finally responded to one of Charles's messages. He agreed to meet him for coffee. Even sitting in Randy's office, he could picture the shop, and smell the roasting coffee beans in the air. He could see the burning excitement in Charles's eyes when he presented Jason with an expensive Omega watch. He could also see the other patrons turn their heads to stare as he angrily refused the jewelry.

"Please, Charles. It has to stop. You're ruining my career and my life. We're nothing to each other. Nothing. Please stop calling me."

Charles just sat there, hands around his cup of coffee, smiling beatifically. "Oh, my beautiful Jason, I get it. I understand that you need me to prove how much I love you. I'm ashamed for these foolish gifts I've been bringing. Of course you don't need another watch. You need a man who understands you and who loves you unconditionally. That's me, Jason. I'll be there for you forever, as long as it takes for you to know that you can trust me."

Jason put his face in his hands and ran his fingers through his hair. He tried for dignity as he said, "Leave me alone, Charles. I don't want you. I don't love you, and I never will."

Charles just smiled and tsked at Jason's words as though they were nothing but a challenge.

Then came the break-in at his apartment. He relived the horror of finding Charles naked in his bedroom surrounded by monstrous dildos. Sweat trickled down his back when he remembered his panicked run to the front desk in his building. He could smell scorched coffee in the police station as he filed the complaint and sought a restraining order.

The two weeks that followed felt like a victory. His new phone numbers and his piece of paper directing Charles Rumson to stay at least five hundred feet away from him at all times seemed like magical talismans. Jason actually began to relax a bit, to think it might be over. He might be safe.

Until the ambush a block from his apartment. No, Charles never actually threatened to harm Jason or the man he brought home with him. But Jason could see it in his eyes—the betrayal Charles believed he had suffered, the sense of righteous fury. If Charles had not been stupid enough to approach them in public, Jason honestly believed someone would have died that night. He remembered the sense of relief when the police appeared and arrested Charles. And again he actually thought it might be over. That time it *would* be over.

As with the restraining order, though, relief was fleeting. By morning the local newspapers had picked up the story. The only son of one of the wealthier men in Seattle stalked the photogenic son of another wealthy man. Jason was summoned again to his father's office. Mason berated him for his foolishness and for the damage he had done to the family business.

"Not only are you a faggot, but you're a pussy as well," his father screamed. Spittle flew out of his mouth. "Unable to handle one pissant like Charles Rumson. Jesus Christ. If you couldn't fuck him, you could at least have found a quiet way to take care of this. Beat the shit out of the little pansy, or hire someone to do it if you don't have the balls."

Jason tried one more time. "He would have stabbed me if he got me alone," he said flatly.

Mason's face showed all the scorn he felt. "Then you would have deserved it, and we would be the wronged party instead of Nathaniel Rumson."

Jason got up and walked out. He hadn't spoken to his father since.

August Drake called him in the next afternoon, and Jason knew what was coming. A secretary showed him into the corner office, where he found August sitting behind his desk. Newspapers were spread all over the surface, and his own face looked up at him from a half-dozen tabloids. He waited.

"Jason, how our lawyers conduct their personal lives is germane to our practice here," August said. His steel gray hair was perfectly cut and arranged, and more steel glinted in his watery blue eyes. "The firm must instill confidence that our lawyers are men and women of good judgment, sound legal ability, and profound discretion. I wish I could say this business of you sleeping with men was irrelevant. In truth, I find it revolting. Regardless, that's not the reason for our conversation. This publicity is."

He gestured at the tabloids. "You have made a spectacle of yourself, and by extension, of this law firm. A quiet end to our association would be in everyone's interests. You may remain on the rolls for, let's say, three months while you find employment elsewhere. In exchange we expect you to make your exit quietly. Nondisparagement on both sides is assumed. Are we agreed?"

Jason left without an argument. What would have been the point?

He kept to his office as he began his job search, but it did not go well. Headhunters in the Seattle area knew his name and could give him no assurances they would be able find a new placement. They suggested he look away from Seattle—perhaps New York or London. Even then, with his family name, they weren't confident another law firm would take the risk.

Then came the suicide. There was endless footage of Charles as he climbed to the hood of his Porsche and read poetry and odes to Jason all over Seattle. Then the wreckage of the Porsche at the bottom of the cliff. The police and ambulance removing the body. Pleas from the Rumson spokeswoman to respect the family's privacy in this dark time.

Despite the disintegration of his personal life, all Jason could feel was relief. Perhaps when the coverage died down, he could begin to rebuild a career and find a place for himself again. Money wasn't an issue at all thanks to his trust fund and ownership interest in the family business that his paternal grandfather left him. With those and his savings from the law firm, he could wait it out. He just needed a safe place to lie low and regroup.

Then his mother called. "Jason," she said, "this business has taken a terrible toll on your father. I got your note about coming back to the house to live for a while. I don't think that's in anyone's best interest right now."

"Are you serious? That's my home."

"You're a grown man, Jason. You've made choices, and now you have to accept responsibility for them, instead of running home to hide."

"I was the victim, Mother. I didn't ask Charles Rumson to come after me, to ruin my career and make a tabloid freak of me. Why does no one understand that?"

"You chose to let that man into your bed. Everything after that is a direct result. Nathaniel and Nan have lost their son. Try to have a sense of proportion."

Jason remembered feeling physically ill. "And now you're willing to throw away your son so Father can try to get a business deal with Rumson Global."

She sighed. "You were always so dramatic, Jason, even as a little boy. When will you grow up?" And then she hung up on him.

He had sat on the sofa for hours, staring out the window and trying to understand how his life had come to that. How the golden child had ended up so alone. Did he deserve to lose his family and his career because he brought Charles home one time? In his heart of hearts, he started to believe it.

When the apartment got dark that night, he turned on a lamp

and the TV for company. The lead story was about Senator Grace Gilbert being in Seattle for some event. Inspiration dawned. It was worth a shot, so he reached out to her constituent office and dropped his family name for all it was worth. Grace met with him the next day. They hit it off and she launched the vetting process for him to join her staff. At the end of May, he relocated to Washington, DC. Thomas Scarborough started to build a new life on the ashes of the one Charles had destroyed.

Thomas differed from Jason in more than name. He didn't even realize how much. When Zachary laid into him after their second time together, he exposed the lies Thomas had told himself. In the weeks since, he often found himself thinking about the man he had become. Where Jason was casual and relaxed in his sexual encounters, Thomas was controlling and predatory. When he wanted sex, he made the overtures. He guided the action, and he made *damn* sure the men he pursued and caught understood the rules from the beginning—he didn't date, and he didn't do repeats.

He even tried for a while to give up sex. That was when he found that years of being the golden boy had ruined him in a way he never expected. He *craved* the attention and the adulation his looks brought him. After his parents threw him away, he needed even more to feel desired and wanted.

And yet, almost as soon as an encounter began, when he reached that delicious moment of knowing the man he had targeted was his, he began to panic. What if he missed the signs again and the man turned out to be like Rumson? No matter how sexually fulfilling the experience, a part of Thomas always had his eye on the clock and an exit strategy in sight. He refused to let anyone stay the night, in case that was the secret of where it really went wrong with Charles.

His rational brain decried that superstitious thinking, but the rules gradually calcified. Thomas couldn't give up the validation he got from sex, but he would no longer even consider the possibility of a relationship. Perhaps he was punishing himself by pushing men away as quickly as he drew them in.

Until he met Zachary and found himself asking him to stay for the night. Until he surrendered to the longing he saw in Zach's eyes and his own desire and brought him home a second time. Until he relaxed his tight control and gave himself to Zach in a way he had never done with anyone else, man or woman. Until he found himself daydreaming about an Italian vacation with a lover who could have stepped from a Renaissance painting.

Even if that dream would never come true, Zach had given him hope again. Maybe someday there could be another like him, who would cut through his bullshit and help him repair the damage Rumson had wrought.

.   .   .

HE WAS EVALUATING his options, waiting for Randy to return, when his phone chimed. At a glance he saw the message was from Zachary, and another wave of remorse swept over him. He was probably still angry and needed to vent. Well, Thomas had it coming, so he sighed and looked closely at his phone.

But when he read the message, he frowned:

Do you think about me?

Thomas narrowed his eyes. That wasn't the kind of thing Zachary had ever said to him—in person or by text. Before he could think of a response, his cell chimed again with another message:

I think about you all the time because I have nothing and you are everything.

His heart began to pound and his palms to sweat. Thomas ran to the office door, opened it, and called loudly for Randy as a third message chimed.

You know how much I like selfies because I'm so shallow and vapid.

Randy reached the office. Wordlessly Thomas showed him the cell phone, and an image popped up. It was Zachary, lying on his stomach, his shirt off and—oh God. Thomas saw his hands bound by rope, his eyes closed, and his mouth slack.

"No, no, no…," Thomas moaned. Randy gripped his shoulder hard. Before he could say anything, another image appeared. That one again showed Zachary shirtless and the top of his hips, also bare. Blood pooled on the floor beneath his head.

Randy lunged for his office phone, but it rang first. Cursing, he picked up the line and barked, "Vaughan. I'll have to…." He froze at the words he heard over the line, and he turned to face Thomas. His eyes were wide. "It's for you."

Thomas took the phone with a trembling hand and brought it to his ear.

"H-hello?"

"Hello, Jason."

Thomas sagged to his knees and dropped his cell phone as he did. It was Charles. The same fervor lit his voice, the same—

Another text chimed. Randy picked up the cell, and they both stared in horror at the image. The angle of the picture showed Rumson smiling up into the camera as he straddled Zachary's nude form. His hair was auburn, the beard gone, but there was no doubt.

From the phone still against his ear, Thomas heard the hated voice. "Do you like my selfie, Jason?"

"Please don't hurt him," he begged.

"I've missed you so much, Jason. All the tests you placed before me. All the other men you pretended to want until I understood what you needed me to do with them. Oh, my Beloved. It's almost time. I'm almost ready for you. I'm almost worthy." Thomas heard the quiver of excitement in Charles's voice.

Randy asked quietly, "How did he know you were here, in my office?"

Thomas nodded. "Charles, how did you find me? How did you know to call me here?"

Charles giggled. "I always know where you are, Jason. Now, that is. Technology and money are wonderful things together. Here, look."

A new message popped on Thomas's phone from a source that identified no cell number. It was a still image of the bar at Mata Hari and of Randy serving a customer.

Randy looked at the phone over his shoulder and said, "This was ten minutes ago. I just served that guy a martini."

Charles giggled a second time. "And how about this one?"

The next picture showed the inside of Thomas's apartment, looking toward his living room from near the door. Thomas moaned. Charles had been in his apartment again.

"And my favorite." That image showed a map of Washington. A line in blue connected the Senate office building where Thomas worked to the parking lot outside of Mata Hari. That was his route today, Thomas saw. Charles was able to track his car too.

Focus. Focus on Zach. Thomas fought to keep his voice under control and not to scream his frustration and fear into the phone.

"How did you get Zachary there with you?" he asked.

Charles giggled again—a high-pitched, watery sound that grated on Thomas's nerves. "I invited him for dinner, and he came right over." His voice grew mock-stern. "He was a naughty boy and wandered around my home while I was being a perfect host."

"Why do this, Charles? What do you want from me?" he asked, trying to project calm.

Perhaps it worked because Charles's voice was softer, more controlled, when he spoke again. "What I've always wanted, my Beloved. Jason, we belong together. Ever since we were little boys. It took me so long to solve your riddles, but I understand now. I know how to show you how much I love you. Just a few more preparations and we'll be ready. But Jason, you have a soft heart." His voice dropped lower, and his tone held a quiet menace. "I don't want you to do anything foolish like calling the police. This creature, Zachary. He would suffer. Do you understand?"

Thomas nodded and said aloud, "Yes. I understand."

"Good. Don't disable my cameras. Don't stop using your cell phone. Don't change cars. I'll know, and I'll be very, very cross with this cretin."

Thomas heard the sound of leather striking bare skin and the faintest moan of pain. It came from Zach. *He's alive.*

"Of course he liked that," Charles said, scorn and disgust in his voice. "He's going to love what I do to him, just like the others did. I'm doing it for you, Jason, so you can see why these stupid, stupid men aren't good enough for you. You'll see how much he loves it, and you'll understand why I had to show you."

"Charles, please stop. Please don't hurt Zachary."

There was an element of pain in Charles's voice when he answered, "I watched you, Jason. I saw your face. I heard you." A slight hitch of breath, and then he spoke again in a more even tone. "This one means something to you—even more than all those other men you took into your bed. That's why I have to go further. I have to *show* you, Jason. I have to prove to you how worthless he really is. I'll call you when I'm ready, and I'll tell you where to come. No police. Nothing. Not that bitch who's been investigating. Tell me again you understand."

Thomas swallowed hard and said, "I understand. I won't call the police."

"Good. Good. Now, Jason, my Beloved, I'll be in touch." The call ended, and Thomas looked up at Randy. His throat was dry, and his eyes burned.

"What do I do?"

Chapter 24

"**B**EAT THE SON of a bitch. That's what we do," Randy answered. His Secret Service training kicked in as he looked at Thomas's bleak face. He tapped his fingers furiously on the desk. "We need to know where he is. That's the most important thing."

Thomas gasped suddenly. "He said Zach came for dinner. Is it possible Charles is the man he's been dating?"

Randy picked up the thought and ran with it. "That could be right. He'd have to use an alias, in case Zachary ever mentioned him. Do you know the name?"

Thomas shook his head. "No. It wasn't something Zach and I talked about."

Randy scrunched his eyes and thought. "I remember him saying… Sam. Just Sam, though. No last name."

"Would he have talked to Joe or Terry about this? Maybe they know his name," Thomas said, desperate for hope.

Randy nodded slowly. "Yes, good thought. But before we call them, I need to know something." He opened his office door and looked back at Thomas. "Stay here and don't call anyone."

Randy went to the front of the bar, where only a handful of patrons remained. He signaled to Miss Ethel to stop playing, and then he turned up the house lights. "Folks, I'm sorry, but we're having a plumbing problem. No johns, so I have to close early."

The few people still in the bar grumbled but started to collect coats from the check room. "Come back tomorrow, and your first drink is on the house," Randy called. He went to Malcolm and said in a low voice, "Check out early, kid. I'll call you in the morning."

He helped Miss Ethel into her coat a few minutes later. As she was the last, he showed her out and locked the front door behind her.

Immediately he moved around the room and tried to picture the angle from the photo of him serving a drink. He paused along one wall of the room to look at the bar from where he stood. The sight line seemed nearly correct but… too high. He crouched to get the right height and looked under the counter that ran around the wall there. He found the camera right away.

He was careful not to dislodge it, but he studied the mechanism. It wasn't his specialty, but he was reasonably sure it was image only—no sound capability. With his cell phone, he snapped a picture of the camera so he could check further.

He continued to search the perimeter of the bar. Eventually he found a total of four cameras, all positioned in such a way that they could see the bar and two of the side rooms. The mounting was amateurish—basically double-sided duct tape held the small cameras in place. That told him Rumson had acted in a hurry with each installation. Tape would wear out, so it had probably been there no more than two or three months. That added up— he hadn't seen the man with the shaggy blond hair and silver-framed glasses in several weeks. If Rumson had eyes in place, there was no need for him to risk discovery by returning.

Randy went back to his office and searched again while Thomas watched him with wide eyes. He checked under his desk and in every corner, but he found no other cameras. He looked at the phone on his desk and considered it. If Rumson had been unable to place a camera in his office, it was highly unlikely he had a way to tap the phone. No point in taking chances, though. He'd stick to his cell.

Thomas watched him, clearly desperate for guidance. Randy spoke with all the authority instilled in him during a twenty-five-year career in law enforcement. "Right. There are four cameras in the bar, but I don't believe Rumson could hear what went on. Image only. Nothing in here either."

"But my car. My apartment." Thomas seemed close to shock.

"Yes, those are bugged. We should assume he had more time and possibly better equipment. We're going to want to check that."

"He said no police."

"Exactly. What does that tell you?" Randy asked. He wanted to engage Thomas, to keep him focused and to keep him from giving in to his fear.

"He knows the police were here. He mentioned the 'bitch'…. He must have seen Detective Torres come in a few times."

"Good. Agreed. But he only said 'police.' If he knew my background, he would probably have said something else, like no FBI."

Thomas looked up at him sharply with a spark of hope in his eyes. "Can you get help there? Do you still have contacts?"

"I do. Some, anyway, that might help me. Here's what I'm thinking. The office isn't bugged, and I don't think my cell phone can be bugged either. No opportunity. I want to try Joe first about a last name for Sam, and then call a former colleague of mine in the Secret Service. Use her as a conduit to Torres. But I'm making this plan as I go along, Thomas. I need to know if you're on board."

"If we're wrong, he'll…. Oh God, he'll hurt Zach."

Randy held his gaze. "Thomas, he'll definitely hurt Zachary if we do nothing. Maybe more than just hurt. This is a risk, but it's what I've got. You tell me what you want me to do."

Thomas stared at him for a moment, weighing and calculating. Finally he stood up straight and gave a sharp nod of his head. "Do it, Randy."

Randy called Joe on his cell first and put it on speaker.

"Joe Mulholland." They heard the soft Boston accent.

Randy said, "Joe, I'm sorry to be abrupt, but I have an important question. Did Zachary Hall tell you the name of the man he's dated recently?"

"Zachary?" Joe asked. "Let me think…. He said Sam, I believe."

"No last name?"

"Not that I can recall. We tried to make dinner plans, actually, before the situation with Terry and me. It never happened." Alarm crept into Joe's voice. "Randall, what's this about? Is Zachary safe?"

"I'll tell you more as soon as I know anything. I have to go." Randy disconnected the call, knowing Joe would forgive his rudeness. "Strike one," he muttered as he dialed his cell again and prayed Lily would pick up. The call connected, and he heard her voice.

"Hey, RV. Twice in such a short time. That has to be a record," she said.

"Lily, I need help badly. I'm putting you on speaker." He pressed the button on his cell and set it down on his desk. "I'm here with Jason Scarborough from the Rumson investigation. Rumson is still alive. He just called us here in my bar."

"Holy shit," Lily exclaimed. "How did we miss it?"

"I don't know. Question for tomorrow. Right now, we know he has a hostage. It's a personal friend of Scarborough's. We believe he may have killed at least two people. He's monitoring Scarborough, but I believe this is a safe channel. As soon as we disconnect, I'll send you an image of the camera he used here in the bar. I'm hoping you can check the model and its capabilities to see if that gives us any clue. I don't think he's gotten devices into my office, but we're on a clock here."

"What else do you need, Randy?" she asked. Right to the point—no bullshit—as he'd hoped.

"Rumson knows we've been in contact with the Metro police. We can't take a risk on contacting them directly because we don't know what precautions he's taken. I'd like you to call Detective Maria Torres and be our liaison. Here's her number," he said and read off the digits from her business card.

"Got it. What does she need to know?"

Randy described as succinctly as he could the relevant information from the call with Rumson.

"Okay. Monitoring devices in Scarborough's home and car," she summarized. "I'd add most likely his phone as well."

Thomas seemed shocked. "I have a pretty high security clearance, and the phone I use is government-issued. How would he get through the encryption?"

Lily answered, "Mr. Scarborough, no technology is perfect. With our protectees we like to scan phones at least once a month. We compare to previous scans and identify any anomaly that might have appeared. We also change up tech and security on a random basis to avoid hacking. When was the last time your tech support people examined your phone?"

"It might have been two, three months ago. Maybe longer. I'm chief counsel to a Senate committee, so I'm not normally at high risk for hackers."

Randy jumped in. "We can worry about the details later. For now I agree, we have to assume your phone is compromised. Lily, are you able to run some checks for us?"

"You're looking for possible locations for Rumson?" she

guessed.

"Exactly. He came into the bar in disguise, starting over two months ago. It's possible he's transient or staying in different hotels, but he grew up wealthy. Right, Thomas?"

Thomas nodded and said aloud for Lily's benefit, "Yes. His family estate was very large. I went there once for a benefit. And Randy, the money link you told me about…."

Randy said, "Lily, remember I asked you about Rumson's finances? Over six million dollars moved from his personal accounts shortly *after* the date of his death. His mother told the officer who pursued that not to worry about it. We're just speculating at this point, but we should assume he's extremely well-funded. And he's used to comfort."

"So a house, apartment, or long-term lease of some kind are possible. He wouldn't use his own name, though. What do I search?"

"We think our friend Zachary has gone out with Rumson under an alias. He mentioned the name Sam." Randy looked thoughtful. "Let's try combinations of Charles and Sam and Jason with Rumson or Scarborough. He's focused on you, Thomas, so maybe he pretends you're married or something."

"Try Milliken too," Thomas added. "That's his mother's maiden name."

They could hear Lily's pen scratching, and she said, "Got it. Anything else before I call Detective Torres?"

"Just make sure she stays away from the bar and from Thomas's apartment and doesn't call directly. We don't have enough information to know what's safe."

"Understood. I'll get back to you as soon as I can."

"Thanks, Lily. This is above and beyond," Randy said.

She sounded grim. "If we fucked up our investigation, I want to know how. I'll take responsibility for cleaning up the paperwork later."

She disconnected, and Randy sent her the image he'd taken of the camera hidden in the bar. Thomas paced the office as Randy typed.

"What if he's hurt Zach already?" Thomas asked. "Randy, I have to do something."

"I know, buddy. Look. I'm reaching here, but this is different from Gallagher and that other one. Daniel Owen. Rumson chose to reveal himself to you and to let you know he has Zachary. I think that means something."

Thomas stopped walking and stared at Randy with haunted eyes. "Like he's going to make me watch him hurt Zach?"

"Maybe. But I think it means at least that he's not going to do anything yet. Not until he contacts you again."

Thomas's eyes flashed. Randy could see him wrestling to apply his intelligence to the nightmare instead of running like a rabbit. "I need to go home, Randy. Right now."

"What?"

"He's only one man. Even if he has everything bugged, it's going to be hard for him to track both of us if we're in different places. Add in the possibility that he's monitoring Torres somehow. That's three streams he has to watch if we separate."

Reluctantly Randy nodded. "That makes sense."

Thomas thrust his hands into his pants pocket and chewed his lip. "Should I look for cameras in my apartment?"

"I think so," Randy agreed slowly. "But be careful not to disturb them. He stuck on the ones here with tape."

"Okay. I can do that."

Randy looked around his office and cursed. "I don't have a gun in here. There's one out by the bar, but he'll likely see it if I try to give that one to you. Do you own a gun, Thomas?"

"No, I never saw the need."

"Another thing I'll try to figure out. If... *when* I get any information from Lily, I don't want to risk passing it along to you by phone or text."

"Let's do this," Thomas suggested. "Call my cell every hour and let it ring just twice if you have no information. If you let it ring three times, I'll pick up to let you know I'm there. I'll find a pay phone or something to call your cell back."

Randy nodded and put a hand on his shoulder. "This is good. We're doing everything we can, Thomas. We'll get the cocksucker."

Chapter 25

Zachary felt himself being dragged. His back burned along a broad stripe where it met the hardwood floor. His head pounded, especially on his left temple, and his mouth was dry. He couldn't focus or understand what was happening.

His arms and legs felt like lead. His arms…. Were they tied? He tried to move his wrists and realized he couldn't. Then he tried to force his eyes open. Everything seemed blurry, and he was so tired. So tired….

He felt himself heaved up onto a different surface. It squeaked under him, and someone positioned him and moved his body around so he lay on padded leather. The stripe across his back burned more as he was shifted around, and he tried to protest.

He felt a hand bend his left leg, and something soft was wrapped around his ankle. The same thing happened to his right leg, and he realized he couldn't move either one. When he tried to sit up, his head immediately began to swim, and he muttered, "I think I'm gonna be sick."

He heard a chuckle above him and tried again to focus his eyes. It dawned on him that he was naked and cold. Something was happening across his chest. He felt more leather and a metal buckle pressed against his skin. A strap was tightened and locked into place. He couldn't move his upper body.

A pad was placed around his left wrist, and then he heard a

click. The rope that had bound his wrists together was removed. He tried to flail with his freed right hand, only to have it grabbed and forced down. Again something soft wrapped around his wrist, there was another click, and then he was unable to move his arms.

"There we are," a satisfied voice said. "Almost ready."

"S-Sam?" he asked, and he heard another chuckle.

"Sam doesn't live here anymore."

Zachary tried again to get his eyes to focus. He saw Sam leaning over him, and a wide grin split his mouth as he stared down. Something dark and terrible burned in his brown eyes.

"Sam, what's happening?" He pulled at his legs and his arms and only then understood he was completely immobilized.

"We haven't been properly introduced. Call me Charles," Sam said. Or Charles did? Zachary's head hurt so badly he couldn't think.

"Why can't I move?" he tried again.

"You can't move because I have a present for you, and I need you to be in just the right position to enjoy it." Charles's tone was one might use for a small child. He adjusted the strap across Zachary's chest and pulled it tighter, pinching his skin and making him groan.

"I'm naked."

"Yes, you are, you little whore. I need Jason to see you for what you are before I give you my present."

Charles? Jason? Zachary understood nothing, and he moaned. "Please let me go, Sam."

Charles slapped his cheek hard. "Not Sam. Charles. I won't tell you again."

The sharp sting helped Zachary focus for a moment, and then he wished it hadn't. Charles, Sam, whoever—he had to be the one who killed those two men. And he had Zachary trapped.

He trembled in cold and fear. He pulled on his arms and legs with all of his might and rocked as he tried to make the surface he was strapped to fall over. It barely budged, and Charles smiled with deep satisfaction. He sat back on his heels and ran his eyes over Zachary's bound body with malice and glee.

"Perfect," he muttered. "Jason will finally know what a piece of trash you really are."

Zachary thought he needed to try to be calm. Get Sam, or Charles, talking. "Who… who is Jason?" he asked.

"Jason, Thomas…. It doesn't matter what he calls himself. I found him again."

"Thomas is coming here?" Zachary asked as a surge of hope rushed through him.

"Eventually. I need him to see what a disgusting display you'll make. How you'll beg for it. That's important before we're done with you and able to move on." Charles's voice trembled slightly, and his eyes were lit with a manic glow.

"You don't have to hurt me, Charles. I'll go away and leave Thomas, uh, Jason alone." Zachary made his eyes wide as he tried to convince Charles of his sincerity.

Charles just sighed and projected insincere regret. "Ah, Zachary. If only that would work. But Jason thinks he loves you, don't you see?"

Zachary shook his head frantically. "No. He never told me he loves me. We only got together a few times."

"Well, you don't know him like I do." His mouth grew hard. "*Nobody* knows him like I do. With the others I knew he was just testing me. He'd fuck them and send them away. But I knew. He was marking them out for me as a way to test whether I really loved him. To see if I would do what needed to be done. And I finally understood, but I was careless. The first one led too easily back to Jason."

"Gallagher? The one Thomas, uh, Jason slept with?"

Charles grimaced ruefully. "I was too eager, having finally found Jason again after so long. I saw that creature leave with him one night, and the next week he was back, panting again after Jason like a bitch in heat. I think Jason knew I was there, though, even in my disguise. He turned the creature away—dismissed him like I knew he would. Then that boy had the audacity to challenge him. He threw a drink at Jason before he left. That could not stand, so I showed him the error of his ways. I showed him why Jason could never be his."

Got to keep him talking. The longer he talks, maybe Thomas will come and help me. "What about the other one? Owen or something? Thom—Jason said he never met him. What was his error?"

Charles sighed. "That was my own devising, rather than a challenge that Jason set for me. When the police showed up at Mata Hari, I realized my mistake. I needed to draw their attention away from Jason. I did feel bad, though. The boy really had done nothing wrong. But he was a convenient age and build—a bit like the cretin who had accosted Jason—and he left that bar alone." His face hardened as he met Zachary's eyes again. "I regret it, but there is nothing I would not do for Jason. Nothing."

"Why me? Charles, I learned my error, didn't I? I stayed away from Jason?"

"Oh no, silly man. You went back and interfered with his pleasure with the handsome young black man, and that was error enough."

Marcus. He means the night Thomas was going to leave with that man, Marcus, but changed his mind.

"I was so close to getting you that night," Charles said as he shook his head. "You were alone in the parking lot, drunk like a whore, staggering toward the street. I got out of my car and then"—his voice trembled in rage—"Jason followed you."

Zachary remembered it so clearly, even through the haze of the alcohol he had consumed that night. He remembered the nearly deserted parking lot, the bottle rolling on its side. He heard again the sound of a car door opening. *Oh God.*

"Of course I could do nothing in front of Jason. I simply wasn't ready yet. But I followed your cab. I saw you both go up to his apartment." Charles's voice became steadily more strident as he recited Zachary's crimes. "I listened to your *violation* of Jason's body. I heard you throw him around and use him. Every breath, every move. After all of that, you finally had the decency to leave. Then I heard him give you words he denied everyone else."

Charles pressed a button on his cell phone, and a recording of Thomas's baritone played over the sound system. "If I could let anyone in, Zach, it would be you." Zachary's vision blurred with tears.

Ah, Thomas. You really did feel something for me.

He deeply wanted to apologize to Thomas for the terrible things he had said in their last conversation. Was it only yesterday? But despair sapped his strength, and he sagged against the leather bench. Once he would have done anything to hear those words. Now strapped and helpless, he recognized them for a death sentence.

Charles nodded at Zachary's tears. "You're a clever one. I saw that early on. You understand what this means. But I also knew I had to handle this more carefully than I had the other one, that Gallagher."

"Were you… were you trying to make me love you?" Zachary choked out. "To love Sam?"

"It seemed so simple, with your febrile tastes. I went through your books and your movie collection, found what you liked, and then I pretended to like those same things."

"You were in my apartment?" Zachary asked, trying to make sense of what he heard.

"Of course. Simplest thing in the world. Identify a construction or a maintenance team going in. Slip some money to join the crew. Break away once inside the building. Piece of cake," Charles gloated. "Once I was in, I planted a few cameras, added some software to your computer, that sort of thing. That's how I knew about your work trip to New Orleans, of course. I simply showed up as Sam and took things from there."

"But why go to so much trouble?"

"I needed Jason to see how faithless you really were," Charles said with a grimace. "I wanted him to see how easily you'd abandon him for another man. Otherwise he'd simply pine for you, and I couldn't have that. No. When Jason comes to me, I want all of him, every bit of his attention."

"Did you delete that picture from my phone from when we went to the *Captain America* movie?" Zachary asked, desperate to keep Charles talking.

"When you went to the bathroom and left your phone in your jacket. I couldn't have you show that around, just on the off chance Jason would see it before I was ready."

A piece shifted into place for Zachary. "You knew Jason went to the shelter sometimes. That's why you didn't want to come there."

Charles scoffed. "Obviously. Besides, I had no sympathy for those children—weeping and wailing because their families didn't want them. I survived that on my own." Anger glinted in his eye. "Family is a trap. Only love can save you, and that never comes from family. All family gives you, ultimately, is disappointment and punishment and disapproval."

Zachary tried a different tack. "Couldn't you have loved me? I really believed in you, as Sam. We had so much fun together." He tried to put longing into his tone.

Contempt dripped from Charles. "Don't be ridiculous. Jason is the only man for me, and he'll understand soon that I'm the only man for him." He smiled cruelly then and asked, "Now would you like to get a look at my present?"

Charles moved out of Zachary's line of sight and wheeled over a device. A silver-colored arm protruded from a Lucite box. The gears and mechanism inside the box reflected the lights in the room along hard edges and sharp corners. Charles pressed a button on a remote and the gears began to turn powerfully. They thrust the rod forward and back and picked up speed until it punched the air.

Charles shut down the mechanism, stepped away, and returned with a long box. He reached inside. With his eyes on Zachary's face, he removed a dildo longer and thicker than Zachary had even imagined existed. It had to be more than a foot long and bigger around than a beer can. And covering the head of the dildo were....

"Nails," Charles said in satisfaction as he bent to bring the monstrous thing closer to Zachary's face. The nail heads protruded all around the rubber head, each to about a quarter of an inch.

Charles returned to his machine and fitted the end of the dildo over the steel rod. He looked Zachary in the eye again as he pressed the On button. The gears started to churn once more. The arm thrust the phallus with its evilly glinting glans forward and back through a smooth piston motion, faster and faster.

Zachary gasped as he understood. Soon it would ram into his body—Charles's ultimate punishment for daring to have had Thomas. The nail heads would rip and shred him from the inside. He would die horribly.

His bladder voided suddenly, and Charles chuckled in appreciation. "See. I knew you were clever," he said. Then he picked up a ball gag and leaned over Zachary's head.

Chapter 26

THOMAS CLIMBED INTO his Maserati where he had parked it next to Mata Hari. He slumped in the darkened car for a minute and tried to process that Charles had come for him again. He pictured poor Brian Gallagher. He was just a horny young guy looking to have a little sex, and Thomas fit the bill. If Thomas had turned him down, had never taken him home, he'd still be alive.

He remembered the scorn heaped upon him by his father and then by August Drake when he pushed him out of the law firm. They blamed him for the stalking because he was too foolish to see the danger. At the time it seemed monstrously unfair.

But two years older he confronted the consequences and knew they were right. Others paid for his mistakes far worse than Thomas himself. He had believed so firmly in his own intelligence and savvy. He was *sure* he could spot a danger a mile away. So confident in his own charmed life, it had never occurred that his promiscuity could lead him to bring home a man as dangerous as Charles. Brian Gallagher suffered for that blind spot. Somehow Daniel Owen suffered too. Though Thomas didn't understand the connection, he had no doubt the responsibility fell at his feet.

And worst of all…. He clenched his jaw and pounded on the leather-wrapped steering wheel of his car. Worst of all Zachary would pay for Thomas's hubris. Zach. The other man he never saw coming. The beautiful and happy transplant from Utah had burst into Thomas's life. Without even trying, he'd caused Thomas to dream of abandoning his careful rules. Zach gave his time to abandoned gay and lesbian teenagers. He sang torch songs he was too innocent to understand, and liked *Star Wars* and *Star Trek* and God knew what else. Yet he could turn that naïveté and charm around to dominate Thomas in bed.

Zach had brought Thomas to question everything he ever knew about himself and his desires. Thomas absolutely craved more. His eyes welled with tears. He wanted more of Zach, but Zach was going to be hurt or killed by Charles. Because he made the huge mistake of sleeping with Thomas. Thomas had indeed *infected* Zach with his bad judgment, and made him a target for a madman.

He started his car, drove out of the parking lot, and headed toward his apartment. He leaned his cheek on his left fist and held the steering wheel in his right as he made his way through the quiet night. Childhood prayers rose in his mind. He prayed first and foremost for Zachary Hall—that he might be spared from evil.

His phone rang in his suit-jacket pocket, and he assumed it was Randy. When he pulled the phone out, however, Zachary's name appeared. Heart instantly pounding, he accepted the call on speaker mode.

Charles's voice filled the cabin of his car. "I'm ready at last, Jason," he said, and excitement made his voice quiver. "It's been so long, but I found my way back to you. I can't wait to show how Zachary deceived you. You'll finally understand that no one can love you as completely as I do."

Thomas fought down the urge to scream and to rage at Charles. That had failed every time before. Begging for Zachary's life would get him nothing either and might drive Charles to harm him sooner. "What do you want me to do, Charles?" he asked as steadily as he could.

"I need you to come to me, Jason," Charles said. Fervor shaded his tone as he recited an address off Pennsylvania Avenue. "I hate to make our reunion tense, but I must remind you not to tell anyone where you're coming. Not the police detective, not your friend at Mata Hari. Nobody. Do you understand?"

"Is Zachary alive?" Thomas asked, unable to keep his voice from cracking.

"Oh yes. You'll see him soon."

"I'm not coming until I know he's alive." Thomas held his breath and hoped he hadn't pushed too hard. "Please, Charles. Give me some reason to believe you," he requested in a softer tone.

The phone was silent for a moment, and he heard Charles snort. "Fine. You'll receive a video as soon as we disconnect so you can see the creature is alive. Now you're about fifteen minutes away from my apartment. If you aren't here at my door in twenty minutes, I make no promises that the creature won't suffer early. Are we clear, Jason?"

"Yes, Charles. We're clear."

"Good. I'll see you very soon, Jason." Charles's tone was kind, and that was almost worse.

Thomas disconnected the call and drove toward the address near the Capitol. Throwing his phone onto the passenger seat, he waited for the promised proof. In moments, the phone chimed. He reached over to activate the video attached to the message.

It started with a close-up of Zachary on his back. His eyes were wide and afraid, and a ball gag was in his mouth. Off camera, Charles recited, "We're giving Jason assurances that you are currently alive. Nod for the camera, please." Thomas saw Zachary hesitate and then nod slightly. Charles continued, "Now let's give Jason a little preview of what a whore you are, shall we?"

The view pulled back to show Zachary naked and strapped to a leather bench by a band buckled across his chest. Restraints on his ankles and his wrists connected together by hooks of some kind and forced Zachary's legs up and back. What was Charles doing? It made no sense to Thomas.

A horn honked, and he swerved the car as he jerked his eyes back to the road. He had nearly driven over the line into coming traffic. His heart pounded as he pulled sharply over to the right shoulder to play the short video clip again. He tried to understand the way Zachary was held. He couldn't, but the threat was clear.

He froze the video on the close shot of Zach's terrified face. As he stared at it, certitude gripped his heart. More than anything in the world, Thomas wanted Zach safe, at whatever cost to himself was necessary. He looked at the road and the oncoming traffic. If he thought it would save Zach, he realized, he would drive into a median or over a railing. If Thomas's own death could distract Charles enough.... But no, that would accomplish nothing. Charles would still blame Zach and kill him before anyone could find them.

Thomas selfishly wished he could tell Zach—just once—how much he had come to mean to him in such a short time. This terrible situation was Thomas's fault, and Zach could never love him back after the danger Thomas had brought to him. But dear God, he wished he could at least beg forgiveness.

None of that mattered while Zach remained in danger, though. Thomas was wasting precious moments on the clock Charles had set for him. He pulled back onto Massachusetts Avenue and continued toward the address. It was in the Newseum, a few blocks away from the Capitol itself.

He had no weapon in the car and no time to stop and get

one. Yet Thomas would do anything in his power to prevent Charles from hurting Zach. He would strangle the maniac with his bare hands if he got the chance and take the consequences gladly. If he had to pull Charles out a window with him, it didn't matter.

Charles would not harm Zachary. No. Fucking. Way.

Chapter 27

RANDY PACED AROUND his office. His mind worked like in the old days when he was planning a trip into a hot zone for his protectee. His resources were limited. His lines of communication were little better than tin cans tied together with string. He was acutely aware of the fact that he had no official role anymore. But Thomas was his friend. And despite Randy's natural reticence, he genuinely liked Zachary too. If twenty-five years of training could help save that good kid, then Randy would do what he must and apologize later.

He jumped at his cell phone when it buzzed with the ringtone he had set for Lily. "What do ya know?" he growled into the phone.

"I talked to Detective Torres. She understands the situation and she's combing through the file again for anything that might help. All searches for name combinations with Rumson, Scarborough, and Milliken had turned up nothing relevant. The only name that did hit checks out for a seventy-five-year-old man who's lived in the same place for forty years. I have a call in to the Seattle PD myself in case Secret Service jogs something loose that they forgot to tell a DC detective. Any other ideas, RV?"

"The mother has to know he's still alive. Can we do anything there?" Randy asked.

"Yes, she likely knows Charles is alive," Lily said cautiously, "but we have nothing concrete yet. The Rumson family is too well connected in Washington State politics. If I make a call to her without going up the chain first, the shitstorm will wipe us all away."

Randy had to agree. "Okay. Dead end for now. Even if she knew he survived the crash, it's gonna take work to connect her to some murders two years later."

Lily was quiet, and Randy recognized a peculiar quality in her silence. It was why they worked well together for years when she was his deputy. "Out with it, Lily. What are you thinking?"

"If Rumson is alive, then he faked the suicide. Right? So whose body did Mrs. Rumson identify?"

Randy felt the hair on his arms stand on end as he let the ramifications wash over him. "Brilliant, Lily. Run with that thought. How would you come up with another body?"

"You'd need someone unlikely to be missed," Lily said slowly as she worked her way through the puzzle. "Homeless, maybe. But he'd have to have enough similarities to Rumson to make the initial ID plausible. Let me dig a bit, and I'll call back."

Just as Lily hung up, his office door opened, and Randy yelped as his barback, Malcolm, stuck in his head. "Holy shit, Mal," Randy gasped. "What the hell are you still doing here? I thought the place was empty."

Malcolm laughed. "I guess I was taking out the trash when you looked. Sorry, boss. Do you need me to do anything else before I go?"

Randy leaned forward eagerly. "Mal, do you have a cell with you?"

"Sure, boss. Why?"

"I need to borrow it for the night. I know that'll crimp your style, but it's a matter of life and death. No shit."

Malcolm pulled a cheap phone out of his back pocket and handed it over, his eyes wide. "Fuck, boss. What's going on?"

"Not tonight. Thanks, Mal. I'll get this back to you tomorrow," Randy said. *I hope.* Using Malcolm's phone, he immediately dialed and hoped she would pick up despite the strange number.

"Torres," he heard over the line.

"Maria, it's Randy at Mata Hari. I'm using a different phone I don't think Rumson can know about."

"Good. That agent friend of yours is hell on wheels."

"She really is. Do you have anything new?"

"No. I've been through the case file twice, and I can't find anything we missed."

"Lily pointed out that if that wasn't Rumson's body on the slab two years ago, maybe the key is to find out who actually was pulled from his Porsche that day."

"Hang on, that...." She went silent, but Randy could hear pages flipping on her desk.

Malcolm was still standing in the door, and Randy asked him, "You know where I keep the Magnum?"

Malcolm nodded.

"I need you to get it and bring it to me, but try to hide what you're doing. I'll explain later, but there's a camera aimed at the bar. Can you be cool about this?"

"On it, boss," Malcolm said and slipped away.

"Here it is." Torres spoke in his ear, and Randy could hear excitement. "What you said reminded me of a note in the log. Before the body was officially ID'd, the processing officer noted that another officer had contacted him about a missing person case. She wanted to bring the person who filed the complaint to the morgue. He wrote the word *Ryder*, but I can't tell if that's the second officer or the missing person. Our guy notes twenty minutes later that Rumson had been claimed. He apparently either didn't respond on the missing person case or failed to note it. That happens all the time, Randy, when there's a John Doe brought in."

"Anything there we can use to follow up on the missing person report—a case number?"

"I'm checking… Wait. It's Agent Woods calling on my other line."

"Maria, can you patch us all in together?"

"I'll try, but I'm terrible at these tech things. Hang on. Okay. Randy? Agent Woods? We all on?"

"I'm here," Randy said.

"I'm here, and call me Lily, please. I've got something. The same day Rumson crashed his car, Seattle PD recorded a report for a male escort who went missing. He was five foot nine, about one fifty, brown hair, and brown eyes."

Torres said, "Those stats match Rumson."

"Right," Lily continued. "The boyfriend said this guy had gone out on a call two days earlier and never returned or answered his phone. The case file still indicates the missing person is open. Since he was a prostitute, you can guess how much police resources went to follow through."

"What's the escort's name?" Randy asked, knowing already that was the lead they needed.

"Sam Ryder. R-Y-D-E-R. I'm checking now to see if that name turns up in DC."

Torres jumped in. "I'll check too." Randy could hear both women quickly typing into computers, and he cursed his uselessness.

Malcolm returned to Randy's office and pulled the holstered .357 Magnum out of his waistband, where he had concealed it behind his bar apron. Randy took it carefully until he was sure Malcolm hadn't released the safety. "Thanks, Mal."

"It's all good, boss," Malcolm said with a grin. "What else can

I do?"

"Go home. Really. I'll explain this tomorrow." Randy confirmed the gun was loaded and grabbed additional bullets from his office cabinet.

"Got something," Lily crowed in his ear, and Torres muttered a curse. "Sam Ryder, Newseum Residences, phone activated three months ago. It's a top-floor unit, and that's a swank building." She read off an address and unit number.

"Maria, how do you want to play this?" Randy asked and gritted his teeth as he typed *Newseum Residences* into his computer's search engine. His instinct was to take over, but he had no official status.

"No time to get a warrant, but I've got probable cause. If we're right and Rumson hears sirens, he could panic and kill Hall. I'll get backup, no red and blues, and try to surprise him."

"I'm coming too," Randy said as he sent an image to the printer. "I know what I'm doing. Twenty-five years of experience, and I'm still in excellent shape. I won't interfere, but you may need more help than you can get together this time of night."

"Okay. I don't have time to fight you. Meet me at the Newseum and we'll coordinate there."

Randy grabbed his printout and ran through the door with Malcolm's cell phone to his ear as he headed for his pickup truck. "I'm going to try Thomas to see if he's heard anything further from Rumson."

Lily said, "I'll keep working the Ryder angle. I also want to see if there are any other missing-person files worth checking in case this one doesn't pan out."

Torres muttered, "I'll be at the Newseum in ten, Randy," and disconnected.

Randy dialed Thomas's cell from his own, and it rang three times. Then four. Then five before voice mail picked up. Randy frowned as he started his truck and peeled out of the parking lot toward the Capitol. He tried again. Same thing. Call went to voice mail. He knew Thomas wouldn't have left his phone sitting somewhere else or ignored that many calls during a crisis. That led him to one conclusion.

Rumson had already gotten to Thomas.

Chapter 28

THOMAS PARKED HIS Maserati on the street in front of the Newseum residences and steeled himself. He ignored the multiple calls from Randy. He couldn't take the risk that Charles would know. As he exited his car, he summoned an image of Zach to mind. Not the terrified face on his phone but the shining man in the National Gallery. Zachary standing next to a portrait that was more than five hundred years old.

That day he saw Zach's lack of awareness of his own beauty. He read shy certainty at first that Randy and Thomas were teasing, and quiet pride when he met Thomas's eyes. He believed, for a moment, that maybe he was special to Thomas. That was surely when Thomas fell in love with him. He knew it much too late, but that was the only weapon he had. Thomas was certain that he was in love with Zachary Hall and was prepared to kill or die to save him.

He stepped into the lobby and asked the concierge for the apartment number Charles had given. She picked up her house phone, dialed, and then announced, "Mr. Ryder, a Mr. Scarborough is here." She nodded at Thomas as she hung up, and directed him to the elevators.

As he rode up, adrenaline surged through his body. He hadn't been in a fistfight since he was a boy, but his muscles coiled, and he clenched his fists and jaw. On the top floor of the building, he stalked down the hall to the designated door, rang the bell, and crouched slightly. He prepared to throw himself on Charles as soon as the door opened.

Footsteps approached.

He pulled his right elbow back, ready to swing.

But when Charles opened the door, Thomas's eyes were drawn immediately to his left hand. Charles held a remote control of some kind, high and visible. His body blocked the room behind him.

Charles took in his posture and smiled. "Do you know what a dead man's switch is, Jason?" he asked.

Thomas nodded and—suddenly unsure—stood straight and consciously relaxed his fists.

"Good," Charles said. "My machine is already activated and raring to go. The only thing that keeps it from fulfilling its function is my thumb pressed down on this little trigger. If I drop this remote, then I'm afraid Zachary will be the first to know." He stepped back and opened the door wider.

Over his shoulder, in the middle of a large living room, Thomas saw Zach strapped down. A large machine was parallel to the wall of windows and positioned to aim between his legs. An enormous dildo at the end of an arm hovered mere inches away from invading his body. Lights on the machine indicated Charles had powered it up; Thomas could hear the hum of a motor. Zach still had a ball gag in his mouth, and his eyes on Thomas's shimmered with fear and pleading.

Charles gestured at the machine. "It's a work of art, isn't it? I'm quite proud. I built it myself, you know. It's already turned on, as I said, so all that's keeping the creature from being introduced is this device." He waved the remote in the air and cackled. "If I drop it, then Zachary switches from being a living man to a dead man. I guess that's why it's called a dead man's switch."

"I understand," Thomas said over Charles's peals of laughter.

Charles calmed and then turned his full attention to Thomas once more. "Now. Let me look at you, Jason." Satisfaction dripped from his voice.

He stepped behind Thomas to close and lock the apartment door. Thomas met Zach's eyes as Charles moved behind him. Wordlessly he tried to tell Zach that everything would be all right. He had no idea how to keep that promise. He mouthed the words "Be strong."

Charles put a hand on his shoulder as he walked around Thomas to stand again between him and Zach's bound body. "Jason," he sighed. "My Beloved. I've waited for this for so long."

Thomas swallowed and licked his lips. He had to buy time to think of a plan. No one even knew where he was, so he was Zach's only hope. "I have so many questions, Charles," he began, but he heard the weakness and tremor in his own voice.

"Ask me, Jason. You put me through so many tests." Charles looked vacantly into space. "So many tests." Sadness tinged his voice when he continued. "I was alone for so long. Your tests were very difficult for me." He bowed his head momentarily. When he looked up again, he gave a beatific smile Thomas longed to wipe off his face. "You deserve to know how I conquered them to make my way back to you."

Thomas forced himself to speak more assuredly, as though he were in court. Although hatred churned in his belly, he said evenly, "I'm very proud of you, Charles. You've worked hard to convince me that you really love me. Tell me first—how did you pull off the suicide?"

Charles grinned at him. "That *was* clever, wasn't it? I realized what you wanted, after my parents threw me out. You must have obtained the restraining order as a way to force me to stand independently from them. That was the only thing I could think of, about why you would humiliate me that way. And you were so right, Jason. I realized I didn't need them, though I could still use them."

"Wait. Your parents kicked you out?" Thomas asked. "When was this?"

"When the police arrested me for that misunderstanding on the street. You remember how the tabloids picked up the story? Oh, there was much gnashing of tooth and claw at the Rumson manor that night, I can tell you. Mother slapped me in front of the servants, and Father was apoplectic at the scandal. He *raged* at me for hours. Oh, what this would do to his business dealings. How it would look at the country club. How sharper than a serpent's tooth it was to have a faggot child.

"Of course he didn't say it that way. Father isn't very literary." A strange light grew in Charles's eyes. "But Mother... oh, she was almost poetic when she came to my room later. She was quite clear that I had to make the situation go away quietly. Then I needed to find a different place to live." Charles narrowed his eyes at the memory.

Thomas swallowed hard and said, "I'm sorry that happened to you, Charles. I never meant for you to lose your home like that."

"You hurt me, Jason," Charles said quietly. "I couldn't understand why you had done that. Why you pretended in public that you didn't want me when you had to know we were perfect together. When Nan told me to leave.... It was a very long night." A glisten appeared at the corner of his eye, and Thomas tried to gauge whether to reach out. Before he could make a move, though, Charles snapped back to awareness again. "I was shocked at first, of course, but I understood quickly what I had to do. What you needed me to do."

Thomas licked his lips. He dreaded the answer to the questions he had to ask, but he needed to keep him talking for Zach.

"What did you realize, Charles?" he asked.

"I had to leave behind the Rumson home and name and stand on my own feet if I was ever to be worthy of you. I saw that right away, so I left the estate and moved to the Olympic Hotel until I had a plan. It took a few days to get things lined up and to find the right sort of substitute to put in the car. All in all, I was quite pleased with the way it came off."

"Substitute?" Thomas asked. Light dawned, and with it, horror. "Of course. You put someone else in the Porsche before you drove it off the cliff."

Charles nodded, and satisfaction showed in his face. "I did. It was easy. All I had to do was search the escort ads until I found someone who looked enough like me to pass scrutiny. Then I stashed him near the park, and I was very, very visible all over town until I needed him. He filled the part of Charles Rumson, and I became Sam Ryder."

Charles frowned. "I wonder if that was his real name or just what he called himself as an escort. You know, Ryder? Like rider? A bit on the nose, if it was a fake name." Charles's manic grin again stretched his mouth. "But an interesting example of the power of a name if he was actually born Sam Ryder. Don't you think so, Jason? Like Rumson. I think that's what they would say in England. I was a rum son. I was made very aware of that."

What was Charles trying to tell him? "Did your parents...?" Thomas paused as he recalled the thin white scars on Charles's back and buttocks. "Did they hurt you?"

A stern look appeared in Charles's eyes. "She could never hurt me. She just wanted me to be strong."

"Who wanted that, Charles? Your mother?"

He nodded. "Father would get so angry with me, and so Nan came to my room sometimes. After he beat me. She would make

me lie there while she rubbed lotion on my skin. She would…
use things on me. *In* me. She said it was important because it
would make me a better man."

His face was flushed, and his hand drooped. "She had a bam-
boo rod, and she used it to help me learn how to get past the
pain. You see? For every stroke I took, she would give me a kiss."

Thomas swallowed and flicked his eyes to the hand holding
the dead man's switch. "When did this start, Charles?"

"What? Oh, I suppose I was eight or nine."

Jesus. Her own son....

Thomas knew Nan Rumson. He had seen her brittle smile,
carefully arranged platinum hair, and glittering eyes at many
events. She had a reputation for ruthlessness in her various
charitable committees, true. But this was beyond anything he'd
imagined.

"Did you tell anyone?"

"Tell? That my mother loved me? Oh no. That was our special secret." Charles gave a sad smile. "I remember once she found
me with the son of our head gardener. I was probably twelve years
old, and I think he was about six. We were in the shed down near
the pool house, and I wanted to share with him some of the
things I'd learned so he could grow up strong. One of the yard
boys saw me lead him into the shed, and he summoned Mother. I
hadn't done very much when she came in—just a little probing.
She was very upset that I'd tried to share my lessons with others.
That was just for us, she said."

He shivered. "Once she dealt with the gardener and the one
who had reported me, she said it was my turn to be punished.
That was our last special visit because I'd made a mistake and she
couldn't trust me any longer. She made the last lesson quite
thorough. I couldn't sit down for days afterward because she
loved me that much."

"Charles, that wasn't love."

He smiled hugely. "Of course it was. Mother wanted me to be happy and to feel good and be strong. You tried to do that for me that night you chose me and brought me to your apartment in Seattle. I wasn't ready then, but that's what you'll do for me, Jason. You'll help me keep getting stronger."

Thomas nodded cautiously. "I admit I didn't understand what you were up to." He swallowed the bile that surged into his throat, and he continued. "You were so clever, Charles. I didn't realize how clever until now. The public appearances—were those just about drawing attention to you?"

"That was part of it. I needed evidence that I was acting irrationally, although of course I was in complete charge. I knew exactly what I was doing." A malicious smile touched his lips. "A delightful bonus was making a scandal that would live on to torture Father. I admit I was annoyed that it didn't last longer. Maybe a week. Then some Kardashian or another got pregnant, and my death was no longer as interesting."

"Were you counting on the car exploding when it went over the cliff? I mean, how did you think no one would identify the, uh… your substitute?"

"Okay. That was a slight miscalculation," Charles said dismissively as he waved his hand with the switch. Thomas tracked that hand carefully. "Maybe I watched too many movies, but I thought cars always exploded. I assumed that, with my very public displays, there would be no reason to study the remains. When the car failed to catch fire, however, I made a quick call to dear Mother. She had already seen the footage of my declarations around town. I warned her that if she really cared that much about the Rumson name, it would be wise to get herself quickly to the morgue. She should get 'my' body before anyone could look too closely."

Charles giggled, and admiration appeared on his face. "Nan Milliken Rumson is a resourceful woman. She must have handled it all with aplomb, because 'I' was cremated within the day." Charles smirked when he added, "That was what I'd actually intended, anyway, just with the Porsche as my coffin."

"So Nan helped you?" Thomas asked.

"Well, not happily, of course. She didn't want to let me go, but by then I knew it was time to move beyond her. We've never spoken since I made that call on the day of the suicide. There must have been other things she did to help disguise my tracks, though."

"So where did you go for two years? Why did you come out of hiding now?" Thomas asked. Inside he tried desperately to figure out how to grab the remote from Charles's hand. He had to do it without the machine going off and killing or maiming Zach. Squeeze his hand closed? It was a tremendous risk, but did he have an alternative?

He found no opening, and he flicked his eyes past Charles's shoulder to try to see Zach. The wall of windows gaped behind Charles's back, and Thomas could see the National Gallery as his mind worked. If he could hold Charles's hand closed, maybe he could propel them both across the room and out the window. *No, that won't work. The switch would trigger with our fall.*

"Two years. Ah, well, that's almost funny," Charles said with a grin. "You should understand. One of the advantages of having a family in real estate development is there are many, many less-than-reputable contacts one is able to make. So I had little trouble getting a new identity established once I had the driver's license from Mr. Ryder's wallet. I set up a room at a different hotel under my new name before the suicide, of course. I stopped there just long enough to dye my hair and disguise myself until I got out of Seattle.

"I flew to England. Then I went on to France for a time. I needed to learn, Jason. To be *better* for you. A better lover, I mean." He reached out with the hand that didn't hold the dead man's switch to stroke up and down Thomas's arm. "I thought you'd come find me, Jason. I knew you'd be able to feel that I hadn't really died." His voice grew sad again. "I was so lonely. Waiting."

He shook his head, almost angrily. "I was weak. Again. I waited for you to rescue me, but then I finally realized it was part of the test. I had to use my time to become a better man for you. You were so patient with me, but you deserve much more. More than these *creatures*"—he indicated Zachary with a toss of his head—"could ever give you.

"So I found places where they taught me things." Charles shivered, and his eyes were half-lidded. "Many things. Dark things." His voice trailed off at the memories—whether they were good or bad, Thomas couldn't tell, but Charles's hand sagged again. Thomas suddenly panicked, afraid Charles would drop the remote in his reverie.

"You did that for two years?" Thomas prompted loudly, and Charles snapped back to attention.

"What? Oh. No. I was in Europe for a few months. The thing was when I came back, you'd managed to set another test before me." Charles gave a self-deprecating grin. "I couldn't find you.

"Changing your first name, getting a completely different job, and moving to Washington—remarkably effective. I obviously couldn't call your family and ask where to find you. And when I tried searching public records for Jason Scarborough at a law firm, I struck out. I suppose I could have hired someone, but I was determined to solve the puzzle on my own. While I searched for you, though, I kept up my self-education. I learned about electronics, lock picking, all *sorts* of useful skills. I joined a theater company in Bellingham for a while. That's where I learned about makeup and costuming.

"And then, wonder of wonders, do you know what happened?" Thomas shook his head. "I was in an airport a few months ago, getting ready to fly to China, when CSPAN came on. They were doing a piece on your Senate committee, and there you were, sitting behind the chairwoman." Charles closed his eyes for a moment, and ecstasy lit his features. "My heart simply stopped."

Thomas tensed and prepared to move. But before he could make up his mind to act, Charles opened his eyes and fixed them on him once again.

"Well. Once I had that connection to you, of course, the rest was easy. I moved to DC, I rented this apartment, and I began to follow you as I learned your new habits. That's what led me to Mata Hari."

Thomas shivered at the thought of Charles following him through the Washington streets, always watching him. He softly asked the question he dreaded above almost all others. "Was Brian Gallagher the first man you killed?"

"Well, other than that escort back in Seattle, yes. It took time to connect the clues, you see, and for me to understand what you wanted."

His jaw dropped open. "What *I* wanted?"

"Of course. I saw the pattern right away, but not the required response. You'd pick up a boy and take him out of the bar one night. Then, the next time he'd appear, you'd give him a brush-off. Once I got the cameras installed in your home, I'd study the recordings over and over. I'd listen to you make them moan and beg for more. The ones who left you alone after that? Well, I understood you had just used them, and everything was fine. I could hardly begrudge you simply fucking these boys after the things I had let men do to me in—well, never mind.

"But then I'd notice that they didn't all follow your clear and fair rules. Some of them would come back for more, push at you, try to get you to be unfaithful to me. They wanted what was mine. I finally understood that you dangled them in front of me, like a mouse in front of a cat. You waited to see what I'd do to keep you. I prepared and I watched until you told me to act."

Charles's voice grew louder, the anger clear on his face. "That one creature, Gallagher. He was unforgivably rude to you in the bar. What if he'd hit you with the glass he threw?"

Charles trembled in rage, and the fire in his eyes alarmed Thomas more with each second. "But I waited to take my cue from you. I saw how calmly you handled it, and I knew. It all came together for me in that moment. You were calm because you trusted me to chastise him for you. When he left the bar, I followed him home, and I took care of the situation. I showed him his error." Thomas's heart raced. The delusion Charles was reliving threatened to overcome him. Any second he would turn that anger on Zach, so Thomas did the only thing he could think of.

He dropped to his knees, and he made himself say, "I'm so proud of you, Charles, for finally understanding me."

Chapter 29

RANDY PULLED HIS truck to a rough stop at the Newseum, and as he jumped out, he spotted Thomas's blue Maserati.

Shit.

Well, that just confirmed what he had guessed.

Maria Torres hurried over to him with two men in police uniform, and she pointed at Thomas's car. "Randy, is that…?"

"Yeah. Rumson must have told Thomas to come here. He's not picking up his cell, so my guess is Rumson instructed him not to alert anyone. What's your plan?"

Torres looked at the lobby entrance with her eyes narrowed in calculation. "I don't think I have any choice but to break in. I have every reason to believe that a crime is in progress right now up there. It may already be over. I have to get in to either stop Rumson or to secure the scene and try to limit the damage."

Randy ran his gaze up the front of the building as Torres pointed to an apartment on the top-floor corner. Light spilled out over a balcony that was fronted by a metal mesh. Randy took a look at the wrinkled page he had printed from his computer and clutched in his hand all the way over. It was a floor plan of the Newseum Residences from the rental agency's website. "Yeah. It looks like it should be that one," he confirmed, tapping the diagram.

Randy again scanned the facade of the building and focused on the balconies. He estimated the distance between them. It might be doable to make the jump, he thought, but risky. It was almost impossible without drawing the attention of someone inside. That is, even if he didn't miss and plummet to the pavement below. His palms began to sweat at the thought of making the jump. Then a more practical problem presented itself. How would they get into the neighboring apartment without a warrant?

His eyes travelled up to the roof of the building. Was that a terrace up there? He looked again at the diagram and said, "I have an idea."

.   .   .

CHARLES GAZED DOWN at Thomas as the fire in his eyes slowly softened to something like worship. From his vantage point, Thomas could see Zach's face turned toward him and the tears in his eyes. His stomach roiled at the betrayal Zach must feel at his words of praise.

He couldn't think about that. It was *for* Zach.

"Charles," he croaked and tried to show some of that puppy-dog expression that always worked on men. "I've waited so long for you to come to me this way. Thank you for not letting my little games drive you away."

Charles breathed heavily, and his face and neck were flushed. "Do you mean it, Jason? I did the right thing? I had so many doubts over the years. I'm sorry."

"Shh, Charles. Shh. Don't apologize. I had to make it hard, you see, so you could really prove that you love me." Thomas spread his arms and tried to control the trembling there. He prayed Charles would get close enough that he could grab his hand and seize the dead man's switch.

"And you did, Charles. You did it. You've shown me that no one else could ever love me as much as you. I love you for it, and

I can't wait to show you how much you fill my heart." He wanted to vomit at giving those words of love to Charles. They belonged to Zach.

Charles quivered, and his jaw was slack. His pupils were wide and black. "It's like Christmas morning, Jason."

"I know, Charles. For me too. I've been waiting for more than two years, and now you're finally here. You're so close. I can't wait to have you in bed again so you can show me all the things you've learned."

Charles's pants had tented at Thomas's words, but it wasn't enough. He moved no closer. So Thomas tried a different approach. He lowered the timbre of his voice and said, "Tell me about the machine. What is that for?"

Charles turned his head to look at it and then turned back at Thomas, and his smile stretched his mouth like a rictus. He moaned slightly and brushed his free hand over the front of his own pants.

"I was inspired by one of the places where I trained. Heinrich, the Dom there? He had something like this, but not as elegant or as powerful. He called it a *fickmaschine*. A fucking machine.

"His was just an ugly box, though." Charles wrinkled his nose in distaste. "He liked to make me stand over it, and then it would work me open. It thrust in and out, no matter how much I begged him to stop. He had different toys he would put on it, depending on what he had planned for me." Charles shivered. "One was the size of a fist. I hated it so much." He paused, and then he whispered, "I loved it."

A moment's recollection claimed Charles, but then he shook himself. "I knew I could do better, build a superior machine," he continued in a stronger voice. "I increased the horsepower, I added various speeds, and I made a work of art."

"It's beautiful," Thomas agreed and licked his lips. Charles focused on his mouth and unconsciously licked his own lips as well, so Thomas took his chance.

"There's no need to go further with Hall now. I've made you take too many risks already. I don't want you to go too far and get caught—not now when we're finally going to be together."

It was too much. He knew it immediately because suspicion flared in Charles's mad eyes.

"You want me to let him go after what he did to you?"

Thomas frowned. "After what he did to me? Charles, I don't understand."

"He *fucked* you. This creature took control like Heinrich and the others took control of me. He used you. He *humiliated* you, Jason."

Oh God. Of course Charles was listening that second time with Zach. He heard everything.

"I know he confused you," Charles continued. "I've had it happen too, when your body gets used so badly, so wonderfully. And you think you've broken through to some new emotion, to some new *dimension* inside of yourself. But it's a lie. For them it's just bodies and fucking and hurting you. They never love you, no matter what they say. It's all just to make you into something weak they can control. Like Heinrich. Like Nan.

"That's what this creature did to you, Jason. I knew it when I heard you say you'd like to let him into your life." Suddenly Charles's expression crumbled. In a softer, almost sad voice, he asked, "Why him, Jason? Why would you want him? I tried so hard, for so long, but you never made it easier for me."

For a moment Thomas could see in Charles's eyes the young man he'd grown up with in Seattle. The vision paralyzed him with how to use that. He began tentatively, "I'm sorry..." But Charles lowered his head angrily and cut Thomas off.

"It doesn't matter. It has to happen to this monster, Jason.

The only way I can show you how wrong you were, how *confused* you were to think you love him, is to show you what a little slut he is," Charles raged. His face turned red and spit sprayed out of his mouth.

The madness was back, and Thomas's heart raced again. He had badly miscalculated. Charles was going to lose it. His vision narrowed to Charles's hand and Zach behind him, helpless on the bench. Could he lunge in time to seize the hand holding the device?

Charles's fists were clenched, and he loomed toward Thomas, down on his knees, but the remote was still out of reach. "You'll see. When my machine is fucking him, you'll see how much he loves it. He'll be crying in his excitement, and you'll see that's all you are to him too. Something to fuck away his boring little life."

"No, Charles. You made a mistake," Thomas cried out hoarsely. "Of course I don't love him. I love you. Only you. That's what these tests were all about. You know that."

Charles shook his head furiously. "This is important, Jason. We have to see this through so we make sure this creature is out of your life and your mind for good."

Thomas held out his hands toward Charles and projected calm despite his own panicked breathing and pounding heart. He pleaded with his eyes.

Past Charles, through the wall of windows, Randy appeared. His friend dropped from somewhere above to land in a crouch on the balcony outside Charles's apartment.

He tried so hard to keep Charles's focus he almost couldn't register what he saw. Hope warred with the fear in his gut. Thomas knew he had to keep Charles's eyes on him. He cried out, "Charles, my sweet man, my love, what have I done to deserve someone like you? You understand me so well. Maybe better than I understand myself."

Randy stood up carefully and scanned the room as he appeared to assess the situation. He would see Zach on the bench, Charles with his back to the window, and Thomas on his knees.

"Charles, I need you to kiss me. I've waited so long." He forced desire into his voice and crooked his arms to beckon Charles to come to him. Charles hesitated, and his eyes glazed as he stared down at Thomas. Fantasies unspooled across his face. He started to lean down to meet Thomas's mouth in a kiss.

Thomas saw Randy raise a very large handgun. Randy had no way of knowing that if he shot Charles, the dead man's switch would trip and Zach would be killed.

"No," he bellowed as he lunged to his feet and the world slowed down.

Wrestling Charles back and to the ground, he reached with both hands to enclose the fist holding the switch. He struggled to keep his fingers pressed around it so it wouldn't go off. He heard the roar of a pistol blast, the shatter of glass, and a pang of metal hitting metal. The dead man's switch fell out of Charles's hand and hit the ground, and the gears on the machine began to whine.

"Oh no. Zach, please," Thomas cried as he held Charles down and steeled himself to look at where the poor man lay bound. He expected to see blood and terrible things, and he prayed with all of his heart.

It took him a moment to understand what he was seeing. The machine thrust forward and back, and Zach was still bound, but—there was no blood. No muffled screams. The huge dildo lay on the floor, pulverized where Randy had shot it off the end of the steel piston. Without the rubber phallus in place, the steel arm got no closer than a few inches from Zach's vulnerable body.

Randy crashed through the window, his gun trained on Charles while Thomas clambered to his feet. He ran to the machine and kicked it over and away so it ground on its side and scarred the hardwood floor. The front door burst in at that moment, and Maria Torres swept the room with her pistol held in both hands. Two police officers flanked her in the hall.

"We got him, Torres," Randy called out. "Hall is alive too. I think we're good."

Thomas clawed the ball gag out of Zach's mouth first. He tried to ignore the tears he saw as he focused next on the strap across Zach's chest. His fingers trembled so badly he could barely work the catch. By the time he had unbuckled the leg restraints, Randy was by his side with a blanket to cover Zach's nude body.

Thomas couldn't help himself any longer. He pulled Zach into his arms and held him tightly as Zach shook and sobbed. He buried his head against Thomas's chest and trembled violently in his arms.

Thomas pressed his cheek against the top of Zach's head and rubbed it against Zach's soft blond hair. "You're safe now. We've got you. You're safe," he murmured over and over.

Charles wailed behind him from the floor. "Jason, no. You love me. You love *me*." He heard the scuffle as Charles tried to rise, only to be forced back to the ground by the two burly police officers.

Randy put a hand on his shoulder and said, "Thomas, let Zachary up now. Are either of you hurt?"

Thomas let go and leaned back as Randy scanned Zach's body for injuries. His wrists and ankles were chafed from trying to break free of the restraints. The buckle on the chest strap had rubbed a raw, bloody patch on his chest. The ball gag had left red marks on both sides of his face, and his lips were chapped from the rubber ball itself. A nasty bump on the side of his head had bled and scabbed over, but that appeared to be the worst of it.

Zachary said in a hoarse voice, "I don't think I'm really hurt.

Randy, the machine—you shot it."

Randy crossed over to where the evil device whirred on the floor and crouched to his knees. He found the manual off switch, and it powered down. When he walked to the remains of the dildo, he said in a low voice, "Oh, that sick son of a bitch." Torres joined him and her eyes went wide at the sight of the head of the sex toy.

"Nails. The fucker used nails," she said on a shuddering breath. "That's what ripped Daniel Owen to pieces." Zachary gasped behind her, and she whirled. "I'm sorry, Mr. Hall. I shouldn't have said that. The important thing is you're safe. Rumson can't hurt you anymore."

Zach turned his head to Thomas, who still had one hand on his shoulder, and said in awe, "You saved my life."

Thomas shook his head in denial. "Randy and Detective Torres saved you."

"*You* saved me, Thomas. You came here knowing what that monster had done. You tried to get him to let me go. You kept him talking. You saved me."

Randy came back over and holstered his .357 Magnum as he joined them. "You did good, Thomas. You bought us time."

Thomas suddenly sagged. The enormity of that last twenty minutes washed over him and the adrenaline began to fade. He hung his head as he dropped to his knees in front of Zach and said, "Don't act like I did something brave. I'm the reason you were in danger, Zach."

Zach just stared at him, his eyes wide and confused. Torres said, "That's a peculiar way to look at it, Mr. Scarborough. From where I'm standing, the only person to blame is Charles Rumson."

At his name Charles began to cry. "Jason, make them understand. You know why I did these things. For you. Because I love you, Jason. I love you."

Thomas suddenly forced himself back onto his feet and crossed the room to where Charles had struggled to his knees. He looked down at Charles, who was cuffed and flanked by the two officers, and the blood boiled in his veins. The fatigue of moments before was wiped away by a rising tide of red heat. Three men dead. Zach tortured and nearly ripped to pieces. The years of torment and guilt Charles had brought into his life burned through his brain.

Fury surged through his body like lightning and sent his leg swinging in a roundhouse kick to the side of Charles's head. He bellowed, "My name is Thomas."

Charles sprawled on the floor, and Torres said to her police officers, "That happened when he was subdued." Both men nodded.

Chapter 30

THE NEXT FEW hours were a blur of activity. While one of her officers blocked off the hallway and door with crime-scene tape, Torres called in her department. Randy updated Lily on the situation, and she sent a team from the Secret Service and the FBI as well. A brief turf war erupted over whether Rumson was a federal prisoner or belonged in the District of Columbia system. The agents and detective present agreed to shelve that for the night and just get Rumson behind bars. He was escorted away by a uniformed officer and an FBI agent for holding.

One of the other federal agents found clothes strewn in the corner, and Zachary claimed them. The agent photographed the pile and turned over the clothes. A doctor was rounded up to evaluate Zachary in private in the master bedroom. He diagnosed a mild concussion. Other than the surface abrasions and the bruise on his head from the lamp, Zachary had escaped worse harm—at least physically.

Zachary returned to the living room fully clothed. His face was haunted, and Thomas knew Zachary would need time to recover from much more than his bruises and scrapes. The terror he had suffered, the betrayal by someone he thought cared for him but who was manipulating his good nature and innocence.... Those wounds would run deep. Thomas sat by Zachary's side on the sofa as he was interviewed by both the FBI and the local police. He was afraid to touch him, but he needed to give his support. Zachary recounted as well as he could the things Rumson had told him. Then Thomas filled in pieces where he was able.

When Thomas mentioned Nan Rumson's role in the faked suicide, Randy called Lily again. Thomas heard him tell her, "You're going to want someone to look at Rumson's mother. At least as an accessory after the fact for the murder of Sam Ryder. Maybe other things. Fraud on First Washington Bank, probably."

Torres brought some evidence bags into the room. "Look at this shit," she said to Randy. Thomas joined them to look at a blond wig, glasses, a prosthetic nose, and an elaborate makeup kit. "See these thin rolls of cotton?" she asked. "You can use these inside your mouth and along your gums to alter the shape of your face some. With this nose on and covered with a layer of concealer, and those pieces of cotton, it's no wonder you couldn't be sure it was Rumson in those photos that Mr. Hall found."

About three in the morning, Torres and the federal team finally told Zachary and Thomas they could go. "Do you want a police car to take you home, Mr. Hall?" Torres asked.

Zachary said in an exhausted voice, "The doctor said I shouldn't be alone. The concussion…."

Randy looked quickly between Thomas and Zachary and said, "I'd bring you to my place, but I think there's more to do here. Let's call Joe. You can stay the night there, I'm sure." Thomas made the call and nodded at Randy when Joe indeed insisted they bring Zachary to his apartment. To Zachary Randy said, "I have my truck downstairs. I'll drive you to Joe and then come back here."

Thomas hesitated and said, "Zachary, could we talk for a minute before you go?" Zachary nodded, and Torres indicated they could use the kitchen for some privacy.

Thomas and Zachary faced each other in silence. Thomas

flexed his fingers and grimaced as he tried to find words. But before he could, Zachary burst out, "This is why you wouldn't admit what we had, isn't it? Because of Rumson?"

Thomas nodded and cleared his throat. His voice was husky as he said, "I'm sorry I didn't explain everything. If I had, maybe you wouldn't have been lured in by Charles, or—I don't know. Maybe you would have been able to get away sooner."

Zachary tilted his head. "Get away? From Sam, I mean Charles?"

"No. From me. I'm a disaster. This is my fault, like you said."

Zachary reached out and touched Thomas's shoulder. "It's the fault of that sick fucker, not you. I'm sorry about the STD comment I made. I was shocked, and I didn't take time to think what this must mean to you."

"How could you when you didn't know half the story until tonight? Neither did I, really." Thomas sighed as he looked at the kitchen floor and trailed his shoe back and forth over the tile. "Even when I thought Charles was dead, he controlled my life. Every time I met someone, I was afraid he'd turn into another stalker. I had always slept around, but after Charles, my fear hardened into a rule so I could keep anyone from getting close. I thought that would somehow protect me, but it was magical thinking, I guess."

He looked up to find Zachary watching him intently, and he continued, "Charles won in so many ways. He ruined my life in Seattle. Then he poisoned everything that's happened since. I couldn't see the gift I'd been given when you came into my life."

Zachary exhaled hard. "Thomas, I felt something for you from the night we met. But you pushed me away again and again. I don't know what I'm doing right now, and I certainly don't know how to feel about... well, you." He paused and said, "No, that's a lie. I know how I feel about you and what I want. I just don't think I can make a rational choice right now."

Thomas nodded and returned his gaze to the kitchen tile. "I understand, believe me. I know I've hurt you, and this shit is going to take time to process." He looked up and reached out tentatively to touch Zach's face. Zachary leaned slightly into his hand. Thomas swallowed hard. "If you come out the other side of this and you find that you still want me, Zach, I promise I'll be there. I won't say the words you may think you want from me now because it wouldn't be fair to you. But this is as real for me as it was for you."

Zach nodded, and then Randy stuck his head around the corner. Zach and Randy left together without another word.

A few minutes later, Thomas thanked Detective Torres again and drove himself home to an empty condo. All he could do was hope Zach was all right and that he would reach out if he needed—or wanted—anything Thomas could give.

● ● ●

ON THE STREET Randy unlocked his truck to let Zachary in the passenger door. He muttered as he yanked a parking ticket off his windshield and then climbed in.

"I'd like to pay that," Zachary said. "You helped save my life, Randy." Suddenly his careful control slipped, and he found himself crying and sobbing into his hands. Randy awkwardly put an arm around his shoulder.

"Hey, kid, hey. You're okay now. It's over, and you're safe," he murmured until Zachary calmed down. When Zachary leaned away, Randy withdrew his arm.

"Geez. I'm such a baby," Zachary said as he ran the heels of his hands over his eyes to wipe the tears.

"No. You're a survivor," Randy growled. "Not only that, but you kept it together and gave the police what they needed.

Rumson won't be able to hurt anyone again. That's on you, Zachary. You beat him, man. You won."

Zachary flushed with gratitude and squared his shoulders a bit. "Thanks, Randy. For everything."

Randy turned back toward the steering wheel and started the engine. "You're welcome, but it wasn't just me."

Zachary looked out the window as Randy navigated through the dark streets to make his way toward Joe's place. Finally he said quietly, "Thomas came there to help me." Zachary looked quickly at Randy for confirmation.

Randy nodded. "He did. You brought something out in Thomas that I didn't even know was there, and we've been good friends for a few years now. When Rumson came after him in Seattle, by his own account, he was practically paralyzed. He couldn't do shit to stop it from happening. But when he knew Rumson had you, fuck if he didn't grow balls of steel." He flicked a glance at Zachary. "You mean more to him than anyone."

Zachary nodded, but his lips were sealed tightly together. He finally said, "It's crazy. I knew he was out of my league when I met him. For weeks, I kept up this insane idea that maybe he saw something in me. I finally gave up, though, because he seemed so..." He looked at Randy. "Impenetrable."

Randy barked a short laugh. "That's a good word for him, I agree. Or it used to be. I don't know when it happened, but he fell for you." He glanced again at Zachary and asked, "Is it too late for the two of you?"

Zachary looked out the window. "I don't know what to think about him. About anything, really."

"For what it's worth, kid, I'd say just give yourself some time. Don't jump to call Thomas or talk it through or any of that usual bullshit. I know Thomas. He's not going anywhere while you process this crap that happened to you."

"Okay. I'll think about that."

Randy continued softly, "Hey, kid, you also need to get ready for the public onslaught that's going to come your way."

Zachary whipped his head around in alarm. "What do you mean?" he asked.

"Rich, gay, psycho murderer took you prisoner and nearly killed you too. It's going to hit the news," Randy observed.

"Shit," Zachary said with a sigh. "I'm going to have to warn my parents."

"Is that a problem?"

"I've never even told them I'm gay. Now I have to tell them I was nearly fucked to death with a nail-studded dildo gun." Zachary shocked himself by laughing and covered his mouth with his hand. After a moment to compose himself, he dropped his arm wearily and sagged against the seat. "It's like every one of their terrible ideas about gay people come true."

Randy took a hand off the wheel to punch Zachary lightly in the arm. "You might want to think about a different headline for that story. Something like 'Mom, Dad, I'm alive.'"

"Yeah, maybe. You're right, Randy. I'll call as soon as I get to Joe's, in case it's on the morning news shows."

As though Randy's words were a prophecy, Zachary's phone suddenly rang with a number he didn't recognize. Randy must have seen the puzzled look on his face. He said, "Better let it roll to voice mail if you don't know the number."

Zachary took that advice, but immediately a strange text popped up asking him to call. Then the phone rang again with a different number. Zachary looked at Randy and said, "I think it's starting."

By the time Randy reached Joe's apartment building, his cell phone indicated thirty-five calls and dozens of text messages and e-mails from people whose numbers or names he didn't know.

"I have some experience in media frenzies from the Secret Service days. If you need help handling this, give me a call." Randy asked. "If nothing else I can put you in touch with people able to guide you through it."

Zachary leaned across the seats to hug Randy. "Thank you again. For all of it." When he sat back, he had lifted the parking ticket from Randy's shirt pocket. He waved it in his fingers as he jumped out of the truck. "I've got this."

Randy chuckled and rolled down the window. "Okay, kid. Take care of yourself, but don't be a stranger."

* * *

JOE USHERED ZACHARY into his apartment and fussed until he got Zachary settled in an overstuffed armchair.

"Dear heart, I'm aghast this has happened to you. You must be exhausted so I won't ask you about it tonight."

"Thanks, Joe. I'll tell you everything tomorrow. I'd really like to get some sleep, if you don't mind."

"Of course, you dear man. I was just finishing the sheets on the guest bed. Give me a moment." Joe rushed off, and Zachary started to doze. A knock came at the door, and Joe hurried back to open it.

Zachary heard Terry's voice. "I didn't want to let myself in, but is he all right?"

Joe answered, "He seems to be. Come along, Terry. Of course you should let yourself in."

Terry came into the living room and crouched next to Zachary's chair. "Are you doing okay, Zachary?"

"Hi, Terry. Yes. I think I'm going to be fine."

Terry looked sheepishly at Joe. "Randy called me. He thought I'd want to know. I'm sorry for just… barging in like this."

Joe seemed nervous and twisted his hands. Zachary suddenly

had a feeling he knew why Randy had called Terry. He stood up.

"I can't thank you both enough for taking care of me this way. You were the first friends I made in DC, so it means a lot you'd let me stay the night here."

Joe reached to take Zachary's hand in both of his. "You'll stay as long as you need, dear heart. This evening has been terrible for you. Would you like a drink, perhaps, to calm your nerves?"

"The doctor said I shouldn't have alcohol, but some water would be good. I'm supposed to stay hydrated. Oh, and maybe some dry toast?" Joe scurried toward the kitchen, and Terry led him to the guest room. Zachary's head was still aching, so he asked Terry, "Do you have any aspirin?" Then Zachary shivered as he recalled asking Sam—no, Charles—for the same thing. He began to tremble harder, but Terry got him in bed and pulled the comforter up. He sat on the edge and stroked Zachary's head gently until the tremors stopped. When Terry went to the bathroom to retrieve some Tylenol, Joe brought in a glass of water and a plate with a piece of toast.

Soon Zachary was settled, the light was off, and the door was cracked. He could hear Joe and Terry talking quietly in the living room.

Finally alone, he should have been able to rest, but the events began to catch up to him again. All Zachary could think of was how ordinary Sam Ryder seemed to him before the bottom fell out of his reality. He thought about Thomas and the despair in his eyes when he saw Zachary trussed up on the padded bench. He remembered Thomas going to his knees, begging for Zachary's life. He *knew* he was going to die, and then somehow Randy, Thomas, and that police detective saved him.

Zachary found he was shaking again and on the brink of tears. Maybe he should have asked Joe to keep him company, though he could still hear the quiet voices from the living room.

He chewed on the inside of his cheek. He really wanted to call Thomas right then and beg him to come over. Randy's advice warred in his mind with his need to understand what Thomas felt and what he was offering.

Finally he shook his head. Randy was right. In his state, he couldn't trust himself to make a good decision. He didn't want to fuck up what might be a real chance with Thomas.

He jumped when his cell phone buzzed with yet another message, so he focused on that. Right. He needed to call his parents. It wouldn't be fair for them to turn on the news in the morning and hear their son's name.

His stomach tightened again, and he felt nauseated. He had to make that call, but the blood rushed in his ears. What if they disowned him for being gay? He had kept his secret from them for so long. Every time he went to Rainbow Space he saw those teenagers who had been discarded by their families for being different. Every time he thought of the homeless kids in the soup kitchen in Ogden, he wondered. Would that have been him?

Then he thought of Joe and Terry taking him in. He thought of Randy storming into Charles's apartment, gun drawn to protect him. He thought of Thomas. Not the Thomas who begged Charles for Zachary's life on bended knees, but the man he met that first night in Mata Hari. That Thomas, on the basis of one evening's conversation, told Zachary he was stronger than he knew. Zachary's heart rate slowed as he pondered that idea.

Even if the discussion with his parents went badly, he was a survivor like Randy said. He had friends who fought for him. He'd survived a monstrous deception and physical attack. He'd made it through Charles Rumson, so he could certainly risk the disapproval of Jerry and Martha Hall.

Zachary wished he could do it in person, but it simply wasn't possible. He clenched his jaw, picked up his cell, and pressed their number as he glanced at the clock glowing on the nightstand. Even with the time change, they had probably been in bed for hours.

His mother picked up. She must have seen the caller ID because she said sharply, "Zachary? It's so late. Is everything all right?"

"Not really, Mom, but I'm okay. I'm sorry to call like this but this is really important. Is Dad there? Can he pick up too, or can you put it on speaker?"

He heard his mother say, away from the mouthpiece, "Jerry, pick up the line in the kitchen. Zachary needs to talk to us. He says it's important." He heard the bed creak as his father got to his feet.

A moment later the line clicked as his father picked up the extension. "What's up, sport?" his father asked sleepily.

Zachary took a deep breath and again followed Randy's advice. "The first thing you need to know is I'm alive. I came close to getting killed tonight, but I'm okay."

He heard his mother suck in her breath as his father exclaimed, "What's going on, Zachary? Were you in an accident?"

"Not like that." He swallowed hard, and his heart thumped painfully. "God, this is hard. Dad, Mom, I'm gay."

"Were you gay bashed?" his mother asked immediately, and her voice cracked in alarm.

His father barked at the same time, "How were you nearly killed?"

In broad terms Zachary haltingly explained what had happened. He had been going out with a man who turned out to be a killer. That man had planned to kill Zachary until he was rescued by the police and by two friends.

"There's going to be a lot of media attention, I think. This might get picked up on the national news," Zachary said as he concluded his story.

His mother cried. "You could have been killed, Zachary. Someone wanted to hurt my little boy." Through her tears, she declared, "I'm coming out there tomorrow."

"Or maybe you should come home to Utah right away," his father added. "Before the media finds you."

Zachary felt a burst of warmth, and the muscles he had been clenching suddenly relaxed. He fell back against the chair in Joe's guest room and covered his mouth with his hand. Their first instinct wasn't to blame him for being gay. It was to protect him.

"Thanks, Dad, Mom," he finally got out, though emotion nearly robbed his voice. "I think I can handle it. I was really scared at the time. Well, I'm still pretty freaked, but the doctor who checked me out"—his mother wailed again—"he said I'm physically fine. I have a few bruises and a headache from getting knocked out. I have a mild concussion, but I'm staying with a friend who can keep an eye on that."

"How will you deal with the reporters?" his father asked.

"And Jerry, what should we say if they call here?" his mother chimed in.

Zachary said, "I'm laying low for now, and I know someone with experience. I'm going to ask him or the police detective who helped me how to get a handle on this. I won't talk to anyone else until then."

His mother said, "I'm glad you have friends until I can get there, Zachary. You always did make friends so easily. You shouldn't be alone with this."

"I'm not alone." Zachary felt a sob of relief try to force its way out of his chest. He struggled to control his voice as he said, "I'm sorry I never told you I was gay before. You both have strong feelings about that, I know."

His father said, "We do, and I won't pretend I understand.

We can talk about that later, though. Our boy was nearly killed, but he was spared. That's enough to focus on for now."

His mother spoke up too. "Come home if you need to get away or hide from the press."

"I will," he said as one of his oldest fears began to fade. They still loved him. Maybe his parents would never fully understand him, but they wouldn't throw him away. He still had a home.

Chapter 31

Six weeks later....

THOMAS SLID INTO his once-usual seat at Mata Hari. Randy gave him a quick nod from the other end of the bar as though he'd never been away. Of course they talked or met often. But Thomas hadn't felt able to return to the place where Charles launched so much misery and pain. Six weeks after Charles was stopped, he was finally ready to get his life moving again.

He didn't spot Joe when he walked in, but suddenly the little man was at his side and reached out to hug him.

"Thomas, my darling. I've missed you," Joe exclaimed. "Are you holding up all right, dear heart?"

"I am, Joe. Thanks. I went back to work a few weeks ago. I think I'm going to be okay."

"Oh, I'm glad. To find that a monster was so close and hurt so many people.... Well, I admit my faith has been shaken. But the Lord protects. I truly believe that. He put you and Randall in a position to save Zachary."

"I wish I shared your faith, Joe. I kept wondering if I could have done anything different. Would those other men be alive if I'd, I don't know...."

"Exactly," Joe said. "You don't know because there is nothing you *could* have done. Evil comes into our lives for many reasons and in many different ways. It's madness to imagine we have control or that we can single-handedly stop it. All we can do is face it and fight, and you did that. I was so proud of you and Randall when I heard the story."

Randy joined them and slid a drink toward Thomas. "I'm with the recovering monk here. The Seattle police, the Secret Service, we were all fooled. But once we knew what to look for, we got it solved. If all of us, with all our resources, got tricked, I don't see why you blame yourself for falling for it too."

"Thanks, guys. I hear you. Hey, Joe, Randy told me that you and Terry patched things up. Is that right?" Thomas asked.

Joe nodded, and cautious optimism showed on his face. "Frankly it's also because of Charles Rumson. When Randall brought Zachary to my apartment, Terry rushed over to see him. The thought of how easily that sweet young man could have died brought us close in a way that we'd been struggling with for a while. We went back to couples' counseling, and we're working it through."

Randy rapped twice on the bar and said, "I'm glad something positive came from that prick. The place wasn't the same without you and Terry rounding up strangers and making them feel at home."

Malcolm passed behind Randy with a container of empties just then, and he said, "Hey, look. It's about that guy." He nodded toward the television mounted on the wall. It showed a news anchor's face and stylized text about Rumson the "gay stalker."

Randy grabbed the remote to turn up the volume. The anchor intoned, "…has agreed to a plea of guilty but mentally ill to three counts of murder and one count of attempted murder. In exchange, prosecutors will recommend that he be confined in a psychiatric treatment facility. As viewers will recall, Rumson's mother, Seattle socialite Nan Milliken Rumson, is presently facing criminal charges of her own for her role in helping

Rumson stage a suicide and stay hidden for two years. Rumson's defense team argued that her sexual abuse of Rumson meant that he was not to blame for his criminal acts because he couldn't recognize right from wrong. In agreeing to plead insanity, Rumson will avoid a lengthy and probably horrific trial regarding the details of his sexually motivated murders. Sentencing will take place next month."

The newscast moved on, and Randy turned the volume down again. "The vultures were probably looking forward to months of trial coverage with all the sordid details," Randy muttered. He looked at Thomas and narrowed his eyes. "You aren't surprised," he said.

"The prosecutor told me about it this afternoon," Thomas confirmed. "I was going to be a material witness, which I was *not* looking forward to. She called as a courtesy so I'd know I don't have to face that. I may still need to go to the sentencing, but even that's unlikely."

"I'm so relieved for you," Joe said. "Randall, please join us in a toast to Thomas's very good health."

An hour passed, and Thomas sat at the bar and talked to Randy. Joe visited with Miss Ethel as she played, and a half-empty drink sat next to Thomas's elbow. Randy was drying a glass when he looked up a bit and smiled broadly.

"What?" Thomas asked, and Randy tilted his head. Thomas turned and saw Zach standing by the front door. His hair was a bit shorter, and the weather had turned mild, so he was dressed in a light-blue polo shirt and dark jeans. He was stunningly handsome.

Thomas jumped off his stool but then made himself walk slowly to Zach. No, *Zachary*. He was afraid to reach out or do anything, so he stood for a moment. They stared at each other, and hope flickered in Thomas's chest at the warmth he saw in

Zachary's open, bright face. Finally he said, "I'm glad to see you. Can we get you a drink?"

Zachary told him, "It's over."

Thomas's eyes widened, and his heart cracked a little as the optimism of moments earlier drained away. Well, it was no more than he expected after six weeks of silence.

But Zachary clearly saw the emotions in his face. He hurried to say, "Charles or Sam, whoever he was—that's all over now. He's gone away for good. The prosecutor called to tell me about the plea and to see if I had any problems with that, since I'm one of the victims. I think she contacted the families of the others as well."

"What did you tell her?" Thomas asked as he fought the urge to pull Zachary into a hug. Thomas had only been notified as a courtesy. To have an actual say in Charles's fate would be a terrible burden.

"I told her I was at peace with it. He *is* insane. No doubt in my mind. There's a vengeful part of me that wanted him dragged through a public trial for what he did to me and to the others." Zachary paused, and his eyes were clear as he met Thomas's gaze. "And for what he did to you too. But I realized something." He gave a little chuckle, and Thomas crooked his head in question. "When you kicked him in the head, that was all the vengeance I really needed. So thank you for that. Now we can hope justice takes over."

"You're a better man than I am," Thomas said, and his fingers twitched. Zachary saw the movement and smiled a bit. Then he reached out and took Thomas's hand.

A flash of heat surged through Thomas from their clasped hands. He took a step closer to Zachary as he said, "I saw that interview you gave. That was smart, to take the media pressure off that way. And I was glad your parents were there. I remember you were afraid of coming out to them."

Zachary nodded toward the bar. "Randy showed me how to deal with the press inquiries and helped me select an interviewer. It was his idea to have my parents flown in so we could do the interview together."

He smiled at a memory, and Thomas was amazed at how solid he seemed. As though the trauma of six weeks earlier had done nothing to damage his spirit.

Zachary continued, "You should have seen my father's face when we all met at the television studio. Randy made a big impression on them. Jerry—that's my dad—was just in awe of Randy's confidence and, well, manliness. When he found out how Randy helped save my life, he actually hugged the guy. And *then* Randy outed himself as a gay man. Well, Jerry and Martha Hall suddenly had their world view rocked—hopefully for the better."

"I'm sorry I missed that," Thomas said with a small chuckle. "How is it going with your parents? I mean dealing with both the gay thing and the attack...," he prompted.

"I'm hopeful they'll get it one day, but I'll tell you more about that later." Zachary bit his lip nervously. "That isn't why I'm here. Can we maybe talk somewhere?"

Thomas led them to a side room that was empty. He was aware that Randy tracked them with his eyes as they walked out. Thomas tried to prepare himself for whatever would come out of Zachary's mouth. They sat in adjoining wingback chairs, and Zachary angled his body toward Thomas. He leaned forward as he seemed to gather his thoughts. Thomas felt his heart constrict with anxiety.

Finally Zachary spoke. "What I'm here to say, Thomas, is this—I know you stayed away to give me time, and I appreciate that. I started to call you so many times. I was afraid if I did, we'd both always wonder if it was just a reaction to what happened that night. Now, though. I've had therapy these past weeks, and a lot of time to think. The agency was great. They gave me all kinds of leave, no questions asked. I could really figure out how to move past Rumson and toward what I want."

"What *do* you want?" Thomas asked, almost afraid to breathe. *Please let it be the same thing as me.*

"I want what you promised me, Thomas, the night you saved my life. I've come out the other side. Now I want the words." More softly he said, "I want you."

Thomas felt his eyes burn as he said without hesitation, "I love you, Zach. I think I've been in love with you maybe even from the beginning. And I'm sorry about all this shit I put you through. Not just Rumson. Pushing you away, pretending I didn't want you when every fiber of my body was calling out for you." He reached for Zach's hand again and gripped it hard as he asked, "Can you see yourself with me after all that?"

Zach smiled at him, and it was like dawn had come early to Mata Hari. He leaned across the divide between their chairs and kissed Thomas on the mouth. His lips were together, but his kiss pulsed with strength and courage. He sat back and said, "Oh yes. I can definitely see myself with the kind and generous soul who supports the kids at Rainbow Space and helps his friend start a bar and risks his life for someone he barely met. You already know how handsome you are to me—don't you dare smirk—but I think you're even more beautiful inside. There's so many details we don't know about each other yet, but I can't wait to find out, if you're willing."

He paused and swallowed hard. "I do know this already, Thomas. I love you too."

Thomas stood up, pulled him up into a hug, and pressed his lips against Zach's ear. He whispered, "Please be a little patient with me. I have two years and more of bad habits to break, but I want you to know *me*. And I want to know you."

He released Zach and reached into his jacket pocket. "There's something I've been carrying around for a few weeks now, just in case we, uh, ran into each other." He presented an envelope to Zach, who gasped as he pulled out two first-class tickets to Rome. Thomas explained, "You probably can't go away right now, since you're just getting back to work. But they're open tickets, so they can be used any time. You just call the number on the ticket— there—to schedule the flight. Maybe later this year, you'll be able to work some vacation."

Zach looked puzzled. "Me? There's two tickets. Wouldn't you be going with me?"

Thomas grinned self-consciously. "I really hope so, but I don't want you to feel any obligation. These are for you to share with someone special." He bit his lip and heat crept into his eyes. Zach reacted visibly at the look there, softening and leaning forward slightly. Thomas said in a low voice, "I should warn you, if you use the ticket on me. I've dreamed about driving along the Amalfi coast with you since we went to the museum with Randy months ago."

Zach stroked Thomas's cheek lightly, and Thomas tilted his head to press against Zach's palm. Zach smiled shyly. "I actually have another two weeks of leave before I have to go back to the office. Thomas, I have these two tickets to Italy. Would you please go with me? Maybe we can get to know each other better there."

Thomas matched his grin and said, "I can make that work." He hugged *his* Zach again, even more tightly. "I found a hotel in Positano where we'll wake up looking at the sea. I hope you'll like it."

Zach tapped the envelope against Thomas's chest and pretended to be confused. "It sounds like we'd be sharing a hotel room. Does that mean sex is back on the table?" He grinned as he lightly stroked a hand up Thomas's back and then down to the curve of his ass. "I swear that's not the only reason I want to be with you. For the last few weeks, though, I've had some, uh... very *explicit* dreams. They featured the most handsome man in the world. And can I just say about our sex—Oh. My. God."

Thomas laughed and grew hard at Zach's touch. "It's back on the table, all right," he said. He felt Zach's cock against his hip as well, and Thomas moved against it with anticipation. "But I'd like to start this on a new note. Can I be old-fashioned and take you on a date before I let you have your way with me again? Or take me out of the country."

Zach pretended to pout, but then he grinned widely. "Okay. Have it your way, Mr. Scarborough. I haven't had dinner yet tonight, if that would count."

"Well, it might not satisfy Emily Post. But then, she doesn't know how hard up I've been." Zach looked at him with a question in his eyes. Thomas said softly, "This makes up for none of the crap I put you through, I get that. But I need you to know. I haven't been with anyone else since the first night with you at my condo back in February."

Zach gave a strangled cry and hugged Thomas fiercely. "Thank you. Thank you for that."

Thomas said in his ear, "I can't take back all the one-night stands I had before. Once we connected like that, though...I didn't want to settle for less."

Thomas felt Zach's erection throb against him as they hugged. "Damn, you smell good," Zach murmured with his head against Thomas's neck. "Maybe we'll have to make that dinner date a Big Mac to go. Let me just say hi to Randy and Joe, and we'll get out of here."

They walked out to the bar, hands clasped, to find Randy grinning and Joe beaming with his hands clasped together. A round of shots already waited for them all.

As they approached the bar, Zach leaned close enough to whisper into Thomas's ear. "It isn't how many one-night stands you've had before me that matters, Thomas. It's whether I'm going to be the last on the list."

"I think you are, Zach. I really think you are." Thomas smiled.

Epilogue

ZACHARY LEANED BACK on the lounge chair to bake in the Italian sun. He lay on a private terrace at their elegant hotel. No other rooms looked down on theirs, so they might be the only two people in the world.

It all felt like a dream. The first-class flight to Rome, a night in that amazing city, and then the drive to Naples and along the Amalfi Coast. Thomas's rented 1963 Alfa Romeo Spider had brought them to Le Sirenuse. It was the most spectacular hotel Zachary could imagine. On their second day in Positano, he let himself relax in luxury. He gazed out at a view completely unlike anything he'd ever seen in Ogden.

Before him the lovely little town glistened in the sunshine. Colorful houses built into the side of the cliff seemed to tumble down to the Tyrrhenian Sea below. Green and red majolica tiles on the Moorish dome of the cathedral anchored his view. The dome brought balance and harmony to the beauty around him.

And speaking of beauty…. Naked and burnished, Thomas stepped onto the terrace from their room and brought with him two small glasses of limoncello. Thomas stopped to lean against the doorjamb and provocatively ran his eyes over Zachary. He lay there equally naked except for his sunglasses, all splayed out for his lover's eyes.

His lover. Zachary sighed in pleasure at the thought as Thomas crouched down next to his lounge. His *lover* handed him one of the chilled glasses full of pale-yellow liquid and then kissed his lips.

They tipped their glasses together and sipped their limoncello. "Is it just me, or does this stuff taste like sunshine?" Thomas mused and lay on the adjoining chaise longue. "Would you mind rubbing some lotion on my back?" He made his lounge go flat and rolled over so he was facedown on his white towel. Zachary moved to the edge and ran a hand over Thomas's tanned and muscular shoulders. He continued along his back, and to the white swell of his ass. Then he reversed direction and trailed his fingertips up smooth skin again toward Thomas's neck.

Thomas turned his head so his cheek rested on his crossed arms as he looked up at Zachary, his blue eyes alight. "I love you, Zach," he murmured. "No matter how many times I say it, I don't think you know how much."

"That you can say it to me at all after the things that have happened to you means more than you know," Zachary told him. "I understand you so much better now."

The long drive from Rome had proven perfect for that conversation. Thomas kept his eyes on the road as he told Zach about Rumson, about his parents. He even shared his revelations of how he'd been hiding from himself with so many men, and only twice glanced over to gauge reactions. Zach wanted to wrap Thomas up in his arms to reassure him. He had to limit himself to resting a hand on Thomas's on top of the gearshift until the poison drained from his heart. But when they arrived at the hotel, the bellman had barely closed the door to their suite behind them before Zachary pulled him down onto the bed. He showed Thomas that he need never be lonely again.

Zachary shivered pleasantly at the memory and bent over to kiss Thomas's neck. Then he opened the bottle of sunscreen and applied it to Thomas's back. "I'm glad that we've talked about your past, so we can begin fresh."

"I think you let me off too easily," Thomas said as he closed his eyes and relaxed under Zachary's touch. "Even now I wonder how you can forgive me for putting you in danger and for being such an ass to you."

Zachary used both hands to knead the firm muscles of Thomas's back. He spread lotion with the heels of his hands and pressed his fingers into knots of tension. "Ah, Thomas. You're so smart, but you could use a little more trust," Zachary said quietly. "I mean it when I say nothing Charles did was your fault. If he hadn't fixated on you, it would have been someone else."

Zachary straddled Thomas's legs so he could apply sunscreen to his lower back. He moved his hands slowly to stroke the muscle underneath Thomas's taut skin.

"I was scared, no lie, but you rescued me. You knew the danger you were facing when you came to the apartment after Charles called you. You said anything he wanted to hear to buy us time. And then you saved my life. You and Randy and Torres—my three musketeers."

He moved his hands lower to spread lotion on the pale, untanned flesh of Thomas's buttocks. "But speaking of ass...," Zachary muttered. Thomas groaned slightly as Zachary pressed into the firm muscle there. He worked the heels of his hands on each side, pressed his thumbs into the dimple at the top of each cheek, stroking downward. Gradually he moved his thumbs closer together and then traced along the trench of Thomas's backside.

"That feels so good," Thomas moaned. Zachary looked around quickly until he was satisfied no one could see into their terrace. Then he spread the cheeks between his hands and bent forward to run his tongue up and down the cleft. The smell of sunscreen, sweat, and musk, was set to the cry of seabirds and the afternoon chimes from the cathedral's carillon. It all made his heart pound with love and desire while he licked circles against Thomas's tight rim.

As Thomas sighed and relaxed further under him, Zachary used his thumbs to push against the opening. He slid the end of each a little inside and alternated left thumb, right thumb, left. Thomas pushed back against him, and Zachary smiled. He had learned so much about Thomas's body—what made him gasp or pant or moan or sigh in pleasure. He knew how to make Thomas's eyes go dark as twilight by lying on his back and spreading his thighs for Thomas to fuck him. He knew how to make Thomas surrender his control. To quiet the self-recrimination in his head, and let his Zach give him pleasure.

That was what Zachary wanted—to show Thomas how much he was adored. He used his thumbs to spread the pink hole wide open. "I'm going to make you feel so good right now," he growled in the voice that brought out Thomas's submissive side. "Because that's what pleases me. And you want to please me, don't you, Thomas?"

Thomas groaned his agreement and raised his ass to press back against Zachary's mouth. He loved that no one else had ever discovered that aspect of Thomas. He couldn't wait to explore all the ways to make him come undone. He used words to inflame, but he tingled happily to think of other things they might try together.

"So shameless, Thomas, and it's all for me. No one can see us. It's just you and me, and we're here under the Italian sky, where you brought us."

He let a bit of spit leak into Thomas's opening. Pressing forward with his tongue, he forced it an inch inside the delicate folds. That taste of Thomas was intoxicating. He worked his tongue around and around and felt the hole relax. He wouldn't even need to use fingers this time.

He raised his head slightly and bit one white cheek hard enough to make Thomas gasp. "I'm going to fuck you now, Thomas. I'm going to roll on a condom, and I'm going to work my long cock inside you, inch by inch. And then when I'm all the way inside you, I'm going to fuck you hard and deep until you come all over that soft towel."

Thomas trembled at his words and then visibly relaxed even more as he surrendered completely. "Ah, Zach. The things you do to me and the things you say. I love it so much. I love *you*."

"I believe you, Thomas. Do you believe I love you?"

Thomas nodded. "I do."

"Good. Someday soon we're going to go get tested together. And when we find out what I already know, that we're both healthy, I'm going to do this to you again. Without a condom. Would you like that, Thomas?"

Thomas's breath was ragged. "I want that, Zach. *My* Zach. I want to feel your hard dick shoot inside me."

Zachary smiled and reached for a rubber from the strip he'd brought outside earlier with his book and his towel. He used lotion on his sheathed cock to get it slicked and ready. Rising up slightly, he positioned the tip against Thomas's ass.

"I want it too, Thomas." Zachary sighed with pleasure as he pushed past the tight opening. He was slow and deliberate. He fought the urge to plunge into Thomas in one thrust so he could prolong the exquisite sensation of sinking into him. "I want your beautiful, naked cock deep inside my ass too, just like I'm inside you now, until you fill me up with your come."

Thomas moaned as Zachary brushed against his prostate and continued to slide in. He said hoarsely, "I never knew before you how good this could feel, to just get *fucked* by a beautiful man with a big dick."

"It's all for you, Thomas. Just for you now." Zachary was almost all the way inside, and his thighs strained from the slow descent. Already he was close to coming from the sheer bliss of penetrating Thomas.

"Give it to me, Zach. Let me please you with my ass and with my body." Thomas pressed his hips back and tried to get all of Zach inside him.

Zach finally bottomed out. His thighs rested on either side of Thomas's hips and his groin pressed against the pillow of Thomas's ass. He sighed in pleasure and let his body drape across Thomas's back until his nose was against Thomas's hair. Then he worked his arms under Thomas's chest, and they clasped hands as he began to move. His strokes grew faster as Thomas grunted and pleaded beneath him for more.

"Zach, can I...?"

"What do you need, sweet man?"

"Can I roll over? I want to see your face when you come."

Zach stopped his thrusts and slowly pulled out to the sound of Thomas's groan, which made him even harder, if that was possible. Then he helped Thomas roll onto his back. Raising Thomas's legs to his own shoulders, he lined up the head of his cock again. Thomas reached out to Zach's hips and pulled him inside. He rolled his eyes back when Zach was fully seated and used his hands to hold Zach deep.

After a long moment, he opened his blue eyes again and stared earnestly up at Zachary. "I didn't even know I was lonely until I met you, Zach, and now I can't imagine being without you. You bring me such joy, and I'm glad that I never told anyone else that I loved him."

His eyes darkened for a moment, and Zachary knew he was recalling the lies he'd told to Charles that terrible night. Zachary thrust his hips slightly to stroke his cock deep inside Thomas and bring him back to the moment. It worked, and Thomas brightened again, like the sun emerging from behind a cloud.

He said, "That's at least something I've saved just for you—telling you from my heart that I love you."

Zachary blinked back emotion, nearly overwhelmed by the adoration in Thomas's face. What Rumson had tried to *take*, Thomas freely gave to Zachary. It was the most amazing gift he'd ever received.

Zachary began to move again, but it was no longer just flesh meeting flesh. Thomas was in his soul as surely as Zachary was in Thomas's body. He felt each thrust and slide with all his muscles and deep in his heart, and his orgasm rushed toward him. Thomas gave him the slightest nod to let him know he was there too. Zachary pulled him close to crush his lips to that succulent mouth.

And then he and Thomas erupted in a glorious mess of legs and arms, of semen and sweat-drenched skin. They became a firework of humanity, sparkling and glistening together beneath the Italian sun.

The End

Thank you for reading *Every Breath You Take.* I hope you enjoyed it!

Subscribe to my newsletter at *robertwinterauthor.com* for giveaways, my latest book news, LGBT romance recs and deals, and more! I won't spam or share your email address.

If you did enjoy the book, **please consider writing a review** on Amazon, Goodreads or other sites that discuss MM romance. I appreciate any feedback, no matter how long or short. It's a great way to let other romance fans know what you thought about this book. Being an independent author means that every review really does make a huge difference, and I'd be grateful if you take a minute to share your opinion with others.

Readers love *September* by Robert Winter

2017 Rainbow Award honorable mention

"September is a book filled with hurt and comfort, moving on and finding love, and living your best life."
—Joyfully Jay

"The emotional pull in this story is unbelievable. … The writing was captivating and the characters were remarkable."
—Love Bytes

"[Winter'] writing and storytelling
ability are both beautifully brilliant, with characters that are full of emotion, and their plight and struggles real."
—Alpha Book Club

Reader Praise for *Every Breath You Take* by Robert Winter

2017 Rainbow Award honorable mention

"[T]he tension that Winter creates and builds combines perfectly with the other areas of the story, always leaving the reader with an apprehension about the next move of the perpetrator. For me, Every Breath You Take and Robert Winter deserve a full five-star rating!"
—Joyfully Jay

"The juxtaposition of the killer's stalking and escalating madness with the growing friendship and attraction between Thomas and Zachary … kept me biting my nails right up until the end."
—Scattered Thoughts and Rogue Words

"This story starts out on a murderous note, with the prologue leaving me absolutely needing to know how its dark events were going to figure in the lives of the main characters."
—It's About the Book

Excitement for *Lying Eyes* by Robert Winter

Five stars
"Every book gets better... This is an easy recommendation, even more so if you're a romantic mystery and/or suspense maven."
—Hearts on Fire

"Robert Winter is now an auto-buy author for me. Spectacular writing!!!"
—Amazon reviewer

"There are pulse-racing action scenes to go along with the intrigue and building romance, and an ending that goes above and beyond to supply gratification to the reader, as well as to the characters."
—It's About the Book

"4.5 stars!!"
—Bayou Book Junkies

"Robert Winter has definitely made it onto my favorite author list. This is his third book, and they just keep getting better!"
—Scattered Thoughts and Rogue Words

Vampire Claus by Robert Winter

'Twas the night before Christmas, but what's stirring is a little more dangerous than a mouse.

Taviano is nearly two hundred years old and never wakes in the same place twice. Weary and jaded, the vampire still indulges in memories of childhood Christmases in Naples. He lingers in shadow, spying on mortals as they enjoy the holiday.

When Taviano spots a handsome young man in Boston loaded down with presents and about to be mugged, he can't help but intervene. Soon he's talking to joyous, naïve, strong-willed and funny Paul, a short-order cook who raised funds to buy Christmas presents for LGBTQ children. Before he knows what's happened, Taviano is wrapped up in Paul's arms and then in his schemes to get the presents delivered by Christmas morning.

A vampire turned into a Christmas elf… What could go wrong?

Vampire Claus is a 30,000-word standalone gay romance about a lonely vampire and a fearless mortal with no instinct for self-preservation. A heartwarming ending, no cliffhanger, and a young man who discovers he has a thing for fangs. Isn't that what Christmas is all about?

About the Author

Robert Winter lives and writes in Provincetown. He is a recovering lawyer who prefers writing about hot men in love much more than drafting a legal brief. He left behind the (allegedly) glamorous world of an international law firm to sit in his home office and dream up ways to torment his characters until they realize they are perfect for each other.

When he isn't writing, Robert likes to cook Indian food and explore new restaurants. He splits his attention between Andy, his partner of sixteen years, and Ling the Adventure Cat, who likes to fly in airplanes and explore the backyard jungle as long as the temperature and humidity are just right.

Contact Robert at the following links:

Website:
www.robertwinterauthor.com

Facebook:
facebook.com/robert.winter.921230

Goodreads:
goodreads.com/author/show/16068736.Robert_Winter

Twitter:
twitter.com/@RWinterAuthor

Email:
RobertWinterAuthor@comcast.net

Photo by Brad Fowler,
Song of Myself Photography

www.ingramcontent.com/pod-product-compliance
Lightning Source LLC
Chambersburg PA
CBHW051525260626
47170CB00003B/784